Praise for

OCD LOVE STORY

"Warning: this book could cause obsessive-compulsive reading. Funny, honest, and real, *OCD Love Story* stars one of the most likable narrators in recent YA fiction. Once you start this book, you will find that, like Bea, you just can't help yourself."
—*Patricia McCormick*, author of *Cut* and *Never Fall Down*

★ "Debut novelist Haydu doesn't sugarcoat the difficulties of OCD or reduce her characters to a symptom list. . . . [That they try] to build a relationship with someone who's seen them as they really are, to move past shame into intimacy, makes the story that much more touching."
—*Publishers Weekly*, starred review

★ "Heartwarming, frequently funny, and wholly honest, this debut novel is, well, compulsively readable."
—*Horn Book*, starred review

★ "Bea is a completely endearing original, and the book manages to subtly steer her narration through denial of her condition to acceptance without ever losing her essential charisma. . . . [She] remains witty, affecting, and ferociously individual throughout, and readers will delight to know her as they understand her—and possibly themselves—better."
—*The Bulletin*, starred review

I WILL NOT STALK THAT BOY. I WILL NOT STALK THAT BOY. I WILL NOT STALK THAT BOY. I WILL NOT STALK THAT BOY. I WILL NOT STALK THAT BOY. I WILL NOT STALK THAT BOY. I WILL NOT STALK THAT BOY. I WILL NOT STALK THAT BOY. I WILL NOT STALK THAT BOY. I WILL NOT STALK THAT BOY. I WILL NOT STALK THAT BOY. I WILL NOT STALK THAT BOY. I WILL NOT STALK THAT BOY. I WILL NOT STALK THAT BOY. I WILL NOT STALK THAT BOY.

OCD LOVE STORY

Corey Ann Haydu

SIMON PULSE

NEW YORK   LONDON   TORONTO   SYDNEY   NEW DELHI

SIMON PULSE

An imprint of Simon & Schuster Children's Publishing Division
1230 Avenue of the Americas, New York, NY 10020
First Simon Pulse paperback edition July 2014
Text copyright © 2013 by Corey Ann Haydu
All rights reserved, including the right of reproduction in whole
or in part in any form.
SIMON PULSE and colophon are registered trademarks of
Simon & Schuster, Inc.
Also available in a Simon Pulse hardcover edition.
For information about special discounts for bulk purchases, please contact
Simon & Schuster Special Sales at 1-866-506-1949
or business@simonandschuster.com.
The Simon & Schuster Speakers Bureau can bring authors to your live event.
For more information or to book an event contact
the Simon & Schuster Speakers Bureau at 1-866-248-3049
or visit our website at www.simonspeakers.com.
Cover design by Jessica Handelman
Interior design by Hilary Zarycky
The text of this book was set in New Caledonia.
Manufactured in the United States of America
2 4 6 8 10 9 7 5 3
The Library of Congress has cataloged the hardcover edition as follows:
Haydu, Corey Ann.
OCD love story / Corey Ann Haydu. — 1st Simon Pulse hardcover ed.
p. cm.
Summary: In an instant, Bea felt almost normal with Beck, and as if she could fall
in love again, but things change when the psychotherapist who has been helping
her deal with past romantic relationships puts her in a group with Beck—
a group for teens with obsessive-compulsive disorder.
[1. Obsessive-compulsive disorder—Fiction. 2. Psychotherapy—Fiction.
3. Interpersonal relations—Fiction.] I. Title.
PZ7.H31389Ocd 2013   [Fic]—dc23   2012021545
ISBN 978-1-4424-5732-4 (hc)
ISBN 978-1-4424-5733-1 (pbk)
ISBN 978-1-4424-5734-8 (eBook)

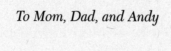

To Mom, Dad, and Andy

♡ 1.

LUCKY FOR ME, I DON'T GET PANICKY IN SMALL dark spaces or anything. I'm a different breed of crazy.

So when the power goes out, I don't do much of anything except try to avoid the horny high school guys trying to feel up girls in the dark. I go to dances at Smith-Latin Boys' Academy two, maybe three times a year, but nothing like this has ever happened before. Electricity must be out all over the town. There is a hit of silence, like a preparatory inhale, and then chaos.

Maybe it's true what they say about being blind: Your other senses get stronger. 'Cause the second the lights and music cut out I realize how disgusting the smell in the gym is. And for a moment the sounds of classmates cackling and tumbling over each other and screaming in fake fear take over. Then I hear a familiar noise, a rhythm I know well. It's the strained, superfast pace of a panic attack. It's coming from somewhere just to my left, so I use that as a kind of lighthouse to find my way out of the thick of the crowd.

The short gasps turn into longer, more strained inhales, and the poor guy having the attack is choking on his own breath. And this is something I know everything about: I've just been lucky enough to come up with ways to stop my panic attacks before they happen. So I sit next to the guy gasping for air; I find his ear and whisper into it. Tell him to slow down and take deep breaths, and I reach in the dark for his forehead, where I can fit my hand perfectly. He relaxes on contact and I do it to myself, too, put my free hand on my own forehead. The touch feels good, this intimacy with a total stranger, so I guess I'm kinda loving the power outage. This is something that would never happen under fluorescent lights. I guess that's true of a lot of things, come to think of it.

"That feels good," his still-choking but less-panicky voice says. "I don't know what just happened."

"Panic attack," I say. I'm ready to list all the symptoms and causes and give him the same advice Dr. Pat gives me when I get them, but just as I'm taking a breath to start talking again he cuts me off.

"Got it." I think it's on purpose, not letting me talk more, but it doesn't sound like a dismissal, more like an attempt to save me from myself, which I've got to appreciate. As a rule it's best if I quit while I'm ahead when it comes to talking to strangers. Although in the dark I seem to be pretty good at reading people. I shut my mouth. Take two deep breaths. Then let myself try talking again.

"Is this your first panic attack?" I say. I'd ask this in full daylight, but it feels even more natural in the dark. His body is still twitching a little in the aftermath of the rush of anxiety, and his skin has a cooled-off, sweaty texture. I let my arm stay against his. With all the craziness going on around us it's good to just have something against me. Someone.

"Guess so," he says. Then nothing.

"I'm Bea," I say to fill the air. It's not that it's quiet: The room is even louder now than it was with the shitty Top 40 jams blasting at full volume. But this guy is quiet and soon the power will go back on and the reality of our visibility will almost certainly make everything more awkward.

"Beck," he says.

"Weird name."

"Yeah, you too."

I stretch my legs out in front of me. Now the silence between us feels more like an agreement, a pact, and less like a struggle.

It's funny how my nerves work: pulsing one minute and retreating the next, leaving me totally spent. If the sense of camaraderie I feel with Beck's heavy breathing and sweaty hands is right, then he must be riding that exact seesaw right now.

"Wanna try to make our way outside?" I say. Nothing's changing in here. Teachers are trying to talk louder than the students and it sounds like the middle of the gym/dance floor has turned into an impromptu rave. If we were at Greenough Girls' Academy instead of at Smith-Latin, I'd be able to find my way to the library, where I could hide out until this whole power-outage thing ended. I'd have everything I like at my fingertips: couches, portable book lights, the smell of those century-old rare books that our librarian is obsessed with. I'm hoping Beck knows a similar location at Smith-Latin. I'm hoping his sense of direction isn't impaired in the dark. I'm hoping most of all that his face matches his voice: low and sweet and a little gravelly. Can faces look like that sound, I wonder? And is this the kind of guy I've been looking for, instead of the mass of ugly-faced, beautiful-bodied high school athletes I keep finding myself with?

"I can't move," Beck says. I reach for his legs, like maybe he has a cast or brace or a missing limb or something. A moment too late I realize this is a really awkward move to make, but as usual I can't stop myself. My hand is too far up his thigh and it stays there a moment longer than it should.

Good lord, I'm awkward.

I swear I can feel his legs tense and maybe something else shift as well.

"You seem okay to me." I slide my hand off his leg.

"You should go outside if you want," Beck says. "I just can't. I mean, won't. I'm not going anywhere until the lights are back on, okay?"

"Nothing to be scared of. You know, aside from really

horny football players. No offense if that's what you are. Or are we avoiding someone? Maybe an ugly Greenough girl you hooked up with by accident?" Beck laughs just enough for me to know he doesn't mind the teasing.

"You're the only Greenough girl I've talked to tonight," he says, and I'm grinning in the dark like a total loser, like some eight-year-old, which is exactly how I would look if anyone could actually see me. There's even a space between my front teeth that supposedly gives me a sweet, little-girl smile.

"Well, in that case I better stake my claim," I say. Things crash around us: people, DJ equipment, school banners. I can't believe I am so heart-thumpingly into the sound of his voice and the idea of getting him to myself for a few minutes, even though I still don't know what this guy looks like. I move my other hand from his forehead to his hand, and when our palms find each other, he squeezes. Then again. And again. After a few more squeezes, he exhales. We settle into the hand-holding for a few moments before he starts to panic again. Then he lets go.

"I'm telling you, you'll feel better with some fresh air," I say. In the dark I can't tell if Beck nods his head or anything, but he definitely doesn't say no, and I'm a glass-half-full kind of girl so I take that to mean he'll leave with me. I pull him to his feet. It takes some serious effort; he pulls against me in an attempt to stay seated on the floor. I don't care. "Are you scared to let me see you? Are you superugly?"

I wait for him to laugh but he doesn't, and it hits me that maybe he *is* really ugly, and not in some subjective way, but truly disfigured. I have a knack for saying terrible truths to total strangers.

"Um, that was a superawkward thing to say. I'm like that sometimes. Sort of awkward. Or, I like to think quirky. Awkward and quirky." This right here, this is why I scare guys away.

"So am I," Beck says. I knew there was a reason I liked him.

The gym is emptying. Teachers are working to herd people out to the parking lot where they can keep a better eye on us. I hear them shouting orders over the chaos. Enough time has passed that most of the other kids are giving in to the request. After all, we're out of booze for sure and the thrill of touching strangers' bodies or bumping into your friends in the literal sense has drained from the room.

"Stay quiet and don't move," I whisper. I have a feeling that if we are patient we'll have the whole gym to ourselves. My best friend, Lisha, and I are always trying to find secret spaces where no one will think to look for us. Like a kind of hide-and-seek with the world. When we were little, we decorated the inside of my walk-in closet with glitter paint and pillows and did all our playing and talking and snacking in there. All cozy and ours. I'm thinking staying behind in the dark gym with Beck would be something like that. Lisha, wherever she is in this dark swarm of heavily perfumed teenage bodies, would approve.

I almost call her name, so she can find us, but I know she wouldn't mind me taking an extra moment alone with the hopefully cute, definitely appealing Smith-Latin boy.

In just a few minutes the gym has gone from mostly crowded to mostly empty and the car lights from the parking lot don't reach the corner we've holed up in. If we stay quiet something great could happen. From the sound of Beck's sharp inhale, I'm worried he's starting to panic again (is this kid afraid of the dark or what?) so I find his shoulder and follow the line of his arm down to his hand again. He squeezes.

I consider leaving it at that. At least until I find some way to see a glimpse of his face.

Instead I walk my fingers back up Beck's arm, wrist to elbow to shoulder to neck until I find his face. And then his lips. And despite the shaky legs holding him up and the heavy ins and outs of his breath, I kiss him. It's a soft thing that he must get lost in for at least a few seconds, because his body stills against mine. Just as quickly as he relaxed, he tightens right back up again and I let my mouth leave his.

He tasted like wintergreen and cooled-off sweat. Minty. Salty. Perfect.

I really had him, for a second.

"Let's stay here," I say. Not sultry, 'cause I giggle on the last syllable. I'm nervous too, just not as amped up as him.

Beck's feet tap and his breath sounds trapped and he steps back so that he is closer to the wall. He stays glued there.

"I can't," Beck says when I take another step toward him. "I should get home. I'm feeling weird. I'm kind of messed up right now." His voice is a mumble. I can feel the heat of his blush, even from a few inches away. I want to reassure him with a touch, maybe even kiss him again, but as I reach out someone else hurtles into me, full force, knocking me over. I scramble up. Beck has moved away.

"I'm messed up too! I'm totally messed up!" I call out after him, and I think he's still in the room; I think he's heard me, but the dark is too heavy for me to see even the slightest movement. I feel for the wall and follow it in the hopes of reaching him, but I don't come across him in any corner or clinging to any doorframe. He's left the gym. I guess somehow he's more scared of me than he is of the dark.

♡ 2.

I GET TO THERAPY VERY, VERY EARLY THE NEXT day. an entire hour early, in fact, because I like listening to the couple that has therapy before me. Some people have reality TV or books about vampires. I have Austin and Sylvia.

There's a spot in Dr. Pat's waiting room where I can hear the mumblings of what's going on in her office. Mostly it's just intonations and occasional spare words. But when Austin and Sylvia are in there I can hear much more. I take my place in the wobbly chair by her office door and hear that they are already in there, right on time as always. I'm instantly calmer, knowing I haven't missed anything.

Truth time: A month or two ago I caught a glance at Dr. Pat's appointment book. She'd accidentally left it on the couch instead of on her desk, and I let my eyes dart over the open page before handing it over to her. It was basically an accident that I even caught sight of their names in the four o'clock time slot.

Somewhat less accidental: Today while I'm cross-legged in

the waiting room chair I'm learning all about their sex life. It comes to me in half sentences and words shouted at uncomfortable decibels. Austin and Sylvia are screamingly attractive, but if the way they speak to each other is any indication, the attraction just isn't enough, 'cause they clearly hate each other. It is mostly Sylvia whose voice breaks through the walls: a Boston accent and a nasal, swallowed tone that is hard to listen to. Without even having to think about it I direct all my sympathy toward Austin and the gentler way he speaks. Also, he's hot.

I have been listening in on them for over a month now and today I brought a notebook. It's a lame patent-leather thing my father gave me for Christmas. There is a shooting star embossed in gold on the cover. A huge, ugly assault on an already ugly notebook. It's a pretty typical gift from my dad. He is equal parts kind and misinformed, so I hang on to his presents but almost never use them.

The notebook is pink, aside from the gold shooting star monstrosity, so there's no chance of anyone thinking to flip through its pages; it's not the kind of thing that looks like it could hold any secrets. It is too flimsy and silly and unbearably *pink* to contain anything of substance.

I start scribbling down what I can hear of their conversation. I don't have a real reason for doing it, but I almost can't help myself. Maybe I'll show it to Lisha tonight if we meet up at the diner for pancakes. I'm also a bit of a collector of information. It's something I've been doing for years, a part of my personality. If I wasn't going to be a costume designer, I could totally be a journalist.

Except I guess I don't tell people much about my information collecting. They don't usually get it. Except Lisha, of course, who gets everything.

There's nothing like writing notes on a fresh sheet of paper in an empty journal. It's like meditation. Or what I would imagine meditation to be like.

Sylvia: . . . no way to treat your wife.

Austin: If you could just pause and breathe every once in a . . .

Dr. Pat: (something very quiet and probing that I can't hear)

Sylvia: . . . you haven't touched me in months. You must be getting it somewhere . . .

Austin: You can't act like a bitch and then just expect me to . . .

Sylvia: . . . do I disgust you? Is that it? I got the boob job but you don't seem to . . .

Austin: . . . I didn't even want you to . . .

Sylvia: . . . just go sleep with some little girl and get it over with . . .

Austin: . . . totally inappropriate . . . I used to think you were the kind of woman . . .

Dr. Pat: (quiet, reflective therapy-speak that I can't hear)

Sylvia: You don't like women. You like girls. Nineteen-
year-old girls, right? I saw your computer . . .
Austin: . . . can't believe you'd say something like
that after all I've told you about my past . . .
(A long pause in conversation.)

It's so utterly engaging writing down everything I hear that I forget I'm in public. The waiting room has started to fill up, signifying the hour change where all the 4:00 p.m. patients leave and the 5:00 p.m. patients come in. With a start I realize I'm strangling my pen and practically breaking through the notebook paper with all my urgency and focus. My hands are cramped and the notes look scribbled. But I'm the calmest I've been all week.

Austin and Sylvia exit Dr. Pat's office and float past me. I try to take mental photographs as they walk by. Sylvia's breasts lead the way and her honey-colored hair is long and thick down her back. She wears so much eyeliner she could be in a teenage indie rock band. Austin has floppy red hair and green, green eyes and tighter jeans than his wife. He has a flannel shirt and a leather bracelet and a Fuck You Curl to his lips.

He's not my type, but he's sexy as anything. So is she.

I've got to come early next week to hear their next session. I know it's a little weird, but they are a book I don't want to stop reading.

. . .

Dr. Pat always takes fifteen minutes in between sessions so that she can compose herself accordingly. I imagine she must get especially distracted after the drama of Austin and Sylvia. They are both tree tall and skinny, and between Austin's furry stubble and Sylvia's Rapunzel-like mane, they are a lot to take in even when they're not screaming at each other.

I want what they have.

And that's how I open my session this afternoon.

"The patients before me are pretty much perfect, right?" I say. It's like an experiment. I want to see the reaction in Dr. Pat's face. It's near impossible to get anything out of her. She keeps a clean, unreadable expression that only ever seems to fluctuate between contemplation, sympathy, and concern.

"Oh, yes?" Dr. Pat says.

"Don't you think so?"

"That's interesting that you are taking note of them." She is a ninja with this stuff. A full-on conversational ninja. I shrug. This isn't going anywhere. "Your mother says you've seemed particularly observant lately. Is that fair to say?" I wrinkle my brow trying to assess how loaded this statement may or may not be. I have to be careful with Dr. Pat. One false move and she'll put me on more Zoloft or make me come in more often.

"They just seem so . . . cool," I say. "Confident. Fabulous. I guess I wonder what it would be like, to be living their lives instead of mine."

"So you take note of them because you'd like to be like them?" Dr. Pat likes to take what I'm saying and turn it a little to the left or to the right. Make it have meaning.

"I mean, I think it would be hard *not* to notice them, right? They stand out."

Dr. Pat nods, but only slightly. I want her to agree so badly. I want her to nod with vigor and touch my arm and tell me that of course everyone feels the way I do. Instead she tilts her head.

"I'm interested in you, not in everyone else," she says.

"What else did my mom say?" Dr. Pat, my mom, and I made a deal back when I started coming to therapy that there wouldn't be secrets kept between Dr. Pat and my mother. It made me anxious to think of them having long phone calls about me behind closed doors.

"You think she had more to tell me?"

"I'm just curious. I mean, I think I'm pretty boring. There can't be that much for her to talk to you about."

"So you think you're boring and that my patients or other people you run into are more exciting?" Dr. Pat says. Therapists are tricky. They'll make connections out of anything. When I first started seeing Dr. Pat, I'd try to talk about casual stuff, but she never let me just have a normal conversation. One time I told her I like pickles in my sandwiches. She reminded me that I mentioned Kurt eating a lot of pickles and asked me what I thought that might mean. Like somehow that proved I was obsessed with him.

In therapy there's no such thing as just liking pickles in your sandwiches. I give a big, audible sigh and Dr. Pat pushes her glasses up her nose. They'd slipped a little; the oversize tortoiseshell frames look even larger when they're askew. "Bea? You seem distracted," she says when she realizes I'm not going to answer her question.

"I guess I'm a little distracted, yeah." The thing is, I like Dr. Pat. I'm doing fine, I don't *have* be seeing her or anything at this point, but it's not the worst thing checking in with her. Her office smells like a vanilla candle and I like the enormous paintings of flowers in close-up that cover the walls. They're calming.

"I was thinking," she says very, very carefully, "that maybe you'd do well in a group setting. Group therapy. Other teenagers, talking about what's going on in their lives. What do you think?"

I'm sure shock registers on my face. I don't hide my feelings well, and she's taken me by surprise. Group therapy sounds like torture.

"Um, I'm not feeling supersocial these days," I say.

"That was something else your mother mentioned." My stomach turns.

"It's not some *thing*," I say. "A lot of people get nervous in, like, social situations."

Dr. Pat pushes the glasses up her nose again. I wonder if she needs them adjusted, if they've gotten stretched out

15

somehow. It could be dangerous, if her glasses fall off when she's driving or something.

"Tell me more," Dr. Pat says.

"That's really it. Nothing more to tell. I just feel a little loner-y lately. I'm sure it will pass."

"It's okay to be having a hard time, Bea," Dr. Pat says. She takes some notes on her yellow legal pad. "It's actually easier if you just tell me what's going on, and then we can address it."

"Nothing's going on though." I look down at my boots. They used to be boring black suede wedges, but I added a ring of fake fur around the top. I'm thinking I'd like to do the same to my cardigan: add fake leather cuffs to the sleeves and change what's regular into something spectacular. "I mean, actually, I'm not even that antisocial right now. Saturday night I went to a dance with Lisha. Did my mom tell you that?"

"She didn't, but that's great to hear," Dr. Pat says, and her smile tells me she means it. Sometimes she nods and smiles with just her mouth, and I think she's probably tired or bored. But other times her smile is a glow, and I remember how much I like telling her things, how easy she is to talk to. I scoot forward on the couch.

"It was really fun actually. And I met a guy." I don't hide the smile. I meet guys pretty easily, but Beck's the only one since Kurt who's made me buzz like this. I'm smiling without thinking. It's a strange sensation because lately I haven't been doing anything without thinking. "I'd like to see him again, maybe. But I don't know what he looks like or, like, his last name. I think he goes to Smith-Latin. . . ." This is probably not helping my case in terms of sounding superstable, so I take a deep breath and remember to actually explain. "I met him during the power outage."

"Aha," Dr. Pat says. "Well, Bea, I think if you can go to a dance with Lisha and meet a boy in the dark, you can probably handle an hour of group therapy a week." There it is again. A patented Dr. Pat ninja move.

The good feelings that were bubbling in my chest drop to my stomach and curdle. I close my eyes to conjure up an image of Austin, thinking it might calm me down. Shaggy hair. Leather jacket. Stubble. I wonder what he's doing now, what he and Sylvia do after their couples therapy.

"People with your way of thinking do very well in group therapy," Dr. Pat concludes. "Some of your behaviors make me think—"

"Fine, okay, I'll go," I say, not wanting her to finish that sentence. I pinch the top of my thigh, over my pants. The way people do when they want to wake up from a dream. It's just a tiny thing, and doesn't hurt, but Dr. Pat's eyes dart to my thumb and forefinger like it might matter.

It's not a dream, and I'm still here, but just barely.

3.

I DO NOT SAY HELLO TO MY MOTHER WHEN I
walk into the house after therapy. She's reheating last night's
dinner and I want her to know from the way I throw my back-
pack on the ground with a *thud* that I'm pissed.

"Everything okay, Bea?" my mom says because I'm being
a three-year-old and stomping my way up to my room. *Bam!*
goes every step on every stair.

"Just awesome, Mom," I call back down. I'm ready for a
screaming match. I half know it's misdirected anger (a Dr. Pat
phrase—I have been in therapy way too long) but hearing the
worry in her voice reignites my anger at having to go to group
therapy.

"It's so *awesome* that you think I'm a weirdo. It's so *awesome* that you are reporting back to Dr. Pat on every single
thing I do."

"Bea, sweetheart, you know I don't think you're a weirdo.
I just thought you seemed a little more anxious lately, and I
think that must be so hard. I'm trying to help. . . ."

"If I'm doing so great, then don't make me do this group therapy thing," I say.

"Honey, have you ever talked about everything that happened with that Jeff boy, that friend of Cooter's, during your sessions with Dr. Pat? It seems like that might be useful information for her to—"

I try to stop her with only my eyes, but it doesn't work, so I break in: "Mom!" Just the name Jeff gives me chills. Kurt's name makes me weak with sadness and missing and shame, but Jeff's name in my ear scares me. It is a word I don't want to hear, a single-syllable sound I wish were erased from the English language. I lift my hands to my ears and wish away this conversation.

"I just was thinking that's when some of your troubles started, a few years ago, and I only mention it because your father and I feel so responsible—"

"Can you please leave it to me and Dr. Pat? Please? If you keep butting in it doesn't give me a chance to—"

"Okay, all right," she says. My mother doesn't like arguments and neither do I, so we tend to stop them before they begin. My father is always more likely to follow through on a fight, but he's not home yet, so we're in the clear. There are so many unfinished sentences between my mother and me, so many unsaid words. I wonder what it would be like to have an entire conversation with her, but we almost never let it happen. "I trust you, sweetie. I'll stay out of it. Just a suggestion.

But I am going to have to insist on following your therapist's advice on the group thing, okay? Fair compromise?"

I choose not to answer. Clearly she and Dr. Pat must have planned this weeks ago. Which is totally crazy, because I don't need group therapy. I mean, I only even went to therapy because of a really bad breakup. I'm not the first girl to do that. Lacey from school went to therapy when her college boyfriend slept with someone else. And I barely even think about Kurt anymore. So should I really have to do this group thing over a year later?

I start to protest, but then press my lips together and stay silent instead. My mother works with juvenile delinquents. She's no pushover, and getting into a screaming match will just give her one more thing to tell Dr. Pat about.

I slam the door to my room. There is nothing my mother hates more. She gives a big, audible sigh and I know we won't be speaking again tonight.

I crawl into bed. It's a perfect cocoon that I've been working on for months. I collect soft blankets: fleece, chenille, down comforters, chunky quilts, it doesn't matter. As long as they are thick and soft and decidedly cozy I'll throw them onto my bed. My mother keeps the house at a ridiculous sixty degrees year-round, so I'm always cold, and I've stopped trying to get her to change her ways. Plus there's nothing more luxurious than crawling underneath a pile of blankets. It reminds me a little of the story "The Princess and the Pea," that princess atop a pile of wildly different but always thick and luscious mattresses. I want to be that decadent sometimes.

The walls are covered with images of fashion photography and well-costumed Broadway shows and period films. A little haven of coziness and the things I love. Thank God for this tiny bit of safety.

Before Kurt dumped me, he used to love coming up here.

"This is the perfect hideout," he said once. "You're the most yourself when you're in your room, you know that?" Then he'd kissed me, one hand snaking around my back and tucking itself under my shirt. I still think about how his hand felt on the small of my back.

I try really hard not to think about Kurt too much anymore, but sometimes even a mountain of blankets and an exhibition of fabulous clothes aren't enough to make the ache of missing someone go away completely.

When I met Kurt I was kind of on edge, like all the time. I couldn't have told you what was making me anxious; I couldn't have named a single specific concern I had. But my body was in a general state of unease. Which is part of what was so great about Kurt: Liking someone that much made the rest of me calm down. I think love does that to everyone.

We had been doing a current events class at school, and we were supposed to read the newspaper every day and bring in articles that interested us, or articles we had questions about. Mostly people brought in political articles, and we'd discuss Israel or Iraq or the Dow Jones. But for our final project Lacey brought in an article about a little local boy named Reggie who had stabbed his ten-year-old sister. He was at the juvenile detention center my mom works at, and Lacey thought the whole thing was so sad, she wanted to talk to the class about it. We spent forty-five minutes wondering aloud how a cute little kid was capable of something so terrible.

The unit on current events ended, but I kept reading the newspaper every day for months after. Sometimes there'd be updates on the Reggie boy and we'd share information on him before class started. We all got a little preoccupied with the tragedy: me, Lisha, Lacey, Kim, and the other eight girls from the class. Some mornings if my mother was especially tired and precoffee, I'd be able to pry tiny pieces of information out of her, and then report back to everyone on how he was doing. Anyway, it was no big deal, but I kept a little notebook with articles and stuff on Reggie. And sometimes I wrote down the things my mom said about him, so that I'd remember what to tell Lacey and everyone. It got pretty full, but we were all really interested in this kid and what he'd done and what was going to happen to him.

Anyway, it was really disturbing for everyone. I met Kurt smack in the middle of all that. So I was a little sensitive at the time; we all were.

Burly, bulging Kurt. Not only was he so soppy sweet that

he couldn't kill a spider, let alone a human, he was also thick in his shoulders, determined, an all-star football player. He was invincible. Being with him made me feel safe. I liked to kiss him. And climb on top of him in his little twin bed when his family was out of town.

Something no one knows: Football-playing popular dudes sometimes fall for quirky smart girls as long as they, you know, have a pretty face and decent body. I think they get sick of the anorexic cheerleaders, and if you catch them at the right moment, you convince them to want something *more*.

Plus, around this time I was really into miniskirts and go-go boots. My mom wasn't thrilled, but she knew it wasn't a phase that had staying power so she let me wear whatever as long as it was retro and from the consignment shop down the block.

I made one big mistake with Kurt. I left him alone in my room for five minutes once and he managed to find my Reggie notebook.

It's funny how something I didn't think twice about looked entirely different when I saw it through his eyes. Weeks before, when I was gluing in articles and printouts from the Internet and taking notes on those bits and pieces of information my mom let slip from her time standing guard over Reggie and his bad-news friends, it all seemed like something akin to scrapbooking. It seemed like something I had to do for class. But in Kurt's hands, pages sticking together from lazily applied glue, scraps of paper poking out of all sides making ragged edges, highlighted paragraphs, manic observations . . . I saw it differently.

Kurt saw it too.

I walked in on the open-mouthed stare of someone who is never going to sleep with you again.

"Dude," Kurt said. He was gorgeous and rippling but not heavy on the emotional depth, and I think those pages were a little much for him to process. "Tell me this isn't yours."

And anyone normal would breezily lie or at least stumble over some sort of acceptable explanation. But I had that itch happening in my throat. My head swam. I tried to say something else. I *started* to say something else.

"Oh. Yeah. No. That's not any kind of . . ." My throat was burning. I am a terrible liar. And being around Kurt slowed me down. I wasn't quick on my feet around him. So I told the truth.

"It's mine. I got really upset about that kid, you know? Like, I just found it really upsetting and actually so did all these other girls. And it's really practically, like, a school project, but I guess I went a little overboard. So weird, I know. Like, *so* weird. But I just, I just feel so bad for the family and it's so weird that he lived so close by and I guess I . . ." I talk too fast when I get nervous. But it didn't matter, because Kurt had already checked out. Where most people express emotions in their faces, Kurt did it in his muscles. I could craft an entire scientific study from the way he flexed or clenched or rippled.

He stopped returning my calls.

And that's it. That's why I went to therapy in the first place, 'cause Kurt was the first guy I had really cared about, and it was so sad to not be with him anymore. There's a picture of me and him somewhere, I think it's in my closet where I keep my notebooks, and on impulse, just beause he's suddenly on my mind, I go look for it. I find it and yeah, I guess I imagine Beck looking a lot like Kurt—muscles and not much hair—but I don't feel that swing of desire and hurt I used to feel when I looked at Kurt's photograph.

There's other stuff in the closet too. Envelopes with legal letters I don't want to think about right now. A yellow legal pad with messy notes about Kurt himself. And stuff from Lish and me growing up, just the kinds of old memories people keep around. Notes we passed back and forth during assembly. Cheesy school photographs with lame backgrounds. Stupid Bart Simpson Valentine's Day cards from my first crush, years before Kurt, the one whose name I want to forget. I wish I didn't remember that Jeff ever sent me a Valentine.

I give my thigh another wake-up pinch. And close the closet with a shiver of memories I don't want to have.

4.

WE'RE READING OUT OF A LAME ORANGE TEXT-
book and I can't stop thinking, like I do three times a week
when I am in this class, that Latin is not the "useful foundation" my mother and the school handbook claimed it would
be. It is not going to help me ace my SATs. It's not even a
spoken language anymore, so when we read paragraphs from
the textbook out loud, we sound like Latin robots. *"Vir est in
horto."* No stressed syllables. No inflections. Robots. Because
if I suddenly needed to speak to some Roman blast from the
past who showed up at Greenough Girls' Academy in a toga,
the first thing I'd want to tell him is a sentence just like that:
The man is in the garden.

I'm a ball of nerves and Lisha's sitting next to me, so she
puts a hand on my knee to stop my leg from jiggling.

Only the really big weirdos go to group therapy, I write
in the margins of her notebook. When Latin class is over, I'm
headed over to my first group session. She winces. Lisha is
not the kind of person who wants to write notes back and

forth in the middle of Latin class. Lisha is the kind of person who believes the school requirements pamphlet when it talks about Latin helping with your vocabulary skills. It is the true sign of friendship that she writes back: *Not true! It's not a big deal. Could be good.*

And I try to believe her, or at least believe nothing could be more painful or pointless than taking Latin for six years straight.

Lisha waits outside with me after class. She's got ballet class in an hour, which sounds a whole lot better than my afternoon plans. My mom's picking me up from school for the first time since I got my license, since she doesn't trust me to go to group therapy on my own. She thinks I'll skip out and go to the diner with Lisha instead, but I don't think I'm cool enough to pull that kind of rebellion off. Neither is Lisha. She's not the world's greatest dancer, but she takes it very, very seriously. When my mom pulls up, Lisha says to call her as soon as it's over and we kiss cheeks three times in a row, which used to be a joke about snooty French foreign exchange students but has turned into the actual way we say hello and good-bye.

Secretly, we both like the delicate femininity of the gesture. Like maybe we could be that elegant and sophisticated.

That feeling of fancy girlishness lasts for the ten-minute drive to therapy and then is torn out of me the second I see what group therapy looks like.

I end up in a room with a girl who has only patches of hair left on her scalp and three other twitchy-eyed, hand-wringing teenagers. I'd like to think I stand out as *too normal* here. At least that's what I was going for when I got dressed this morning. No vintage today. I borrowed Lisha's J.Crew sweater set and my mom's nice leather boots and my hair is smoothed and straightened but not too perfect. Navy nail polish scrubbed off and replaced with clear late last night.

As long as I can keep myself from saying anything truly idiotic, maybe I'll get out of group therapy after a few weeks.

"Ah! Bea!" Dr. Pat says, effectively breaking the silence that inevitably follows someone new entering the scene. The room isn't nearly as nice as her office, but her office would be too cramped for even a small group.

"Hi, Dr. Pat."

"Come meet the group. This is Jenny, Rudy, Fawn, and Beck."

Beck. I'm shaking on the inside now, but the outside of me, the important part, is calm. I look immediately at Beck's hands. They are cracked and dry. They are large and sure. I wouldn't mind holding them again.

It's him. The same Beck from the dance. And from the jump in his shoulders he knows it's me.

I nod my head (no shaking hands or other physical contact—the rules were laid out to me very specifically by Dr. Pat). I repeat the names in my head because I hate the lost feeling of a forgotten name, especially of people I have to tell my deepest darkest secrets to. *Jenny: no hair; Rudy: picks his face; Fawn: tapping fingers; Beck: good kisser.* "Hi, guys," I say, and they all nod and sputter in response and I mean, come *on,* I am so in the wrong group. I am wearing cashmere. I dated a football player. I'm just a little nervous and sad sometimes. I should be in a group of nice girls with tiny problems and pretty hair. Or, you know, any hair at all. Dr. Pat's got her Don't Worry Smile on and Beck is shaking his head a little, so I guess I'm not supposed to acknowledge that we met in the dark a week ago.

I'm not big on astrology or fate or God or any of those kinds of things, but it's just full-on weird to meet Beck again and in this context. I'd call it a coincidence and Lisha would probably say it's destiny, but really it's just probability and statistics, plain and simple. There aren't *that* many therapists in the suburbs of Boston for kids with anxiety disorders, and the whole reason I approached Beck to begin with was because I recognized the fast-breathing sound of a panic attack. So. Here we are. Math at work. Amazing.

"We left off last week with Jenny talking about how she feels when she looks in the mirror," Dr. Pat says.

Like shit, I'd imagine. Her head is a patchwork of bald spots.

I nod too enthusiastically and smile at Jenny. "Have you ever considered just shaving it all off?" I can't trap the words before they come out. If I didn't know better, I'd think I suffer from some sort of Tourette's-autism hybrid, but Dr. Pat insists I can control the impulse to say whatever pops into my head. That it's, like, a defensive mechanism, not a biological imperative. Therapists think everything is a defense mechanism. Just my thinking that in my head, right now, is a defense mechanism.

Now they're all looking at me. Fawn, Rudy, and Jenny have varying degrees of wide-eyed defensiveness. Beck is hiding his mouth and I can't tell for sure, but I think maybe he is stifling a giggle.

"I don't know why I can't stop pulling my hair out," Jenny says. She rubs her head and I think she's trying to pull a piece of hair out even here, even now. "It feels good in the moment. And then . . . this." She gestures to her head, to the weak roots, the sad attempts to cover up the bald spots.

There is absolutely no way I am as fucked up as Jenny. If I start talking through my little anxieties about driving and missing my ex-boyfriend, these people will feel approximately a thousand times worse about themselves. Actually, Dr. Pat is putting them in harm's way by having me here.

Beck is doing exactly what I'm doing: looking at Jenny's knees and lap instead of at her head. But he's also tapping his thigh with really quick jabs and looking a little breathless.

"Dr. Pat, could we talk in private for a—" I try, pitching my voice high and sweet, superpolite.

"Bea? Would you like to talk about your self-image?" She knows I don't, but she also knows I *will*. This is going to be a problem with group therapy. Dr. Pat knows enough about me to manipulate me into oversharing. What she doesn't know is how badly I want Beck to think I'm the almost-kinda-normal girl from the dance. "Or maybe you'd like to share why you're here? We can start there if you'd prefer." Like Dr. Pat recommends, I look at my physical surroundings to stop myself from launching into a stream of consciousness, truth-telling storm.

The floor is covered in a thin layer of dust and all our voices echo in the mostly empty multifunction room. The suburbs are filled with places like this: uninspired and vaguely sized. Ready to be used for graduation parties and AA meetings and Christmas pageants. I'm not entirely sure where we fit into that mix, but I'd guess it's somewhere between graduation and AA. Everyone looks a year or two away from college and a step or two crazier than your average alcoholic.

Except me. And Beck. And obviously Dr. Pat.

"I'd rather not talk right now, Dr. Pat," I say with a smile and a flip of my hair in Beck's general direction.

"We all share here," Jenny proclaims. She is that rare combination of pathetic and aggressive. I hate her immediately. They're all looking at me eagerly, even Beck, chomping at the bit to hear what makes me crazy. I've seen Beck afraid of the dark and I've felt his too-dry hands, so I think he wants to even the playing field or whatever. See why I'm in this room on this awkward metal folding chair, wondering why no one has fixed the wall clock so that it's not stuck indefinitely on 3:25.

"I . . . um . . . sometimes get anxious?" I say. I'm trying it out, to see if that little bit of information is enough. It's not. It's unnaturally hot in here. The only windows are at the top of the wall and probably won't ever get opened. "I don't know how to deal with my anxiety?" I'm just trying to not vomit out a bunch of personal information before Beck has another chance to kiss me. I know I'll lose him eventually when he gets a glimpse of my elaborate note-taking or my jumpy, sweaty driving style. So I'm just hoping for another kiss at this point.

There's a stream of sweat making its way down my spine.

Scab-faced Rudy makes a *tick-tick-tick* noise. Tongue flicking against his teeth and a little puff of breath behind it.

"I think everyone here knows what it's like to be dealing with a lot of anxiety. Why don't you talk about how that anxiety relates to how you see yourself?" Therapists. Always asking the same questions over and over in slightly different ways. They are, like, the Ultimate Thesauruses.

"Uh. I don't know that it's connected to my self-image." They all glare at me. But I'm not lying; I actually like the way my curves surprise my petite frame, the tininess of my waist, the way my hair hangs in brown ringlets like I'm a tap-dancing pageant girl instead of kinda-crazy Bea. I like being smaller than everyone else and always looking up into people's eyes instead of straight ahead. Wispy, ironic bangs. I like the length of my torso: too long for my body. Or I *did* like all those things until I saw Sylvia with Austin and imagined what it would be like to have her life instead.

Rudy pops a zit on his neck. He doesn't wince, but I do.

"I think all of us here sometimes feel unsure about ourselves," Dr. Pat says. It seems dangerously close to breaking the doctor-patient confidentiality code, but I wouldn't be doing myself any favors by pointing that out.

Then my mind is thrumming with the image of Sylvia and the way she held Austin's arm even after the huge fight they obviously had in Dr. Pat's office. I swallow down that thought and grind my teeth so that I don't say it out loud. But there's something in that. Not jealousy. Not desire. But interest.

Followed immediately by the desire to protect them. I don't want to tell a group of strangers about Austin and Sylvia. It feels dangerous, for me and for them, and clamping down on the information, keeping it a secret, sets off a delicious wave of calm in my body. I take a nice, full breath but immediately regret it. The place smells like purple dust and fearful boys who need more deodorant.

"Hello???" Rudy says, and moves his chair back with a huge, metal-against-linoleum screech. I'm so startled, the sound makes goosebumps pop up all over my arms and legs, and I know I have to say something, even if it's not *everything*.

"Sometimes I wish I was someone else," I say. The words have a different meaning for Jenny than they do for me, I think. I just want the drama of Sylvia's Playboy Bunny looks. Or a half second in her skin. "There's this woman I see around"—I have got to keep this revelation as small and normal sounding as possible—"she's glamorous, in a California kind of way. In a swimsuit-model way. I think about what it would be like to live her life. To be as stand-out as she is, to be as substantial. I mean, she can't be denied. She is *there*." I dig my fingernails into the palm of my hand to shut myself up. It works, the same way the wake-up pinch on my thigh seems to be working, and I halt the whole sentence just like that. Fold my lips in on each other. Shrug. Look at Beck.

I don't have any crazy skin or hair-destroying habits, but there must be something in my face, too, that has the look of not-right-ness. I pray, pray, pray that this is enough of a confession for Dr. Pat. And then I wait for what I really want: some kind of confession from Beck. It'd be good to know just how messed up he is, if I'm going to have any kind of crush on him.

"And what kind of compulsions does that thought pattern lead to?" Dr. Pat says. I've never heard her use the word "compulsions" before, and her mouth slows down over the syllables. Her eyes meet mine, her huge glasses finally framing her eyes rather than slipping to the tip of her nose. Fawn has darting eyes and seems to be listening extra hard. A sure sign that she's a virgin. As in a therapy virgin. Rudy on the other hand has probably been doing this since birth. He can't stop his foot from tapping, counting out the seconds until he can get out of here. He *tick-tick-ticks* again, tongue against teeth. He's the kind of guy that can make you feel like you're in a mental institution, not just a Wednesday afternoon processing group.

It's only Beck that I can't read at all. He's more like me: somewhere in between broken and whole. Not desperate exactly, but caught in a cycle that he can't get out of. Probably he thinks he's okay, but his parents are annoyed with how much hand soap he goes through in a week. Or something. I'm just guessing here.

"Bea? I asked you about your thought patterns?" Dr. Pat has an agenda. I'm supposed to own up to something, but I'm not sure what it is. I take notes. I drive carefully. I'm a little nervous sometimes. I know what it feels like to lose your breath from thinking too hard, but none of that is noteworthy in this context. Jenny reaches her hand to the back of her head and her fingers crawl all over her scalp. She stares at her lap and has the focus of a dog sniffing around, searching for a treat.

"I'm feeling private today," I say at last. And it's not a lie. That *is* how I'm feeling. I don't care how doubtful Dr. Pat looks. I'm not going to let her pigeonhole me in this group of crazies. I have anxiety issues. Not exactly unusual. Or a big deal, even.

Beck swallows down a little laugh. I don't think it's ever occurred to him to stand up to Dr. Pat, if the blush on his face is any indication. Beck's even cuter than I would have guessed after our interaction in the dark: hair buzzed so short that there is only a fuzz of black on his head. Huge blue eyes. Not tall, but all muscle, every last inch of him thick and hard. Dude works out. That much is for sure.

"I think it's good for us all to think about how our thoughts create compulsions in our bodies," Dr. Pat says. There's that word again, and the slow-down of speech that accompanies it. She overuses her mouth when she says it, the way you might speak to a toddler. *Com-pul-shun.*

Dr. Pat's looking right at me, so I nod and smile and say "okay" in that very polite way girls from New England are taught to do. A pocket of anxiety opens up in my chest, so I try to cover the space with the palm of my hand. If only I could reach in there and button it up for real.

Instead, I take deep breaths and look out the window at the way the leaves are blowing off the trees: furiously spinning around each other, giving in to the wind instead of fighting against it.

The fall in Boston is beautiful. It's all orange sunsets and leaves under your sneakers and football fields of handsome boys and the anticipation of Thanksgiving dinner. At least that's what it is for me. Inhale. Exhale. Inhale. Exhale.

"That's some good, calming breath," Dr. Pat says, and I jump. I thought my moment was over, so I'd stopped looking at myself from the outside in. The hypnotic power of dry leaves speeding along in the dry, dry wind. Five pairs of eyes observe me with interest.

"Ha, sorry, I spaced out," I say in the lightest voice I can manage. I'm not lying, but it feels like a lie in my mouth. I really *was* just spacing out. "I like the fall. And, you know, long day at school." I smile in Beck's direction, like this is some opportunity to flirt. His smile meets mine but I can't take more than a half moment of eye contact. There's blushing and awkwardness and a slide in my throat, like words might slip out without appropriate notification.

If Dr. Pat can tell, she doesn't show it. It seems impossible that someone could miss the zap of heat and fear between us, though.

"Well, we all expect more from you in the coming weeks. More sharing. More willingness to dig deep. Right, everyone?" Nods all around.

"Beck, why don't you tell us a little about yourself."

"Well, uh, I had my first panic attack last week." Those blue eyes are on me. It hurts, how oceanic they are. How much of his face they take up. The stark contrast between his pale face, shaved head, and bright, bright eyes. He is a lot to take in at once. I can't keep a cough from escaping.

"Your *first* panic attack? You've only had *one?* Then what the hell are you doing here?" Rudy says, exploding from his chair. His face is red, and not just from the scabbing of whatever it is he has been picking off of it. He is a flushed color with spider-bite-like red blotches popping up in the worst spots: forehead, cheeks, chin, neck.

"Rudy, when it's your turn I'll let you know." Dr. Pat never talks to me with any sort of harshness in her voice, but it's there when she speaks to Rudy. A kind of impatience I didn't think therapists were allowed to have.

"Hey, one of those panic attacks is enough for me," Beck says. "I mean the other night was scary. And I guess it made me realize I have these things I like to do. Like Dr. Pat was saying. Compulsions, I guess. I sort of like to wash my hands. My parents say I go to the gym too much. I don't know. Those both seem like good things to do. Healthy things. But . . . when I couldn't do them the other night, I felt so horrible that I had that panic attack thing." Beck closes his eyes as soon as he's gotten all the words out. He's perfect-bodied but has a look of shame on his face like we're all judging him. Meanwhile, I doubt anyone else here has ever even been inside a gym. That's the thing about anxiety: It's a real time suck.

When Beck opens his eyes, we get caught in prolonged eye contact and I start to smile again, because there's something just so attractive about a hot guy with muscles getting all vulnerable. Like the way women think it's hot when men play with puppies or babies. The corners of my lips can't seem to help themselves from lifting around him.

That's when Jenny starts pulling out her hair more aggressively. It's the worst thing I've ever seen: worse than the time I saw my mother's broken ankle all distorted and backward; worse than Rudy's cratered face or the flaky, dry patches of skin in between Beck's fingers. I wince with every tug and Jenny lays each little hair on her thigh before Dr. Pat pulls her chair right up to Jenny's. She holds Jenny's hands and maintains steady eye contact while the rest of us try to politely look away. They sit like that for a few minutes: Dr. Pat and Jenny, knee to knee.

I've never sat that close to Dr. Pat. I tell her everything and she keeps her distance, watching me from her perch on her armchair. The sight of Jenny's strands of pulled hair lined up with the ridges of her corduroys gives my insides a painful squeeze and the Fear I Can't Name blossoms in my chest.

Beck must notice something giving way in my face. Beause before I know it he's sitting in the empty chair next to me and putting his hand on my forehead.

"No touching," Dr. Pat says, because she has the ability to look at five places at once. She may be sitting with Jenny and calming her down, but we're all still under her watch. Rudy sighs and Beck settles back into the seat reluctantly. I liked his hand on my forehead, and the second it's gone the little panic spikes into something bigger. Then a bunch of immediate needs spring into action and start tapping on my brain to get me to pay attention to them. The desire to get out my notebook. The desire to see Austin's face again. To listen in on family secrets of strangers. Then the memories start to invade too. The memory of Kurt's face when he saw that notebook of newspaper clippings. The memory of being twelve and having a monstrous crush on skateboarding Jeff. It's the thought of Jeff, above all else, that causes the persistent desire to keep my hands and mind so busy that I can't think anymore.

Com-pul-shun, I hear Dr. Pat saying in my head, a diagnosis I refuse to listen to.

So then Beck and I are just sitting next to each other not touching, and that is charged too. Beck's eyes are mockingly blue, that's what I've decided after giving it more thought. I have blue eyes too, but mine are more of an impression of a color whereas his are the purest shade, the blue that comes to mind when you hear the word. He's sort of smiling and I think it's because we're both thinking about how totally ridiculous this situation is. How we are little beacons of normal in a room full of crazy.

We're saying all of that (I think) without saying a word.

And there is the thickness of his neck and the way his shoulders reach so far past mine they could be a brick wall.

I don't know that I've ever held eye contact with someone for this long. Especially not a guy who looks like Beck. And the longer it goes on the more blissful it is, until it shifts into being funny. Dr. Pat and Jenny are deep in a breathing exercise while Rudy and Fawn wait it out in silence. But without warning Beck and I are biting our lips to keep in the laughter and then letting it sputter out in gasping laughs and squeezed-out tears. I've wrapped an arm around my stomach to help hold it in and Beck is clamping his palm over his mouth and shaking instead of guffawing.

"Feelings manifest in all different ways," Dr. Pat says with a heavy glance at me and Beck. She can't get us in trouble for emoting but she also doesn't want to promote that kind of behavior. "But we're all here to support each other. I'm sure Jenny could use a little more emotional support, Bea. Beck. Just be present for everyone else in the group, okay?"

"I'm sorry," Beck says, and he sounds like he means it. I feel bad then too, because I really wasn't laughing at Jenny; I was laughing at being in this room with Beck. "It's cool," he keeps going, eyes right on Jenny and hers on him. "You're cool. The way you tell us everything. The way you show up and don't hide . . . anything." Jenny's eyes sparkle from attention. If I could, I'd say something like what Beck said, but I can't come up with the right things. So I nod really vigorously to show how much I agree. "This shit sucks," Beck concludes. His neck bulges a little on the word "shit."

A tiny bubble of tension releases in the room. It's slight. It doesn't change too much. But Dr. Pat tilts her head and smiles at Beck, and the rest of the session feels like a cafeteria conversation. Jenny giggles and Rudy leans forward and looks at everyone when they're talking. Fawn shifts in her seat and yawns.

It's not so bad.

Beck and I do an awkward dance at the end of the session. Not really speaking but not really avoiding each other either. We make eye contact and open our mouths like little fish and walk a few paces apart toward our cars.

I turn away from the way he looks: hand tapping on thigh, half a dimple peeking through from the beginning of a smile, licking lips like he's recalling the kiss from the other night. He gives a little wave even though I'm mostly just looking at the pavement. I wiggle my fingers back at him and let myself look up into his eyes for one half second before getting into my car. I have to wait for him to leave first. I'm not the best driver, and I don't want him to know that yet. Plus, I don't want to nick his car or, worse, his body.

Once he's out of view, crummy SUV shooting down the road, I can start my own engine and drive the few miles home at a snail's pace. If I could drive faster, I would.

I'm here, I text to Lisha. My car found its way to her driveway instead of my own. *Cooter and I made orange mac n cheez, come on in,* she texts back, like it's too hard to come outside and tell me. Lisha's family doesn't lock their doors.

My family didn't used to either, but really that's just not safe.

Lish and her brother, Cooter, are on the couch and *Law &*
Order: SVU is just starting up on the TV in front of them. Even
the music arrests me, that opening *shoock-shoock* noise that
says, *Something terrible is about to happen.*

"If you want some delicious orange food, you're gonna
have to let us watch what we like," Cooter says right away. His
dirty-socked feet are stretched out on the coffee table in front
of him, and he's eating out of a saucepan instead of a bowl.

"Shut up," Lisha says, and hands me the sad remains of
the Kraft Macaroni & Cheese clinging to the plastic mixing
bowl they use almost every night for just this purpose. "Grab
a fork and join us. She's *fine*, Cooter." This isn't totally true.
I hate the *Law & Order* franchise, but I'll grin and bear it if
it means Cooter starts thinking I'm cool again. I sit far away
from the television, at the little breakfast table in the corner
of the large family room.

Lisha raises her eyebrows and joins me at the table. She
takes the chair that faces the TV, and I face away from it,
and it is in this exact formation that we can both get what
we want. "Sorry, it's a good episode, but I swear I'm paying
attention to you," she says. I shrug and she doesn't push the
issue. She knows when to put something aside, which is what
I maybe love most about her. That and her love of Catholic school uniforms. She usually makes it a point to wear at
least one element (plaid skirt or knee-high socks or tight navy

blazer or starched white shirt or even just a little gold cross necklace) of a uniform every day. As far as Lisha's concerned this qualifies as gutsy fashion sense.

No one ever notices. But it makes her feel good, to have a little irony to her prep-school sensibilities. Even if it's our secret. Otherwise, she wears what everyone else at school is wearing and does what her parents tell her to do. Even right now she's in ill-fitting, laundry-day jeans and a turtleneck, but she's got a little vest over the ensemble, and the emblem over her heart tells me it's from St. Mary's School for Girls. Probably circa 1985, judging from the boxy shape and gold buttons.

Shoock-shoock, the television says, and Lisha turns her full attention to me.

"How's group therapy?" she asks, and my face must betray just how awkward my afternoon was, because she leans forward right away. "Oh my God, what? Are they all freaks?"

"You're not going to believe this," I say. I can barely believe it myself. "The Smith-Latin guy I made out with at the dance last weekend is in group therapy *with me*."

Lisha's mouth drops open. Cooter turns up the volume on the Jordan's Furniture commercial.

"I know," I continue. "What are the chances, right? It's basically the most humiliating situation possible."

"Oh my God," she says at last. "Oh my *God*. Okay. All right. So? What does he look like?" There's no mention of coincidence or fate or impossibility, 'cause she knows that would just make me crazy (excuse me, crazier). But I'm pretty sure she's going to consult the stars and the planets and her tarot cards or whatever to see what it means that I've come across Beck again so quickly.

I shrug. *Law & Order* has started back up, but Lisha's focus is on me. I try to block out the doctor's description of the autopsy results and the normal-looking guy who I already know is the killer.

"The Beck guy is cute," I say, when my shrug isn't enough.

"Oh my God, come *on*. Details."

"Yeah! Details!" Cooter says, imitating Lisha's semi-squeaky voice.

"Muscles. Shaved head. Typical Bea territory." I have a type and apparently it's so much a part of me that even in the dark I can find him. I know she's looking for details on his actual face, his smile and eyes. But he's still faceless, even after seeing him at therapy. I can't get beyond the darkness of the blacked-out gym, the strange nontime we spent together. Like a pause button had been pressed but we kept going.

"The bluest eyes I've ever seen. Stupidly, irritatingly blue," I say.

I pinch my thigh. Lisha doesn't notice. *I* barely notice. I mean, it's nothing.

"Did you guys talk? Are you gonna make out again? Do

45

you seriously not think this is the most romantic thing *ever*?" Lisha's practically panting for more information but I suddenly don't feel like talking about Beck. Every time the kiss replays in my head, my heart pounds out of control and my chest gets all constricted. I fill the space with a fork full of fake-cheesy goodness. Cooter didn't even mix the powder in all the way, so the bottom of the bowl is thick with the stuff. Pasty. Delicious.

"Dr. Pat's group therapy for crazy teens is not romantic, Lish," I say with a full mouth.

"You're just scared," Lish says. "That's what Dr. Pat will say when you tell her all the details." Lish has never met Dr. Pat, never seen her or talked to her or anything. But that little fact never stops her from feeling like she knows what Dr. Pat would think. With Lisha it's sometimes a little like some poorly constructed version of Dr. Pat is sitting at the table with us. I'm tired of Dr. Pat. Even fake Dr. Pat who is not here at all.

"Sure I'm scared, I made out with someone more messed up than me," I say. "I mean, he said it himself. He admitted that he's some freak." This isn't quite how it went, the night of the dance. I know that, but I'm not ready for Beck to have a face and a life. He's just some guy who washes his hands a lot and has amazing biceps and issues that I'll hear alllll about in group sessions. That's not the kind of guy I need to fall in love with. There's not gonna be any mystery there.

I like the other Beck too much to give him up. The one in my head. The one in the dark.

"You're not *that* messed up," Lisha says with a big, teasing smile. She knows I don't want to talk about it. I smile too, because when she teases me, it's almost like I'm just a little quirky, and not some total disaster.

Cooter scoffs. *Shoock-shoock*, the TV says. The normal-looking guy is on the stand, of course. He's sweating. He's guilty. People are so messed up. All of us, I mean. We're all so screwed up.

5.

DR. PAT WAITS UNTIL THE VERY END OF OUR SES-
sion to give me the pamphlets. She waits until I have discussed missing Kurt: It happens in waves, and there's nothing
I can do about it, since I'm not allowed to contact him. I have
about a dozen unsent e-mails in my drafts folder. Dr. Pat gives
me a strong warning not to send them, and says she'll have to
tell my parents about them. Legally speaking.

"What made you miss him this time?" she says. Dr. Pat
likes to find reasons for everything. Motivators.

"I don't know. I guess I was thinking about him on my way
home from Lisha's house last night. We watched this horrifying
SVU episode, and . . . I don't know. It didn't make me think of
Kurt or anything, it just upset me, and when I'm upset about
one thing I'm sort of upset about everything, you know?"

She nods her head as I talk. "What was so upsetting about
the episode?"

"The criminal—the rapist guy—he looked like a dad,
you know? He looked like a golf-playing, tie-wearing dad."

"Did he remind you of your dad?" she asks, totally missing the point.

"No, he didn't remind me of anyone. I just think we're all really capable of scary stuff, you know? I mean, even me. Who knows, right?"

"Well, no, not right. We know you aren't capable of anything truly terrible," Dr. Pat says, but she's taking notes at breakneck pace.

"We don't know that. Read the paper, right? They're always surprised when a little kid or a nice old woman or a pretty girl does something awful. They always say they seemed *so nice*."

I'm thinking about that kid Reggie again, the one we discussed in my current events class. I'm thinking about the way his eyelashes were long and that the picture in the paper had him wearing a blue button-down shirt, and that his chin had a little dimple on it. I open my mouth to recount the harrowing story of Reggie, but Dr. Pat's heard it before, and she interrupts since we're almost out of time.

"I want you to look these over," she says. "I just want you to let me know if anything in there resonates. We can talk about it here, or in group if that's comfortable."

"I won't want to talk about it in group," I say. I smile with the words. Dr. Pat and I sometimes joke around, and I love when her smile reaches all the way to her eyes and for a moment I can pretend we are friends.

This time Dr. Pat doesn't smile. She cocks her head to the side and puts the pamphlets in my lap, since I haven't reached for them.

Obsessive-Compulsive Disorder: Managing Your Compulsions, Living Your Life.

I giggle.

It is the worst response. But then I can't stop giggling. It's not funny at all, but the laughs are coming from deep inside my stomach and I can't seem to control the waves. My eyes tear up, and I'm afraid I might do that thing where you laugh and cry at the same time, because strong emotions are all so close to each other that sometimes your body gets confused.

The other pamphlets are more of the same, and just when I think I've gotten the laughter under control, it bubbles up again. Sputters to the surface, so that even when I clamp my mouth shut against it, a little spit and giggle burst through my lips. Hot.

"I'm guessing you're uncomfortable," Dr. Pat says when I have taken a few deep breaths successfully and the giggles have subsided into me just shaking my head and scrunching my nose.

"Um, I'm mostly confused. You think I have OCD? Like, the hand-washing disease? Have you seen my room? Or, like, my general hygiene? I don't even floss." Today I am wearing secondhand huge bell-bottom jeans and a secondhand flannel shirt and (even though I know it is the big taboo) secondhand *shoes*: brown platform boots that are fit for someone else's feet. With every step I am more and more aware of the previous owner. These are not the actions of someone with OCD.

"OCD is really just a type of anxiety," Dr. Pat says. She slides forward in her seat, the signal she uses week after week to alert me that it is time for me to hand over my mom's check. "And it shows up in lots of different ways. Some of the things your mother and I talked about, and some of the little behaviors I've noticed in you myself—"

"A *lot* of people get nervous driving," I interrupt.

"I know it sounds really scary, but it could actually be great for us to put a name to some of your behaviors and fears, don't you think?"

"I don't—"

"I think you'll feel better after you read some of that information," Dr. Pat goes on, speaking over my small-voiced reaction. "I know I'm throwing a lot at you, but I think it's best if you process this alone and then we chat in group about it, okay?" This must be some lesson she learned at therapist school, so I just nod and smile and grip the pamphlets with a violent force I always suspected I had.

On my way out the door I catch sight of Sylvia and Austin heading in. I usually only see them before my Wednesday session, but maybe they've added a second session this week too. Given the decibel at which they yell at each other in there, I wouldn't be surprised.

I grin at the sight of them. Just what I needed. My chest is tight from my session and the car ride ahead of me, but the *clack* of Austin's cowboy boots on the linoleum gives me a shot of relief. And I know I need more where that came from.

My car feels exceptionally small. I turn it on, knowing I'm not leaving the parking lot anytime soon. But I need the heat and the radio tuned to Oldies 103.3 and the saving grace that is "My Girl" playing at full volume.

I read through the pamphlets. But that is not why I wait in the car in the parking lot for an extra hour after my session. Here's what I learn in pamphlet number two, *Your Brain and Your OCD*: Apparently, obsession and anxiety go hand in hand. OCD has gotten a bad rap, but is totally workable. A person with OCD has to face anxiety head on. Compulsions are just a way of delaying the inevitable rush of feeling and fear.

These are the kinds of things people like Dr. Pat say to make you feel like OCD isn't a death sentence.

Austin and Sylvia don't hold hands on their way out of the building when their forty-five minutes are up. But their legs walk in time with each other, spider-long limbs striding across the pavement in record time. Sylvia drives and Austin sits in the passenger's seat, a fact that I sort of secretly love. I write it down in the pink notebook with the star on the cover. Scribble it out, because they zip away fast and I have to follow closely, without crossing the speed limit.

I have one of those innocuous cars that is just the right shade of dusty navy blue to blend in with the pavement or the sky or streets full of other similarly blue cars. There aren't scars of abuse on its surface but it's also never newly shiny and clean. It's like me: not all used up and dirty but not exactly beautiful either. Nice *enough*. Normal *enough*. Pretty *enough*.

But I love the thing anyway, and not just because it gets me around. I have Mardi Gras beads from a great New Year's Eve out in Boston with Lisha hanging from the rearview mirror. Gold and green, my favorite colors, clanging against each other as I drive. The rest of them are in Lisha's car, hanging from her mirror. We decided they're good luck, though so far nothing too exciting has happened in either of our cars. Besides, I think Lisha just being in my life is good luck. Really.

I keep a minilibrary of my favorite books in the backseat, just in case I'm caught without anything to do, or if Lisha's running late to meet me. There's a hardcover of poems by Mary Oliver, this poet who writes about nature. It was a gift. To be honest it's something Kurt owned and gave to me a few weeks before he dumped me. The spine is broken so it automatically opens up to his favorite poems. I try not to think too much about why they were his favorites. And more books too: old-school favorites like Judy Blume. *The Fountainhead*, which is my favorite book of all time. I can open any of them up to any page and get lost for twenty minutes or an hour, depending on what the situation requires. Add a couple of blankets, and my car would be just as fantastic as my bedroom.

It's not a short drive to where they live. We make our way through crowded rush hour traffic from the suburbs into the city. I have to drive fast to keep up with their zippy VW, so my heart's pounding. I hate driving fast. I try to be a hawk, watching for pedestrians and oncoming traffic with the full knowledge that if I'm not careful, I could hurt someone. I find that if I blink my headlights in warning every so often I can deal with the windier roads, the merges, the heart-pounding intersections. So that's what I do, all the way from Lexington to a high-rise on the waterfront. We are somewhere between the old-school Italian charm of the North End and the tourist trap that is Faneuil Hall. I pull over across the street. Austin and Sylvia park somewhere around the block but quickly get back to the entrance of their urban palace. It is all windows, all silver and mirrored facades. It's not the kind of place where people actually live, not really, and maybe that's why they're so miserable that they have to go to therapy multiple times a week like me.

How could you live somewhere so icy cold and imposing, so clearly in conflict with the rest of the city, the rest of the human population, and stay in love? As far as I can tell, love takes place in townhouses and cozy cottages and cramped studio apartments and rundown guest houses. This place might as well be an office building or a spaceship.

Austin clasps the doorman's shoulder on his way in. Sylvia doesn't make eye contact and there's no hesitation when she enters. Nowhere else she wants to be but in her glass apartment high above anything resembling real, feeling, troubling, exhilarating *life*.

I'd be lying if I said I didn't get that.

Maybe I don't need to try on her skin to get how she feels after all.

I stay in my car. I don't drive away immediately because I don't want to see Austin and Sylvia's building vanishing in my rearview mirror. I stay because I'm holding out for the possibility that Austin has forgotten something important in his car and will run back out and I'll get a final glimpse of his string-bean body and the way his feet pound clownishly against the pavement.

I'm half right.

It is not Austin who appears a few minutes later back on the pavement, but Sylvia. She has changed her coat to something warm and full of down and has added a ridiculous Russian fur hat to her ensemble. It's cooled down, even inside the car. I've turned it off to distract from my strange waiting game and though the windows are zipped up tight there's no real fight against the last puffs of winter.

Sylvia leans against their building, and like some old-school movie star she has a cigarette case and a silver lighter and an air of certainty about her importance in the world.

She matters. Watching her is like watching a dancer, but it's not enough, the just-watching, and I get tired of the way her hand with the cigarette in it finds her mouth over and over and over without hitching on her jacket or stopping to consider lung cancer or even just missing its mark. She's a painting and a work of art and a person I wish I could be. But the calm I get from seeing her is short-lived. My mind keeps returning to those pamphlets from Dr. Pat that lie, partly crumpled, on the seat beside me.

Or maybe it's Austin who is the real pull.

He reminds me of someone else. Like another guy I used to like who had the same skinny unkempt-ness, the same ironic T-shirts. It makes my heart swing in my chest. He's not my usual type, I guess, but he does look like that guy Jeff. The first kiss one. The one I don't like to think about. Cooter's old best friend. I push the thought away. The memory of a first kiss sticks to your heart pretty ferociously; I think that's true for everyone, but especially me.

I make my heart stop swinging with a deep breath like Dr. Pat told me to do. I put a good strong wall up around that thought and decide not to go near it again.

Sylvia takes another drag on her cigarette and checks her watch. Doesn't look expectantly at the door to her building, so I don't think Austin's going to suddenly appear.

Then that's it, and as impulsively as I decided to follow them here, I decide to leave again. It's a long drive back when you can't go much faster than thirty miles an hour, and I'm supposed to meet Lisha at our favorite diner for french fries and gossip. I will try not to tell her about my weird little drive to this mysterious couple's building, but Lisha has one of those really nice faces that makes you want to talk. And the girl always says the right thing, or knows when to say nothing at all. I'm an open book anyway, and Lisha is a voracious effing reader.

I go thirty-two miles an hour the whole way to the diner. I consider those extra two miles an hour a tiny victory. Even so, I'm about an hour late, so Lisha's already at the Pancake House when I get there, still in her tights and leotard, hair matted to her forehead and knotted into a high bun, prickly with bobby pins. She's set up with hot chocolate and half-eaten waffles and a plate of french fries drenched in mustard and tabasco sauce that she's been picking at, hopefully not for too long. Lisha's caught up in her love affair with Russian fiction, though, and she holds up a finger when I sit down, telling me she's got to finish the sentence or chapter but hopefully not the whole book before she can focus on me.

"You know you're the latest you've ever been, right? Do we need an intervention?" she says when she finally looks up at me and bookmarks *Crime and Punishment*. I've told her to give up and finally read *The Fountainhead*, but she's determined. About everything. Always has been.

The waiters know to bring me hot chocolate too, and a fork to help Lisha finish up her binge.

"I think I already had one with Dr. Pat."

"So what's the conclusion? Are you crazy?" Lisha says. We don't talk in vague metaphors or evasive questions like the rest of the world. We tell it like it is and add on a healthy dose of self-deprecation if things are particularly shitty.

"Dr. Pat thinks I am. But that, you know, it's no big deal and I shouldn't let it affect my life or whatever." I don't say the word "OCD," because Dr. Pat didn't actually say that's what my problem is, and besides, I can't quite get that terminology out of my mouth. I'm not ready for the *I'm Bea and I have OCD* moment.

I reach into my bag and find pamphlet number three, *Where Anxiety Meets Compulsion: Cognitive Behavioral Therapy and Obsessions.* I slide it across the table and get lost in a waffle instead of looking at Lisha's face.

"Ah," Lisha says after a pause.

"Yeah." I take the biggest possible bite of waffle, and before swallowing, follow it up with three French fries.

"Well, listen. Don't let her lock you up," Lisha says with a grin. She is the only person I let talk to me this way.

"On a scale from one to ten, how weird am I? Be honest. 'Cause I thought I was rocking, like, a four, but I feel like Dr. Pat giving me these brochure things lifts me to at least a six, right?"

"I love you too much to rate you," Lisha says carefully. "I mean, aside from in hotness. In hotness you are a totally solid 8.5 and if you showed off your legs instead of hiding them in those weird hippie pants you'd be a nine for sure." I can't help smiling.

"My legs are stumps," I say, and stuff down a few more fries. Lisha keeps sticking her fingers in her mouth to suck off the stickiness of syrup. Part childish, part sexual. I want to pull the fingers out of her mouth and set them in her lap. She's not a lost cause, exactly, but she loses track of her hands, her words, her facial expressions too easily and it's gotta be at least part of the reason she's still never kissed a guy.

"That guy Beck likes them though," Lisha says, and kicks me under the table.

"Uh, that guy Beck has never seen my legs. *Will* never see my legs." I purse my lips and swallow, because actually I'm not so sure I want that to be true.

"Is he hot? I feel like you're holding back details."

"He looks like Kurt," I say, before I can stop myself. I clear my throat and go in for more waffle, but we have impressively demolished the plate. "I mean, he doesn't really. Just like, body type. Or whatever. Not even. Whatever."

"God, Kurt," Lisha says. "I never think about him anymore." We make eye contact over the empty plates and even emptier coffee mugs. I am supposed to say I never think about him either.

"Yeah," I squeak out. It's not a lie if I just nod my head and say "yeah" a lot. But Lisha's not letting it go. She wants to know, for sure, that I do not think about Kurt anymore. Ever. She raises her eyebrows, waiting for me to say more. When I don't, she fidgets in her seat.

"I mean, you don't talk to him or anything right? Or, like, *see* him?"

"Of course I don't see him. You know I can't see him," I say. Lisha nods too enthusiastically. "I don't know why I even mentioned his name." That thing in my chest grips and without thinking, I pinch my thigh.

Is that a compulsion?

I move my hand under my thigh, sit on it in what I hope is a supremely not-obvious way, and beg Lish with my eyes to change the subject. Lisha knows the look well—we have perfected it, in fact—and she waves her hand like we're going to just erase the last few minutes of conversation.

"Dessert?" she says.

"Ice cream?" I say. Ice cream is safe, and soft and cool. Numbing.

"I'm all over it," Lish says. Her hand motions for the waiter, but her eyes stay on me just a moment longer than they should. I have the impulse to cover myself in makeup—liquid foundation and dark eyeliner and the kind of mascara that glitters. Anything to hide whatever it is she sees on my face. But when I excuse myself to go to the bathroom, I only apply a fine layer of bronzer and ruby-red lip gloss. I don't want to look too long in the mirror, don't want to see what a teenage girl with OCD might look like. But I'm not ready to go back out to the clanging utensils and speed-talking wait-staff either. So I reach into my purse for something even better: my pink notebook. Reread notes from Austin and Sylvia's sessions. Record Sylvia's outfit from earlier today. With every curve of my pen I get some relief, and in a few moments I have a clear head and a not-shaking heart and the belief that everything will be fine: for me, for Kurt, for Austin and Sylvia, for Beck.

Lisha and I split a bowl of chocolate ice cream. The OCD pamphlet sits on the table between us. I guess I forgot to put it back in my bag earlier, and I can't stand to look at it anymore, so we just leave it there. Keep it on the table, like the world's worst tip. But carrying it around will condemn me even more.

I drive home slowly and watch for kids and puppies and the elderly and sharp turns. I just don't want to hurt anyone.

6.

SATURDAY AFTERNOON GROUP THERAPY. DR. PAT said after yesterday's session that if I come to group twice a week I only have to see her once a week, on Wednesdays. The room is just as stuffy as it was Tuesday afternoon, and we're all focused on Jenny again. She's lost even more hair and if I'm not mistaken, she's also down a pale white eyebrow. Today she has to resist pulling out her hair during the session. That's what Dr. Pat has instructed, and it's about a million times harder for her than it sounds. Whenever anyone mentions their parents, in any context good or bad, she raises a hand to her head and we all have to snap at her to stop. Then she gasps for breath and we wait it out while Dr. Pat holds her hands.

Abused. I knew it.

Not that I don't feel for girls who have been abused. But I'm a little jealous of them too, because they know why they do what they do. They know what they're so scared of, what's made their mind such a weird maze of rules and terrors and nutty solutions to problems that can't really be solved. I'm so not that (un)lucky.

I tried saying that to Dr. Pat the other day and she said I may not have something as obvious as a decade of abuse, but that I have my own stories. My own traumas. I hate when she says that kind of thing. Makes me shiver.

Meanwhile, I've driven by Austin and Sylvia's apartment building twice since last night. I guess this is what my free time will be from now on: long drives back and forth from Lexington to Boston, stopping only to double- and triple-check that I haven't nicked any passersby with my car. Then I get to their building, stay for ten minutes just staring at the thing like some pervert.

According to the few pamphlets I did hang on to, these are compulsions. The checking when I'm driving, the checking on Austin and Sylvia, even that little pinch I keep giving my thigh from time to time (more often lately).

Dr. Pat asked me to come in a half hour early, so I'm already strung out on too much therapy.

"Do you have any questions?" she'd said. I had one thousand questions. But asking even one of them meant admitting I might be crazy.

"Is this, like, an official diagnosis?" I said. "I mean, are you saying I have OCD? Like, for sure?"

"I think you have both obsessions and compulsions, Bea," Dr. Pat said very, very carefully. She held her hands in her

lap like she was praying. "And they do seem to be related." I
don't think Dr. Pat has ever answered a question with just a
yes or no. It makes my head hurt. And I didn't intend to cry,
but my eyes welled up with fat tears and my hands shook with
the effort of holding it in.

My brain said: GO CHECK ON AUSTIN AND SYLVIA!

My brain said: WEAR MORE MAKEUP TO MAKE
YOU LOOK NORMAL!

"Are people with OCD dangerous?" I said, fixing my
mouth around the word "dangerous" with effort. It was hard
to ignore the blossom of thoughts in my head, but I felt sure
I could do it. I could be totally, one hundred percent normal.

"Do you need more reading material?" Dr. Pat said.

"Oh. I don't know. I guess? I just was worried . . ." I lost
the words in my mouth and shook my head.

"You're not dangerous," Dr. Pat said. "You're not crazy,
either, just in case that was your next question." And then
Dr. Pat smiled. Her teeth were whiter than usual, like she'd
just had work done on them, but otherwise her face was plain
and untouched. Trustworthy.

Then Beck came in, and Dr. Pat uncrossed and recrossed
her legs, signaling our time together was over and group had
begun.

Now Jenny's creating an earthquake with the force of her
shakes, and she has one hand in her hair. She hasn't pulled

anything out yet, but her palm rests on top of the largest bald spot, and I get the feeling the intensity of the shaking is in exact proportion to how hard resisting is.

"Can we move on?" Rudy says. He has been hiding his face in his hands. Watching Jenny hurts, but no one else would dare say something. Jenny's sobs get harder. She's skinny and her top is too tight, so I can practically see the fear and pain and tears rattling around in her lungs. "If Jenny needs this much help, maybe she should just be in individual therapy, you know?"

"Hey, man," Beck says quietly. "Not cool."

"Not *cool*?" Rudy is all scorn and his face is flaming with infection. "You've got a lot to learn, man."

"What do you mean by that, Rudy?" Dr. Pat says. I've noticed she uses our names a lot. Like, a *lot*. It starts sounding awkward and forced. I'm not used to hearing my name, or anyone else's, used in casual conversation over and over again. It should make me feel less likely to vanish, since it sort of validates my existence or whatever, but now that I realize how often she uses my name in this group, I sort of freak out and decide I have to pinch myself whenever she uses it to make sure that *Yes, I am Bea* and *Yes, I am here.* There's a bruise forming on my thigh. It seems like I just do this thigh-pinching thing a few times, but now that the skin is turning purple I might have to admit I'm doing it more than a little. Maybe almost a lot.

Good thing I'm not hooking up with anyone right now. Random black-and-blues don't do it for most guys.

Rudy makes a growling noise deep in his throat and touches his face. Just a quick touch, his hand practically bouncing off the skin the second it makes contact.

"I feel like Beck's judging me, you know? And this is supposed to be a safe space, I thought. So it's making me upset," Rudy says with a little smirk. He's one of those people who will use your own words against you.

"It needs to be safe for everyone, Rudy. Jenny has to feel safe. Beck has to feel safe. We all need to feel safe. Even me," Dr. Pat says. Rudy rolls his eyes and settles back in his chair. He stares down Beck and when Beck stares back, Rudy just starts picking at his face. He stops himself before Dr. Pat has a chance to call him on it.

"Bea? Fawn? How are you two doing today?" Dr. Pat says. We shrug in unison.

Beck and Rudy keep checking each other out from across the room and Jenny cries a lot and Fawn hides almost her entire face behind the fold of her turtleneck sweater.

It's a long hour.

I don't like to go home right after therapy, group or otherwise. In fact, I like to stay in the parking lot, right outside where the words were said. It's not a compulsion, exactly, it's just a way to let the adrenaline of *sharing* dissipate before reentering the real world. I keep a notebook in my car for just this purpose. A different notebook. Not the pink one, which I've reserved just for notes about Sylvia and Austin. This notebook is one of those mini pocket ones. It looks like an address book but I don't think people really have address books anymore, so now they just make itty-bitty blank notebooks. I sit on the hood of my car and watch Fawn and Rudy and Jenny all zip away, and I take notes on what just happened.

There aren't any cars left in the parking lot aside from Dr. Pat's big blue SUV. But I haven't seen Beck emerge from the building yet, so I list possibilities: he's getting picked up by someone, he lives close enough to walk, his car got stolen, he likes hitchhiking. I write it all down in the tiny notebook. Not just the facts of Beck's life, but also the possibilities, the little ideas I have about what his life might be.

I'm lost in the list-making (Beck has a bike stored somewhere, Beck is homeless, Beck has a girlfriend who is running late, Beck has a girlfriend who got into a car accident on her way here, I ran over Beck's girlfriend on my ride over and didn't notice), so I don't immediately see when Beck does finally emerge. I smile just at the sight of him. I blush, noticing the broadness of his shoulders. I want to lean against them, have them keep me steady. I shut my notebook like it's no big deal, but my knuckles go white gripping it closed.

"We meet again," Beck says. He's so clean it hurts.

"Hey. I'm glad we ran into each other. We never exchanged

numbers," I say. "I mean, after the dance. The other weekend."

"Numbers? Oh. Like, to hang out?"

"Or whatever." I shrug. A reflexive giggle escapes. I've flirted before, but never after therapy. "We could be therapy buddies."

"I'm only here 'cause of my parents," Beck says, not returning my sneaky grin. I was just trying to loosen the post-therapy mood with some of my Classic Bea Self-Deprecation but maybe Beck doesn't speak sarcasm.

"Dr. Pat's great," I try.

"I told my parents I'd put in a month."

I'm missing the vulnerable Beck I met at the dance. I pull my legs in, my knees to my chin, and the hood of my car gives a little under my shifting weight. Neither of us speaks. But he's not exactly walking away either. Then I remember the lack of car, the lack of anyone driving by to pick him up.

"Do you need a ride somewhere?" I say. Lisha will freak out at this story. Me and the mystery man from the Smith-Latin dance, posttherapy, flirting. Trying to. After Kurt dumped me, I said I wanted a guy with more problems than me so that he doesn't think I'm totally nuts. Except I guess according to Beck he's not *really* crazy. Maybe I should go for Rudy instead.

I take that back in my head, just in case thinking it some-how makes it true.

"Would you mind?" Beck says. "It's not far." He's looking

over his shoulder and I can't imagine what he's neurotically looking for until she pops into view: Dr. Pat. When he sees her, he gives her a quick wave and she smiles back, pleased, I think, at her patients' posttherapy bonding. "Wait for her to leave," Beck says, and he's staring at the pavement, at the wheels of my car. Like Dr. Pat cares if I give him a ride home. But I do what he says anyway, whatever it takes for a few moments alone in the car, hopefully with him relaxing a bit. He's like two different people—small and scared and sweet one moment and walled off and rude the next. But I have a feeling once we're in the Volvo listening to the National and watching the gas hover between full and mostly full (the only two options in my car), he'll be the sweet guy again.

I hope.

I'm hoping so hard, in fact, that I convince myself I can drive like a normal person for a few minutes, if it means seeing a little more of Beck. As long as he doesn't live too far away and there aren't any children or puppies running in the middle of the street, I should be okay.

Dr. Pat drives off with another wave, and as soon as she's out of sight Beck gets into my car. I slide off the hood and crawl into the driver's seat.

We wait for the car to heat up. He twists the hanging gold and green Mardi Gras beads around his fingers.

It's quiet, the waiting. Or we're quiet. But it's nice, sharing the same air, and we are both bundled up in coats and scarves and mittens and hats. My car's small enough that it's almost not awkward to share an armrest, which we do. Our big winter jackets touch but the sensation can't get through all the layers to travel to my actual arm.

"Your car fits you," Beck says.

"Oh God, I hope not," I say, but I look over to see if he's smiling or smirking. Dimples. Cartoon spark in his superhuman blue eyes. It's a compliment.

"No, it's cute. I like the way you are. I mean, your vibe. Your clothes and car and stuff," Beck says. I try to remember what's under all my winter layers: white leggings, short blue summer dress, thick white cardigan, fur vest to top it all off. "You're all, you know, cool-seeming," he concludes with an awkward, accidental squeak. I'm grinning like an idiot because there is nothing more charming than a boy tripping all over his words while trying to say something nice. I giggle, I mean literally *giggle*, and for maybe the first time ever feel lucky that it takes this long for my car to heat up in the winter.

Beck shakes his head and blushes hard.

"Don't be embarrassed! That was nice," I say. (Lisha's voice in my head: *People don't like when you point out their every emotion.* Lisha is the only person in the world who can give advice like that without it sounding mean.) "I mean, I like the way you are too." Then we both just stare at the dashboard or out the window and I think I can hear, or maybe just *feel* the way his heartbeat is keeping pace with mine: loud and stubborn and fast as hell.

He picks up the book of poems at his feet and flips through it. I try to forget that it was a gift from my ex, and that there are some notes about Kurt in there. In the margins. On the title page. On the back cover. The same kind of observations I sometimes write down about Austin and Sylvia. Nothing truly insane, but not the kind of thing I can explain quickly to Beck.

"That's not really mine," I say, a weird half lie that I can't explain. He sort of throws it out of his hands like he's done something wrong, and it could not be more awkward in here. Thank God he hasn't seen the other notebooks in the backseat: scrapbooks of newspaper articles, the pink starred notebook, the miniature one I just wrote about *him* in.

Then there's another sound interrupting our heartbeats. The heat turning on at last—a loud thunking and wobbling noise, the clicking and rustling like my vents are full of pebbles. The sounds my car makes are always vaguely discomforting.

"Is your car safe?" Beck says.

"Oh yeah. Just old."

"You know, its no big deal, I can totally just walk home." It's funny how quickly a particular energy can change because of stuff like noises or temperature shifts or a silence extending one second too long.

"It's a *Volvo*. It's totally safe." Beck nods. "Trust me. I'm pretty into safety. You'll see." It's an effort, his agreement to stay in the car despite its rickety state and my possibly-crazy-person status and the encroaching sexual tension.

Beck is sitting with such a straight back I wonder if he's, like, a ballerina or something in his spare time, but then I realize no, he's just in amazing shape and probably spends all his time on his body. He starts giving me directions, left here, right there. He is staring straight ahead but not holding on to the handle on the roof or anything. It's more like he's instructed his body to stay in place.

"You drive slow," he says.

"Didn't you learn defensive driving?" I try to smile through the sting of the observation.

"No, it's good. You're a good driver." Beck still isn't looking at me when he speaks, but I look at him. Take my eyes off the road to glance at the perfect profile of his face. My heart catches in my chest when I realize how dangerous that just was. I slow down two more miles per hour and Beck leans his head against the seat back, like he is relaxing for the first time in hours.

When we do our final turn we're pulling into a twenty-four-hour gym, not his own personal driveway.

"Oh," I say. If there's anything worse than enabling my own craziness, it's enabling someone else's.

"I live near here. Told my parents group therapy was three hours, not one. They're clueless." I nod, but I can't help the drop in my stomach. I thought we'd had a real *moment*, but maybe I'm just a way for him to go to the gym without getting in trouble. "Figured you'd understand . . . ," Beck says. I nod again because he's basically right. I'm already jumping five steps ahead of him to when I can do another drive-by of Austin's place. So I'm certainly not any better than him and probably would do the same thing, given the opportunity.

For instance, right now I'm considering bumming a cigarette from Sylvia in front of her building. You know, if she's around.

"Okay. I have to go in," Beck says. "I'd hang out if I could, though. I just gotta get in there."

Before the disappointment has a chance to seep in, my mind clicks back to the half second that I let my mind and eyes wander to Beck's face. We're in a residential neighborhood and there was a car accident on one of these roads two months ago and focus is the number one most important thing to have when driving defensively.

"Did you notice any kids earlier? When we were driving here?" I ask. But Beck's already opening the car door and there's an invisible, taut string between him and the gym. His fingers tap his thigh. "Sorry, sorry—go."

Beck's finger taps a few times again. Pauses. More tapping. Pause.

"Hey," I say, "I get it, okay?" Finally he looks my way. The shape of his eyes changes, a little squint of recognition narrowing the corners.

"You know," he says, giving me a sheepish grin before shutting the door, "we're the normal ones in that group, right?" His face comes a little closer to mine, and I can smell Dove soap and mint and fresh sweat. For a full six seconds I'm not thinking about anything but his eyes. "I mean, the girl with the hair?" he continues. "The guy with the scabs on his face?"

God, I hope so, I think. His eyes are their very own Crayola color. Does he know that?

I wonder if hanging out with Beck will maybe only make me crazier.

I wonder if these thoughts are, in and of themselves, driving me insane.

I pinch the delicate inside of my wrist.

"Sure, look at us!" I say with a grin. "Nothing too weird about us."

"Most people think I'm really healthy, you know? I mean, didn't cleaning up and staying in shape used to be good things?" This is the second time I've heard him make this exact argument. I catch sight of Beck's hands again and see they are not only dry from all the washing but also scraped up from the weightlifting. Ouch.

"You're kinda huge," I say. The words are itching in my throat. If I don't say what I'm thinking about I'll explode. "I mean, in a good way. Not a fat way or whatever. Just—do you think your biceps are bigger than your head?" I've done pretty well, up until now, in terms of not saying every single thought that comes into my head. But I'm taking him in, all of him, and I'm terrified of what will happen if I don't just say what I see in front of me. "Sorry," I say. And then: "Can I touch your arm?" Beck doesn't answer, so I think that's a no. Or, if I'm lucky, he thought I was kidding.

"I'm really not that big," Beck says. But he *is* and it's even more awkward when he's sitting there denying it. "There's way bigger guys in there."

"How many times a day do you work out?" I ask.

"At the gym?"

"Is there somewhere else you work out?"

"I mean, we have some weights at home. And I go running sometimes. Maybe three or four times a day total?"

I nod and try not to say it but: "That's a lot. A *lot*." And whatever spell we've been under that's kept him in my car falls apart. Was it really just a few minutes ago that we were giving in to little bursts of puppy love?

"Thanks for the lift," Beck says. "Can you, like, not mention it to Dr. Pat?"

I guess I knew he would say that. I could tell him how lying freaks me out, and that it seems unfair to lie about *his* weird habits when I don't even really let myself lie about mine. But instead I shrug. Which isn't a lie or a promise to lie, so it's okay. It's just a quick movement in my shoulders, almost like a shudder, like a quick chill of indecision. Beck nods and gets out of the car. He has a pocket-size notebook tucked into the back of his pants that I hadn't noticed until this moment. I'm dying to know what he writes in there. I like that he has it, that he keeps some sort of record, that he too remains accountable for the things that happen around him.

I smile and wave and he gives enough of a smile back that I think . . . *maybe.*

And that's it; he's gone.

I've got about a million missed calls from Lisha that I don't see until Beck is all the way inside the crazy-big gym. He's right about one thing: There are definitely guys much bigger than him strutting up to the doors, guys with arms so big they don't swing at their sides but hover almost parallel to the ground.

I don't want Beck to end up looking that way. I like his body now: the slightly off proportions of muscles to height. Meanwhile, if Austin were here, he'd stand out against the tightly wound wide bodies. His legs are skinny, his waist smaller than mine, his hair too floppy for a proper workout. For a split second I think I see Austin, but it's a soccer mom with a short haircut and no breasts.

It's a relief to drive away, back to the place on the road where I glanced at Beck. I pull over to take a quick look around, make sure nothing terrible happened while I was trying to reimagine the feel of Beck's lips on mine. No signs of catastrophe, so I take a moment to listen to my voice mail.

"Bea, it's Lish. Where are you? Are we meeting up?"

"Bea, it's Lish. What time is your group over? I'm thinking maybe we shouldn't go to that guy's house . . ."

I'm already regretting telling her I wanted to go to Austin's place tonight, but she'd asked what I was thinking, and it felt like my throat was swelling up when I didn't answer right away.

"Bea, it's Lish. My parents are being freaks. Did you see the Beck guy? Was it awkward?"

"Bea. It's Lish. Okay, we can go check out this guy's apartment, but it's on the record that I think it's kiiiiinda a bad idea."

I laugh, an awkward sound when you're alone on the side of the road.

I almost call back to tell her about Beck, but I can't figure out the right words to say. He used me to go to the gym. We're not even friends. We barely spoke. We are co-patients, and I'm, like, a chauffeur and an enabler. But that's it. There's nothing romantic in any of that.

Except, of course, for the way it feels to be around him. That part is romantic.

I get back in my car and wait a long, long time before getting back on the road. I hate merging, and there's a veritable parade of cars passing by. Cars with children in them. Cars driven by sweet little old grandmothers. My driving instructor always told me to trust myself, but the thing is . . . how?

So I sit there as the cars drive by one by one, and I savor the last few moments of total safety.

I breathe, like Dr. Pat tells me to do. I probably shouldn't spend any more time in the car today. But if I don't drive by Austin's place, he might vanish. Into thin air or a hospital or a foreign country, I'm not sure. I need to write something in my pink notebook and tomorrow is so far away, it might not ever happen.

If I don't check on Austin, *I* might vanish.

Poof.

♡ 7.

BECAUSE SHE'S CALLED SO MANY TIMES AND because I need to interact with a normal human being for at least a few minutes every day, I decide not to cancel on Lisha, and I drive to her house. She's that perfect kind of friend who's always home and available because she has no other friends.

Cooter is in the driveway shooting hoops. He makes me nervous; his face focusing on the hoop spurs the edge of a memory I don't want to think about. We used to play H-O-R-S-E out here: me, Cooter, Lisha, and Jeff. Jeff of the ratty Dr Pepper T-shirt and sneakers colored in with a Sharpie. Jeff with the shaggy, Austin-like hair and the lips that kissed with pressure, opening a little but not searching. Jeff, who was the first guy to call me pretty, and for all the wonder of that tiny moment, I get a gasp of bile in my mouth at the thought of him.

Jeff isn't around anymore. He's not dead or anything, but he's gone.

Cooter dribbles and passes the ball to me without warning. It hits me in the stomach, and I let out a hiccup of surprise.

"Look alive," he says with a smirk, and I know I'm supposed to grin back and push the ball into his chest and wave my arms in his face, which is the only part of defense I ever understood. I haven't touched a ball since Jeff left, and with my mouth open and the ball at my feet Cooter realizes his mistake. "You okay?" he says. Doesn't come to put a hand on my shoulder or anything, but looks like he really cares.

"Yeah, sorry, been awhile. Guess my athletic days are over," I say with the lamest laugh, the kind that is basically just an exhalation of breath. In trying to remember nothing, I remember everything: Jeff's long, skinny arms moving gracefully and his clown feet dancing around me. The flash of his neon-dyed hair making me flutter inside. The way he'd grab me by the waist when I'd get the ball, lifting me up to the basket, and the whooping as I made a slam dunk.

It hurts my heart, and my mouth goes dry at the memory. I pinch my thigh and let myself in to the house without another word. It's not so hard to run past Lisha's parents and their awkward small talk. They're not exactly outgoing, so they call out to me in small silky voices and if I just wave exuberantly and smile wide, they're satisfied. When I get to her room, Lish is fixing a tie around her neck (must be an old-school boy's uniform) but is otherwise innocuous. Her blond hair hits that vague place between her shoulders and her collarbone and she's wearing enough makeup to smooth out her skin and add a little push to her eyes, making the brown pop under mascara-ed lashes. But it's all to make her blend in, not stand out. The tie (navy, skinny, loosely knotted) is a sort of sad attempt to be noticed.

I smile anyway.

"You're all put together!" I say, and check myself out in her mirror to see how we fit (or don't fit) together. I'm all glittering eyeshadow, and the layer upon layer of dress-cardigan-vest is dancing on that line between homeless and hot. Sort of inspired by Sylvia's overdone celebrity style. No wonder I'm totally scaring off Beck.

But I do want to be a costume designer someday, so at least I'm succeeding there. See, it's not all obsession and stalking. Some of it is run-of-the-mill dedication to my craft. Maybe Sylvia is just my costume-designing muse.

"You're really late," Lisha says. She's at her desk, which is made for a child, not a near adult, and she's doing homework for some stupid class that I'm sure she's acing anyway.

"You know how it is," I say.

"No. I don't. Was it group therapy? What was it like? Was the girl with no hair there? Did you and Beck talk?"

Lisha needs a television. Or another friend.

"Did you already go by that apartment? Of that guy? What's his name?"

"Austin," I say, but I'd rather have kept it to myself. "Haven't been yet, so let's do it."

"I think it's a bad idea," Lisha says. I notice she has a pair of scissors out on her desk. Professional-looking in their sharpness. I almost tell her to put them in a drawer where they can't hurt anyone, but the words sound weird even in my head. Still, I can't seem to get my eyes off of them.

"You will love their building. It's, like, from the future. And they are totally fabulous," I say, happy to talk about Austin and Sylvia and drag my mind kicking and screaming from those scissors and their sharpness. "It will be an adventure, I swear. We can get Starbucks on the way." I know if I can at least get her moving, then I'll be able to answer whatever questions she comes up with later.

"Getting in your car and letting you buy me a mocha does not mean I'm committing to going the whole way there," she says. I roll my eyes. She's frowning but getting her coat and mittens on at least, and it's a good thing, 'cause my heart is racing. My mind can't seem to decide between thinking of Beck and thinking of Austin. It's all wound up together. But at least they both distract me from thinking about Jeff. "He's like, hot, right?" Lisha says. "Hot and old?"

"Not ancient or anything. I think he wears eyeliner, which I guess *some people* think is hot," I say. Lisha has a weakness for guys who wear makeup, which is hilarious since she herself barely wears any. Lisha blushes.

"Shut up and buy me a mocha," she says, walking out of her room before I can get a look at the sheepish grin she's never able to get control of.

We get past her parents without much discussion once again. After Lisha got in early to Harvard, they stopped needing to keep track of every little thing she did. Kind of like getting into Harvard was the end of the parenting race, and now anything else Lisha does is a cooldown from that victory. As soon as we're in the car, though, Lisha is all over me.

"Can you just explain it again? How do you know this guy, exactly?" She keeps peering at me like I'm a knot of string to be untangled, but I don't have time or space in my head to go over this. My breathing already feels funny. I haven't felt right since I dropped Beck off at the gym. Maybe it's guilt for having helped him do his OCD thing.

I turn on the radio and zone in on the local news just in case. Something about a fire. *Crap.* I start the car and Lisha reaches to turn the radio to whiny college kid rock, but I clear my throat to stop her.

"That's kinda near where they live," I say. "That fire they're talking about. Can we listen for a sec?" I feel a shake in my voice, but I'm hoping she can't hear it, and I decide to drive as fast as I can, which right now is thirty-three miles an hour, because there's probably black ice on the roads from this morning's chill.

"I've, like, run into him and his wife. I just think they're . . . cool. They go to Dr. Pat. I don't really *know* know them." The car slows as I talk; doing both at once seems dangerous.

"Oh my God, he's like some hot mystery guy! Intrigue. And married? Is she hot too? Are they in, like, marriage counseling? What do you guys talk about? This is kinda sketchy, right? Are you being sketchy?" And I know she's trying to sound judgmental or at least concerned, but she doesn't. She sounds one hundred percent thrilled. The report about the fire has ended with no real details, so I try to push myself to get a tiny bit more speed. Just in case. Lisha changes the radio to the indie college station and takes off her boots so that she can bend her knees up to her chest and get comfortable in the cramped seat. It's the best part of friendship: the familiarity, the little bits of routine that mean everything's okay. Lisha pulls out a granola bar and breaks off a piece for me.

Somehow, my hands won't move from the wheel. I want to just take it from her hand, but my brain is telling my hands to stay on ten-and-two.

"Black ice," I say, "need both hands." I open my mouth and she lets me clamp the bar between my teeth, like it's the most normal thing in the world.

"Anyway, I barely know him. Let's say I'm intrigued," I say. But Lisha's already in a fit of giggles planning my torrid love affair with Austin.

"Oh my God, this is *bad*," she says. Covers her mouth with her hands.

"He seems like a rock star. Charismatic. But fragile. His wife, too."

I don't say: *I'm pretty positive if I don't check on them a few times a week at the very least, something terrible might happen.* I don't say: *If Dr. Pat knew about this, she'd be even more convinced I have OCD.*

"Oh my God, are they divorcing? And then will you move in on him?" Lisha puts her legs up on the dashboard. "Can you speed up, please? This is painful."

"Honestly, he doesn't even know who I am."

"Are you his stalker? I'm not judging, but stalking is a felony. Or a crime. Something. And I'm sorry, you sort of have a history with—" I don't let Lisha finish the sentence.

"Lisha," I say, stopping her with what I intend to be a snap but comes out as a plea.

It's funny having someone know so much about me. Funny and infuriating. But she squeezes my shoulder, zips her lips, takes a breath, and does her best to change the subject.

"So," she says. "What do you know about the wife? Is she pretty? Do you want me to drive, Bea? This is killing me. It's going to take, like, two hours to get there at this pace. The weather is not that bad." It's like she saves all her energy and all her questions and all her enthusiasm for life for just our time together. She's been storing up all this energy and it just comes spilling out.

"It's fine. I'm not stalking. I'm only going to go with you this one time and then I'll give it up."

Lisha nods.

"Hey, did you hear that Mr. Venner is getting asked to leave? Like, getting fired," she says, filling the air with gossip about our Latin teacher that would usually be more than enough to keep my mind occupied. "And it gets even better, because I guess Mr. Venner is involved with a former student." I want so badly to be in a place where this conversation matters. I try to make my mind focus on that fact. If I can just care about this bit of gossip, I will be a normal girl again. It's almost working. I'm about to ask Lisha who found out about it and what the administration is going to tell us and whether or not we know the student, but my mind splinters off just as I'm starting to relax. Kind of like my brain can't stand being calm.

It feels like a big cartoon lightning bolt *crack*.

"Did you see the puppy back there? The black lab?" I say, interrupting Lisha and my own thoughts and totally destroying the tiny moment of normalcy I'd almost gotten my hands on. I'm trying to look in the rearview mirror but that's hard to do when you're also trying to keep your eye on the road.

"Yeah. So cute," Lisha says. "So anyway, supposedly

Mr. Venner started trying to date her like the *second* she graduated, but he didn't realize that her mother was on the school board—" She interrupts herself to turn the volume up on a Journey song that we both love to sing along with.

"No, but did I hit it?" I say, and turn the volume right back down. Then I change it back to news. Enough is enough.

"Um, no?" Lisha says.

"Did you see for sure though?" I can tell from the look on her face—crooked mouth, squinting eyes, wrinkled nose— that I am being weird.

"Bea, you'd know if you *hit a dog*. Are you high?" Lisha tries a laugh and nudges my shoulder. I wince.

"Careful! I'm driving!"

"Hey, okay," Lisha says. She crosses her arms over her chest and slouches a little in the seat. Lisha is not a good punching bag. She doesn't like it when I snap at my mother, let alone at her.

"I just . . . I feel like I lost control of the car for a second there. I'm not driving very well right now." I try to say it like it's no big deal.

"Was group therapy bad? Maybe you're just upset from that or something? Pull over, I'll drive," Lisha says. Her hand twitches, like she might reach it out to me, but she reconsiders.

"Yeah, no, let me just drive back around, make sure I didn't, um, do anything wrong," I say. Lisha takes an inhale but no exhale comes. I am definitely freaking her out.

I turn around and circle back through the neighborhood, ten miles an hour, windows down so I can get a better view.

"Maybe we should just head back home? Order Thai or something . . . ," Lisha says. She bites her lip and shivers as the cold outside air rushes into the car.

"No!" I say too loudly. "I mean, no, I want to show you this place. But yeah, you can drive. That's better I guess. I'm on edge or something. I guess an hour in a room with those weirdos got me a little riled up." I pull over and try to believe myself.

"Fine. Let's just get there," she says. A sigh comes out of her, sharp and sleepy. A sound I've never heard from her before. We get out of the car. Lisha takes the driver's seat and I crawl in the back.

"What are you doing?" Lisha says. There's a growl to it, and I blush hard and red.

"I'm just feeling anxious. Maybe I skipped a day of Zoloft or something. I need to spread out in the backseat, okay?" There is no way, no possible way to make this seem normal, but I am a determined chick so I'm giving it my best shot.

"Dude, I'm not your chauffeur."

"I'll be way less annoying back here, I swear to God," I say, and she shakes her head, but with less disgust than the earlier knife-twisting sigh. I check to make sure my seat belt's secure. Then I undo it and put it back on, just in case.

We're on the highway in about two minutes now that Lisha's in charge.

"Maybe you can just, like, tell me about Beck instead of this Austin dude? Since Beck's not, like, old and married?" she says when we've both calmed down enough to return to normalcy.

"Don't want to jinx it," I say, and smile big, smile pretty, smile the smile my mother taught me to let everyone know that everything is okay.

Austin is not the first guy I've gotten a teeny-tiny bit obsessed with. Lisha never approves but always wants all the details. But Austin's different, and I want to explain that to her. He means more, he's a real interest. He's not like the movie stars I used to send letters to, or like Jeff, who Lisha used to gather intel on from her brother about his favorite TV show (football, which isn't a TV show at all), his favorite color (blue), his favorite food (tacos). And Austin's not anything like Kurt, who gave me the poetry book and then dumped me when he realized what a freak I am. Austin's shaggy and professor-like and battle-scarred and married. Totally, totally married. To a chain-smoking trophy wife with fake boobs. I'm not trying to make out with him or get him to forgive me all my faults and love me anyway. I just want to know everything about him.

Lisha's gonna kill me.

I'm telling her all the turns from the backseat, and I can

basically do it without looking out the window much. I only tell her to slow down twice and it's fine because she ignores it completely both times and I pinch my leg, which seems to help keep the panic at bay.

Lish seems freaked out by how well I know the roads to Austin's house already. "What does Dr. Pat say about all this, anyway?" she asks.

"I can't tell her about this, exactly. Austin and Sylvia are her patients. So, it's like a conflict of interest, you know? But she knows I'm not doing the best job driving in general." I don't mention the pinching myself. I guess that's probably the least weird thing I've been doing lately, but for some reason it strikes me as worse, as a bigger deal. Too close to Rudy's face-picking or Jenny's hair-pulling. So for maybe the first time ever I'm keeping something from Lisha, and something else from Dr. Pat, and I better remember who I told what because not telling the truth is way more complicated than I would have thought.

We're quiet for a long time and when we finally arrive, it's anticlimactic because Lish doesn't seem to think the building is anything special. Not to mention it's huge, so our spying is pretty limited. I guess Lisha thought we were going to a house or a condo or someplace where we could peek in the windows and see what they're having for dinner.

"How do you even know which one is their apartment?" Lisha says. She's wrinkling her nose at the whole situation.

"Do you, like, know which window is their window or whatever? Or what time they get home from work? Like, what am I looking for here?"

"I hadn't even thought of that," I say. "I could look up their apartment number. I mean, if their apartment faces the street I could at least figure out when they're home and whether they have blinds or curtains." I tap my foot, trying to decide whether or not I should get out of my car and risk checking out the name tags on the buzzers outside or maybe even asking the doorman where Sylvia and Austin live.

"Do it," Lisha says at last. "If we're going to sit here, let's at least know what we're looking at." When you really pay attention to the activity in an apartment building, you actually notice a lot: lights go on and off, shadows move through windows, TV screens shift the colors of different rooms from dark to light, to dark, to blue, to yellow.

But Lisha's right: That general impression, that map of activity, is not really enough.

"Can you do it for me? I don't want them to see me. Just, like, talk to the doorman. Make something up. You know I can't lie," I say. But that's the thing about Lisha: She'll encourage me to do this stuff but then she's not really any help in executing it. I think if it wasn't for me, she'd be bored out of her mind; she's such a scaredy-cat when it comes to real *action*. We balance each other out.

Dr. Pat says thinking that way justifies my bad behavior,

and call it what you will, but Lisha is an enabler and that's that. Dr. Pat says the way Lisha was after my breakup with Kurt was problematic. That she should have talked to someone about my behavior. That Lisha should have been concerned at how fixated I got on Kurt and his whereabouts. I still think, you know, everyone deals with heartbreak in their own way. And getting dumped sucked and Lisha was just trying to help it suck less.

I don't know. I sort of wish Lisha would jump out of the car and chat up the doorman and be a spy or a stalker, or even tell me to stop and be a pseudoparent or party pooper.

She shakes her head no. Her eyes are lit up with interest but her head just keeps shaking *no no no*.

Until:

"Oh my God, there she is," I say. The thrill of seeing Sylvia coming out for a smoke is tempered right away by the disappointment that it's not Austin.

"That's the wife?" Lisha says. The appearance of Sylvia's skimpy dress, bundles of hair, thigh-high boots is enough to make us both shut up for a good long moment.

Thank God, I think, like if she hadn't shown up, the world might have ended.

Oh God, where's Austin? I think next.

Lisha doesn't notice any shift in me because if she likes anything, it's a tragic beauty. I nod to confirm that's her, and wiggle my eyebrows, and then we're laughing and talking about Sylvia's sex-kitten style and way of blowing out smoke in long ribbons. She's an entire tabloid story, a socialite gone wrong, right in front of our eyes. "Is she for real?" Lisha says with a huge breath in. "Do you think she's a Playboy model? Or, like, an ex-stripper? Or from Texas?" Her eyes are alight with possibility and the affirmation of all the things waiting for us outside of Greenough Girl's Academy.

"I don't know much about her background. But she had an affair and got a boob job to impress her husband. Oh! And during their last session they discussed her lack of employment. I guess she's living off a trust fund from some racist dad who died. It's complicated."

Lisha's floored. She even pulls her gaze from the smoking sensation that is Sylvia and locks eyes with me.

"Is that legal? You knowing all that?"

"It's not my fault Dr. Pat doesn't soundproof her office."

Lisha's stuck between judgment and fascination. Whatever I say in the next few minutes will push her one way or the other. Old Bea would tell her every little thing I've ever written down about Austin and Sylvia. Old Bea would rant and rave about how I absolutely *have* to get to know Austin. But New Bea stealthily moves one hand to her thigh and pinches until the truth-telling urges stop.

Sneaky and subtle in the backseat, I take out my pink shooting-star notebook and write down everything Sylvia's wearing. I count how many drags she takes per minute. I am positive if I can just get a grasp on these details, I'll understand everything.

"She's like a character from a movie, right?" I say. Look at Lisha with the hope that I am not on this sinking boat all alone.

"Kinda intoxicating, yeah," Lish says.

"Yes! Intoxicating! Exactly." I grab Lisha's arm. My heart flips with love for my best friend. I'm okay. Even Lisha is fascinated. Proof positive that I don't even need group therapy. I say that to Lish, 'cause its too big an accomplishment to keep in. Sylvia stamps out the first cigarette and starts another. Twists her hair into a messy bun at the nape of her neck. No mirror, but it's perfect anyway.

"Group therapy's not the worst thing in the world, right? I mean, maybe you'll end up liking it." She chooses her words carefully. Her eyes are still trained on Sylvia, but I know my gaze is more intent, my interest less casual.

"You think I'm crazy too."

"Would I get into a car with a crazy person?" Lisha jokes, but my chest collapses a little anyway. "Look. I'll think you're all better when you go on a date with that Beck guy or if you can drive us all the way from Boston to Lexington in less than an hour. Until then stick with Dr. Pat." She says it with a smile, but it's that invisible line anyway. I may have more fun than Lisha, but she gets to stay over on the side of sanity and I seem to have one foot outside the border and into crazytown.

"Oh." The word is part swallow, part whisper.

"Hey," Lisha says, maybe hearing the echo of her words and witnessing the pang of hurt on my face. "You're the funnest person I know. I love you to death. You're basically the reason I'm not wasting away from boredom. And I love you like this. It just seems like it could be . . . exhausting. To be you."

Sylvia gives up on her search for another cigarette and heads back inside.

"Listen, you probably shouldn't be spying on these randoms, but I'm not about to stop you. And you *have* to let me know if you're going for it. I mean, if something happens with Austin you have got to tell me." I crane my neck to see if I can catch sight of Sylvia heading to the elevator. It's a long shot but we're parked close enough to the building that I think it might be possible. Maybe I can see what floor she goes to. Maybe the little numbers above the elevator will light up and be visible from this distance. And maybe when that happens I won't need to go any further.

"You'll be the first to know," I say, even though it's so not the point. "Sorry to drag you into this. I know you think it's effed up."

"Hey, I wish things mattered to me the way they matter to you. You create the excitement, you know? Where there's boring crap, you make meaning." It sounds like a thought she has crafted over years of watching me obsess and, let's face it, compulse. "And he may be hot, but getting all into some married guy is stressful, especially when there is some perfectly cute-sounding guy our own age who obviously likes you. . . ."

I squint until my eyes are tiny, watering slits and I think I see the numbers on the elevator go to number six. I wouldn't bet on it or anything. But I just decide it's true. That they live on the sixth floor. That if I count the windows from outside the building and if Lisha would just chill for a second so I could focus, I'd know for sure where they live. Or, almost for sure. She's going on and on about people she's read about in *Cosmo* or whatever who've had lurid affairs with married men. It's making my heart beat even harder so I sort of slap her arm and tell her to be quiet for a second. Every inch of me is focused on the row of windows that are six above the pavement. I'm breathing hard.

Then it's worth it because a window lights up, right on time, on the sixth floor. I can make out a lamp with fringe on the shade and a red glow that must mean their curtains are some sheer pink or orange. Even better: I am certain the tall, skinny form next to the lamp is Austin himself.

And then I can breathe. And then I can feel my heart slow. And then my fingers stop tingling and feel like fingers again.

I pinch my thigh through my pants.

There they are. Here I am.

"I'm just saying, when guys cheat it's for a reason, you

know? So you need to know what that reason *is* before jumping all in. And that's actually really easy for you, I guess, since you are privy to all his deep, dark secrets." Lisha's plotting it out like a romance novel or a really juicy Lifetime movie. I smile at her. It's dark and cold and I owe her a hot chocolate and an all-night movie marathon. Lisha likes crap movies but I can put up with a few hours of teen romantic comedies to thank her for the relief I'm feeling right now.

"There," I say, my eyes lingering on that window for a few more perfect moments.

"You see what you needed to see?" Lisha says.

"I think that's them," I say. "The red window. The glowing one."

"Of course," Lisha says. "You know how to pick them. The glowing fucking window. Of course."

I always laugh when Lisha swears. And she laughs too and I may be a mess but I haven't lost everything yet.

THE FIRST DATE ISN'T A DATE.

I'll clarify: I think it isn't a date, so I wear jeans and my mother's hippie necklace from the seventies and an argyle sweater I found at the Salvation Army near school.

The Salvation Army near school is where all my preppy classmates drop off their preppy clothing. Then I pick up their leftovers and wear them on the weekends. My mom says it's "uncouth" to wear my classmates' discarded clothing to school. That she respects my spirit, but that I can't take it quite that far.

I read a blog by this real costume designer who lives in New York City. She says when she's working on really low-budget projects, the first place she goes is the Salvation Army 'cause you never know what you're going to find there. When I read that blog post, I freaked out, since I've been, like, their number one customer since I was twelve and trying to impress Jeff with my non-Gap, non-Abercrombie outfits. I guess I proved my point, but I also fell in love with the heaps of clothing, the unexpected treasures, the hours lost in that store. Not that I'm an actual costume designer yet, obviously, but let's say you need to look like you're really outdoorsy or like a slut or like a really conservative do-gooder for a college interview or something. That's where the Salvation Army is genius. I can transform myself pretty accurately for about fifteen bucks.

Besides, I look good in hand-me-downs. I know how to take a bunch of stuff that other people find ugly and make it beautiful. Or at least make it interesting.

"Who's the boy?" My mother asks before Beck gets there. It's just now occurred to her to be protective.

"Beck."

"And what do his parents do?"

I giggle at that question because it's so clearly an imitation of, like, a 1950s family that is nothing like ours. When my mom thinks she's not being a good enough mother, she'll break out one of those old tropes and pat herself on the back for acting like we're a real family.

Dr. Pat says this kind of lax parenting is what makes me feel unstable. Not that my parents caused my issues, but that they didn't help matters much. That I'm "looking for stability" or "overcompensating for lack of control."

Beck Facebooked me after last Saturday's session and said that he owed me for the ride I gave him to the gym and that we could grab some lunch before our Saturday afternoon session. We avoided eye contact during group Tuesday afternoon, but he confirmed our lunch on Facebook last night. And when he shows up, he's in a collared shirt and a tie and pants that have been pressed within an inch of their life. It's all just the tiniest bit too tight on him.

"Your pants don't fit," I say. And then immediately realize I'm a jackass. "Neither does your shirt." I swear, if I could stop myself from saying this stuff, I would. But if I don't say the things that pop into my mind, then they might eat my insides out or I might get condemned to hell for dishonesty, so I can't really take the risk.

I know I sound like I'm really religious or a prude or just making convenient excuses for being a bitch. I swear I'm not any of those things. I only go to church when my parents make me on Christmas. I'm not a virgin. I swear (sometimes like a sailor). And I'd way rather be a bitch than a freak. I just hate the way lying dries out my mouth and makes my head swim with anxiety.

"My parents won't get me new stuff since they're not into me bulking up," Beck says, his eyes darting between me and my mom. I think he can't decide who it's more embarrassing to make eye contact with at this minute. "It's, like, the lamest punishment ever." My mother is shuddering at the whole conversation; she is not so good at the awkward moments. She's always telling me that she was a great parent when I was little, and she'll be great when I'm over eighteen, but that she knows she sucks at the teenage years. They make her too uncomfortable: awkward silences and ugly braces and painful skin-breaking acne.

And my guess is this whole OCD thing isn't making her feel any less uncomfortable around me. But she's going to rally even if it kills her. We haven't talked about the new diagnosis, but she has given a lot of supportive and warm smiles in my direction, so there's that.

"You look very nice. Beck, is it?" my mother breaks in at last. Then she goes in for a handshake. It's clear in Beck's face that he's doing a mental calculation, once again, of what will be least embarrassing: refusing a handshake or doing his weird hand-squeezing thing and then running off to the bathroom to scrub his hands. Lucky for him, my mom pulls her hand back and stuffs it into the pocket of her ugly cardigan sweater like it's no big deal. Clearly, Mom has read the OCD pamphlets and knows the deal. She shrugs. Beck shrugs back, mirroring her.

"You kids have fun," my mom says when none of us seems to be moving from our spots in the hallway. Beck puts on gloves before opening the door for me. I wonder if he wears them in the summer, too.

I don't have to mention how super-crazy-clean Beck's car is. There is hand sanitizer in the glove compartment. He tells me about it not once, not twice, but eight times. In a row. The rest of the short car ride we spend in painful silence.

"This place okay?" Beck says. We're pulling up to a white tablecloth Italian joint and all I'm thinking is, *God, this really is a date.*

"I think I'm underdressed," I say. I could have said something way less polite. I'm shaking a little from keeping in the comment about how wannabe-romantic this place is. How it's the sort of place middle-aged divorcees would go to meet their internet dating matches. But I just keep pinching my thigh because Dr. Pat says if I can resist saying rude things for a little while then the anxiety will lower on its own. It's worth a try.

My attempt at quiet, normal conversation doesn't last long. Once we're actually in the fancy joint, Beck's so quiet I can hear every thought in my head and they're all telling me to purge a whole bunch of words and opinions and random thoughts. Not to mention when we're at the table I have a lot of time by myself picking at the bread and sipping at my water. Beck spends an extra-long time in the bathroom before they even take our order. We are so going to be late for group today.

"You have a big hand-washing thing, huh?" I say. I think at the very least, we have our craziness in common. And I may not be into the whole hand-washing, tapping-fingers, meticulous-counting thing, but the basics are the same.

"Yeah. Usually people pretend not to notice," Beck says.

"Oh. Right. I'm so sorry. I do that. I say all the shit you're not supposed to say."

"No, no, I mean, that's cool. I've never been asked." Then

he shrugs, because maybe he likes the idea of me asking him about his obsessions, but in reality he doesn't seem to know what to do in the aftermath.

It's killing me: He got so dressed up for our lunch and is ordering all kinds of fancy pastas for us but otherwise he's deeply quiet. I get preoccupied with the possibility of dirt under my nails and I wonder if anything about me would pass his cleanliness/working-out test. His fingernails are perfectly uniform in size and shape; I can smell soap and detergent coming off his skin from here. It's that smell that isn't a smell: fresh, cottony, soft.

Meanwhile, I am one hundred percent sure I'm sweating, and I washed my hair last night instead of this morning, so there's that, too. I'm so hot in my sweater I'd do anything to take it off, but what's underneath is a pale pink-striped camisole, even more embarrassingly casual and probably getting damp from sweat now, so that's not an option. I'm not having a *good time*, per se, but my heart's jumping all over the place looking at Beck's sad eyes and huge muscles. I want this to work. I just do.

"You on any meds?" I ask. If he's new to therapy and anxiety and stuff, he probably isn't on anything yet, but the thought pops into my brain, so there you go. Beck shakes his head no. I'm not completely socially inept, so I can tell this is not what he wants to be talking about on our "date." But he's not saying much and my mind is itching from the inside. *Talk about something else!* I scream in my head.

"My mom's kind of into new age vegan stuff," he says, "so she wouldn't sign off on that." There's a smile inching onto his face. Like his face is telling me it's okay to say whatever comes into my head even if his words can't quite reflect that. He's just sheepish enough to be safe, but even if he wasn't I'd plow ahead anyway.

"I've been on Zoloft forever. But I can see Dr. Pat's itching to get me on even more stuff. Watch out. She's into that. I went on Zoloft when I was fourteen. I actually don't even know if that's legal. And it's amazing sometimes, but I don't know if it works the way she wants it to." Normally, I don't talk about things like medication with boys I like, but Beck nods along with my words and scrunches his eyebrows and underneath all the nervousness of a first date, there's comfort and intimacy. If we were different people, I'd like to think he'd tuck my hair behind my ear or kiss my forehead or something. The moment is that taut. I think I'm supposed to stop talking now; this is the part of the conversation where I lose people, but Beck's waiting for me to continue. He's not sipping water or fiddling with his napkin or even tapping the table over and over again.

"Keep going," he says at last. He's not asking follow-up questions or even really having a conversation with me but I'm not sure that matters right now. "You look like you have more to say."

He's right, but it doesn't take the shock out. And that's when I realize *why* I have the beginnings of feelings for him.

He's not Mr. Personality, that's for sure. And he's cute but not drop-dead gorgeous or anything. But as nervous as he is, he isn't scared of me. I'm not the weirdest person he's ever met. I'm . . . okay.

I take an inhale and keep going, keep chatting away. I would have anyway. The thing bubbling in my throat is too much to swallow down or hide with a pinch to my thigh or a look in Beck's eyes. My mind has thought of the most embarrassing thing I can say about Zoloft right now and if I don't say it out loud I will fall to pieces or the world will. I fight the urge to say it for one more second but Beck's leaning forward and I can't risk the consequences of not saying the things that are trying to come out.

He asked for it.

"I get night sweats from the medication. I mean that in a really extreme way. I wake up in a fucking lake of my own sweat. Like, so bad I don't even really compute that it's from *me* until I've been up for a few minutes. Sometimes it happens during the day. Behind my neck. I just go wet, all over. Soaks through my shirts. So. There's that."

I may be humiliated, but saying this has made the anxiety subside. The panic has been quelled. But of course the unstoppable force of anxiety is replaced immediately by the horror of what I have just said. Beck's so red he must be running a fever just from the blush. But he's smiling under that red, red burn of embarrassment.

And then: so am I.

His smile turns into a really big grin, a goofy, lopsided thing I haven't seen yet, and it lights up the inside of me. I shake my head at myself and expel a bit of breath that seconds as a half laugh and I think I feel a tiny trail of sweat make its way down my spine. Beck runs a finger along my hand, which I've been resting on the table. I know touching someone's kind of a big deal for him, 'cause before he does it he takes a huge ragged inhale and taps his finger on the table really fast. This time, I count. He does it eight times. Then he raises his other hand to the edge of the table and taps. Again, eight times. Noted.

"Thanks," I say. I don't know what exactly I'm thanking him for. Listening to me? Not leaving after I've uttered the phrase "night sweats"? Touching me? Being here at all? Beck starts to pull his hand away. There's something about drawing attention to the nice things people do that makes them uncomfortable.

Then the moment's over and that's kind of nice too. The idea that the world doesn't stop after you tell a cute guy about your big sweating issue.

There's a hush in the restaurant; it's the kind of place that's all about an unspoken volume control and a lack of other teenagers, even at lunchtime. There are cloth napkins and small white candles that flicker out and get immediately relit, and multiple forks and wineglasses full of ice water. The menus are all leather-bound and it is not my imagination that we are being carefully watched.

"Your mom seems nice," he says, and looks down at his bread plate. He does not start eating. Instead he pulls out baby wipes and cleans off his hands. I work hard to look in his eyes and not at the baby wipes or the humiliated way he's rocking back and forth a little.

"She is nice. Works a lot."

"Doing what?" The conversation is so normal I almost put a stop to it completely. I don't do small talk. But the rest of my mind is blank from excitement and how hard I have to work to not say something about baby wipes and how they are meant to clean dirty baby butts, not hands.

"She actually—she works in a jail. She's a guard. Which is hilarious since my dad's an architect and my mom's from Minnesota and how the hell did she end up here working in a prison? But. That kind of sums up my family." I don't know why this information always sounds like a lie to me. My mother is pretty and feminine but approximately ten feet tall and when she's mad her face contorts into that of a lion. "She got a black eye once." Beck raises his eyebrow.

Our pasta comes and it looks delicious. I reach for a fork but Beck's hands pause over the utensils and I notice a little tremble in his fingers.

"Do those look, um, dirty or anything?" he says. I hadn't thought to look at the fork or knife, but all of Beck's focus is suddenly on them, and so I fixate too.

"I think they're okay . . . ," I say. But the feeling I had at Lisha's place when I saw her supersharp scissors boils up and my breath becomes a little less available. Not gone completely, but a little out of reach.

I don't think the fork and knife look dirty, but God, do they look sharp.

For no reason at all this article I read in the newspaper a few months ago lodges itself in some corner of my mind and then stubbornly refuses to move aside. This blurb about a woman who used a steak knife to do some really horrifying damage to her husband. It was meant just to harm him, she said at the trial, but he bled to death. She wasn't pretty, but she also didn't have missing teeth or serial-killer eyes or anything. I'm sure if you saw her on the street you wouldn't think twice. She had brown ringlets not unlike mine on a frizzy bad hair day. She looked petite: narrow-shouldered, almost a full foot shorter than her husband, if the picture from their wedding day was any indication.

It doesn't feel like such a stretch to think I could be capable of something terrible too, if someone as plain and sweet-smiled as that woman was. I stare down the knife. It definitely, *definitely* stares back.

Beck's waving over the waiter, and asking for plastic utensils, individually wrapped ones, he specifies, and before he has a chance to blush or apologize, I ask for the same. The waiter's in a crisp white shirt and has a just-shaved face and a napkin folded neatly over his forearm. He knows how to hide judgment.

"You don't have to do that," Beck says. "I mean, thank you, but you can eat with normal utensils."

"I actually—I'd rather plastic too. That knife . . . is it bigger than a normal one? Sharper? It looks sort of . . . intense."

"Huh, didn't notice," he says. For a moment an awkward silence threatens us, but then Beck starts to laugh. And I don't know exactly what's so funny, but his laughter is contagious, and I catch the giggles too. "I mean, I notice *everything* but the one thing that bothers you," he sputters out, shaking his head at himself. "I don't know why that's so funny. Maybe it's not funny. I just can't stop—" One hand holds his stomach, and the other, I'm happy to see, is still on the table. No tapping.

It feels good to laugh, and by the time our plastic utensils have gotten to the table, we've worked up quite an appetite. The boy can *eat*. I guess that's what multiple workouts a day does for you.

Armed with the plastic fork, and with the knife cleared off the table, I'm calmer, and my in-knots stomach unwinds itself so that there's room for pumpkin ravioli and veal parmesan and mushroom risotto so creamy it's bordering on soup. I'm still a little distracted by the other shiny knives on the other candlelit tables, but if I watch Beck's beautiful arms or catch his arresting blue gaze, it's a little easier.

"My mom says to move risotto to the edge of the plate to cool it off," Beck says, demonstrating with his fork. "She studied abroad in Italy when she was like, nineteen, and acts like she grew up there." He shrugs, embarrassed to have said so much without prompting.

"Sounds funny." He nods and I nod, and maybe it's silent for a little too long, but it's not the worst kind of silence. I smush the cream rice to the edges of the plate and then scoop it up like Beck does, with the long dull side of the fork. Then we just eat. It's delicious, the array of food he's ordered, and it's too rich and plentiful to leave much room for chitchat. When my mind wanders too much to knives and life's uncertainties, and the nutmeg buried in the ravioli pillows isn't distracting enough, I pinch my thigh. It's a quick fix and doesn't last, but it will do.

I could be wrong, but I think Beck chews each piece eight times before swallowing.

"I had a really good workout today," he says.

"Oh yeah?"

"Yep. Gonna go after therapy too. Then it'll be a really good day."

I'm thinking: *This is the weirdest date ever*, except I don't really feel that way. There's something undeniably intimate about how small the table is, how my foot keeps accidentally hitting his shin when I go to cross my leg, how he keeps looking at my plate to make sure I'm eating.

We don't have time for dessert. As it is, we're already going to be pushing it to get to group on time. The check comes and Beck pays like it's a real, live date, and it occurs to me I haven't actually been on one of these before. The guys I've dated have taken me to lame parties and hooked up with me in their cars. Kurt and I would rent movies and make out on the couch or get ice cream, but he never paid. It's funny how acting like an adult only ever makes me feel like more of a child. It's why I don't bother with nice clothes or leather purses or low, conservative ponytails.

"You know, you're really pretty," Beck says as we stand up. I think maybe he'll take my hand or kiss me, or something datelike. And maybe he even wants to, but he doesn't. I grin from the praise but only for an instant because the joy that bubbles up from that supersweetness is too much, and before it has a chance to really latch on to my mood or my heart or anything at all, I push my mind to Austin.

I fell for you first because of how pretty you were, Austin said to Sylvia a few sessions ago. It made her stop crying. Dr. Pat called it "good work" and sent them on their way.

"Hang on, okay?" Beck says. "Sorry." He puts up one finger, telling me to wait for him. I stand there watching him as he lifts the chairs at our table and the empty one next to us up about a centimeter off the floor eight times each. He does it with as little movement as humanly possible. He tries to look casual, like he's just adjusting the chair, but the movement is exact and unmistakable and people are trying not to look but they're looking anyway. The heat from his face is so strong, so red, I imagine I can physically feel it.

When Beck gets back to me, he's embarrassed but relaxed, like he can breathe again even though he wishes no one was watching him do it.

"I'm so sorry," he says again, like the preemptive apology wasn't enough.

"Let's stop being on a date and let's just, like, hang out," I say. Lisha warned me about saying this kind of thing, which is a testament to how well she knows me, but if Beck's going to go to all the trouble of wearing a tie and complimenting my horribly underdressed self, than I'm going to at least be myself. We have got to be past the formality already anyway, and if he's gutsy enough to do his chair-lifting, number-eight compulsions in front of me and not totally disintegrate, I want him to know who I am too. I am not a quiet girl who keeps my mouth shut. I am not a girl who is capable of even imitating that kind of girl. He deserves to know me, if I'm going to get to know him.

I assume this all must be clear to him, because the logic is all neatly laid out in my head, but there's a frown on his face, a quick reverse of that goofy smile, and I know I've pushed things one step too far. I never know where I am until I've crossed that border. I never anticipate it. I never know it's approaching.

It usually takes me a minute to get what it is I've said that's made someone upset, so I review the last few lines of conversation in my head until I have one of the mini-epiphanies I have about a million times a day.

"Oh my God!" I say to the face that used to be Beck. "No, no, we're on a date, I meant let's not be formal. Or let's not be on a date with a capital *D*. Like, you seem nervous. And I wasn't really prepared for a super formal—I'm a disaster and I just mean we should both relax and—"

Dr. Pat would call this self-sabotage.

"Is it the tie?" Beck asks. His face has relaxed into something sweet again but he still has the flush of embarrassment on his cheeks. "I can ditch the tie. My mom made me—" He starts untying it before I can get a word out, but I guess it is kind of the tie that's bothering me so I let him untangle it from his neck. He's so buttoned up and clean that I expect the process to be deliberate and controlled. But the tie is a mess in his hands; he is knotting it rather than unknotting it and he's so flustered that the whole thing is choking him. I sort of giggle but try to keep it under control: There's something raw about Beck that I hadn't fully understood when we met. He's ready to fall apart at any minute.

When the tie is finally off, he rolls it into the neatest little ball I've ever seen and tucks the whole thing into his pocket. Then he nods to the door because we really need to get to group.

"I don't really know what I'm doing," Beck says in a mumble that breaks my heart.

Do the sweet and perfectly awkward moments from earlier in the afternoon still exist after I've screwed it all up? Or do they vanish into the air? I can't be sure. I do know that for a few minutes there it was something unmistakably romantic, if only to people like me and Beck.

He doesn't kiss me or anything, but I feel like maybe he's thinking about it, because when we get into the car he won't stop tapping his finger against the steering wheel in little clusters of eight.

I look at a picture I snuck of Austin's apartment building on my phone and kinda hate myself. I google "Austin, Boston, MA" on my phone, hoping it will magically come up with more information about him, but without his last name it's a pointless venture. I ask Beck to turn on the news station on the radio, and listen for the names Austin and Sylvia or their cross streets, just in case. When Beck looks over to smile at me, I hide my phone's screen and admit to myself that I do not deserve this nice a date.

I think I'm about to fall for Beck, and it's making me crazier than I was before. I know both of these things for sure: I like Beck, and I'm probably going to screw up in some major way because of it.

And that's how it starts.

♡ 9.

DR. PAT ASKS ME TO STAY AFTER GROUP SESSION,
like I'm nine and passing notes or throwing spitballs, or whatever it is that disobedient grade-school kids are doing these
days. If Beck were a normal guy, he'd maybe give me a hug
after session or even just nudge my ribs and tease me about
getting in trouble with our therapist. But instead his face
droops and he waves and makes a beeline for the bathroom,
probably to give his hands a good thorough scrubbing.

Was it really only an hour ago that we were caught in the
spectacular awkwardness of a first date?

I learned a lot about Beck this afternoon during session because Dr. Pat seemed especially focused on him. For
instance, I learned that baby wipes are something he consid-
ers a very poor substitute for actual hand washing. And that
he would do everything, *everything* in groups of eight if he
could. So I was right to count off the table taps and chair lifts.
But shouldn't he have kissed me eight times, then?

The room is an overheated, dusty mess and I'm dying

to get out of there. I'm *thisclose* to sweating through my sweater and not just the thin camisole underneath. Meanwhile, Dr. Pat is wrapped up in a collared shirt and a cashmere sweater-vest and a bulky light-violet scarf that I'd use as a blanket, it looks that comfortable. She's probably the kind of person who is always in the most appropriate outfit for every occasion. If it had been her on a date with Beck today, I'm sure she would have intuitively known to wear heels and a cocktail dress instead of the homeless-bum-meets-hipster-OCD-chick look I came up with for the occasion.

"You're not talking much in group," Dr. Pat starts off. Unlike in our comfortable, quiet, one-on-one sessions, she's not letting me take the lead. It's awkward to have her speak to me so pointedly. I don't know that she's ever called me out so deliberately and it totally reorganizes our dynamic. I cross my legs and flutter my fingers above my thigh, reminding myself not to give in and pinch the skin.

"I don't know that this is the right group for me," I say at last, like I've been thinking about it very seriously and have finally come to a mature, well-thought-out conclusion.

"I have a feeling there's some stuff you're not telling me," Dr. Pat says. I miss the old Dr. Pat who would just nod and take little notes. This one is looking me right in the eyes and not letting me cut off eye contact for even a moment. When I try to look somewhere else, she dips her chin and moves her head around until she gets me to meet her gaze again. "It seems like there's more going on inside than you're letting on. But this is the place to address those concerns. We still have our private sessions once a week, but I want you to do a lot of your work in group, okay?"

I shrug. I'm so not committing to that.

She doesn't stop. "I'm also worried that we haven't talked enough about your diagnosis since I gave you those pamphlets. I've been hoping you would come to me with some thoughts. I know it's hard to really address how you're feeling about your obsessive-compulsive disorder—" I shake my head. Every time she brings it up I've told her I need more time, but she's getting more aggressive, and this is the first time she's laid it out quite so starkly.

My obsessive-compulsive disorder.

"You can be honest with me," she says. Her head moves forward at an angle that reminds me of a turtle emerging from its shell, and I just know I'm not getting out of here without divulging something.

I'm not going to talk about Austin or Beck or the weird way I'm trying to balance out my feelings for the two of them. But I noticed something else in today's group session that's made its way into my obsessive thought hierarchy.

"Do you think you could ask Rudy not to bring that Swiss Army knife key chain into the room?" I say. It's not what she's looking for and I get that but until I address it I'm not going to be able to say anything else.

"I hadn't noticed he had one," Dr. Pat says. I see for the first time that she has a diamond ring on her left hand. I'm either oblivious or she just got engaged. It's got a nice sparkle but I don't like how much I'm getting to know about Dr. Pat. I think I liked her more when she was mostly furniture and pat statements. "Does it bother you?"

She knows it does.

"It doesn't seem safe. And yeah, okay, I'm feeling a little bothered by really super sharp things lately. I mean, people do really crazy stuff . . ."

"People like your groupmates?" Dr. Pat says. She clasps her hands together, accidentally letting them clap loudly as they come together. It's deeply awkward.

"People like me," I admit with a roll of my eyes and a huge sigh.

"Ah," she says, but she already knew. "I don't think you need to worry about that. You're not going to hurt anyone, Bea." She reaches out to touch my arm and I jump, but I let her do it just to prove that I'm not as messed up as these other kids.

"No, I know I'm probably not going to really do anything, but I think it's distracting for everyone and, like, kind of unsafe to have a knife just sitting there in the middle of the room, you know? And do you really know enough about all of us to totally guarantee we don't have those tendencies? You know, I read an article about a kid who had these really violent dreams and he was told to ignore them and then he killed someone in his sleep."

I'd been holding on to that tidbit for a while. It wasn't a newspaper article exactly, but I read it online and pasted it into that notebook I had for school, thinking I'd talk about it in current events class some day, but I never did.

There's a real relief to having acknowledged it out loud. Maybe now Dr. Pat will lock me away or something so I can't do any real damage.

She nods, writes something down.

"I'm glad you've addressed that with me, Bea. I'm sure Rudy would feel terrible if he knew his key chain was impeding your ability to participate. I know usually you are a really open person, and I think the group is missing out by you being so quiet all of a sudden."

"I thought my oversharing issue was sort of a compulsion?" I say. "So maybe I'm just actually making progress." Dr. Pat grimaces and I pull my hands through my hair in exasperation and then immediately pull them away. Thoughts of Jenny's partially bald head shoot through my brain.

"These people are making me crazier," I say to Dr. Pat. Then I'm flooded with tears because sometimes once I've relaxed a little bit I can't keep anything at all in.

"There we go," Dr. Pat says. "Good girl." She rubs my back for half a second and then says she'll see me in our next session. That's what's so weird about Dr. Pat. And maybe therapy in general. You think you know what they want from you, but when you give it to them they basically shrug it off. And you're left in a pool of your own tears when all you really wanted was to dish about your date or get out of therapy altogether.

I'm not sure who I'll find out there waiting for me. Obviously I didn't drive here myself, so I have to just hope my mom and dad put two and two together and magically realized I need a lift.

That is extremely unlikely. On her days off from the prison job, my mom totally spaces out on the couch with the television blaring and watches girls with boob jobs compete for the affection of douchey guys with muscles. My dad is almost certainly in the garage doing some woodworking, his newest hobby. He blares the Rolling Stones and sings along with the chorus while he delights in all his shiny tools.

I'm already taking out my phone to give them both a call and planning a quick walk to Dunkin' Donuts while I wait for whoever manages to answer the phone.

But Beck's there. He is sparkling clean and pacing around his car.

"Okay. If we're going to do this, you need to tell me more about yourself," Beck says. "I mean, I just said all that crap in group. You need to tell me at least one thing you don't want to tell me." He smiles. No one has ever asked to know *more* about me. If you say everything on your mind up front, there's never really anything left over for people to be curious about.

My mouth itches, wanting to tell him everything. I swallow. Swallow again. Pinch, hard.

"I listen in on people's sessions," I say. "Before therapy with Dr. Pat. I listen to the couple who goes in before me. I'm sort of fascinated by them." It's true, without being all OCD and oversharing. It's enough of a confession to temporarily experience a bit of relief from the overwhelming sensation that I'm going to melt away from not saying enough. It's the bare minimum of what I need to say right this second.

And Beck doesn't bat an eye.

♡ 10.

"I MEAN THIS AS NICELY AS POSSIBLE," LISHA says before second period on Monday, "but you sort of look constipated when you make that face."

I'd be pissed, but I know the look she's talking about. Dr. Pat calls it white-knuckling, and it's what I do when I'm not "doing the deep work," but instead am just focusing really hard on not compulsing. It is not a very effective method of not being crazy. And apparently it makes me look constipated, too. So, kind of a lose-lose way of dealing with my OCD.

"This better?" I ask with all seriousness, and arrange my face into what I hope is a more normal expression.

"You need a time-out?" Lish says, which is code for *No, that is not better at all.* I nod. Time-out means skipping class to hang out in the library, which is exactly what I need. Second period is Life Skills, anyway. And I reject the notion that we have to take glorified home ec when we are modern women. I only signed up for it because it was the closest thing to a class on costume designing. The first half of the semester was okay. We did some sewing and balanced a checkbook, both of which seemed kind of useful and kind of antiquated. But I'm not one to complain about sewing. I stitched a tiny jacket for Lisha's tiny dog and got an A.

Now Life Skills has moved on to baking and I'm over it.

We go to the library, with its fake marble columns and comfortable armchairs and rows and rows of books. There're a few of us who sometimes meet in the lofted area, which features a group table, big windows, and a slightly relaxed "No Noise" policy. Two of the usual crew are up there, Kim and Lacey, and they continue their serious-looking talk but hand us a tin of homemade chocolate cookies and gesture that we should dig in.

Kim and Lacey have Life Skills first period.

All the girls who come to the library loft are in that nebulous world between popular and loser. We're not really a group, but we have a couple of inside jokes and sit together during all school assemblies. Their numbers are in my cell phone.

Kim and Lacey used to chat with me about that kid Reggie, the one we talked about in current events class, but at some point I kept talking about him and they stopped really participating in the conversations. Kim would try to change the subject and talk about the hot new soccer coach. I'd get all flustered and imitate a girl who cared about hot soccer coaches, and I'm not a great actress so I'm sure I didn't pull it off.

Besides, the soccer coach is not that cute, and girls only

like him because they all just like soccer players in general. When I tried that theory out on Kim, she blinked too quickly and got suddenly superinterested in her algebra book.

Lish and I pick books for each other, which is what we always do on our time-outs. Today I hand her an Italian cookbook and she gives me a month-old copy of *New York* magazine, which she knows is my favorite. She must feel really bad for me today, so I can only assume I look like crap. We sit side by side on the floor for the whole period. Our backs rest against the rickety shelves, and I successfully skip over the article about New York's faltering prison system and instead rip out a few pictures from the "Street Style" article: neon armbands, vintage chandelier earrings, high-waisted linen pants, dark green denim.

One of the models reminds me of Sylvia. I pinch my thigh and promise myself I can drive by their place after school. *It's no big deal,* my mind says. *It's better for everyone if I just go check on them.*

"Is this helping?" Lisha says, catching me mid thigh-pinch.

"Totally!" I say, but my teeth grind as I smile.

When the period's over, we part ways with cheek kisses and plans to meet up at the Pancake House later. Lisha has AP Calculus and I have an elective photography class. Guess which one of us got into Harvard early?

My library time-out with Lish chilled me out a little, and

I make it to the end of the school day without incident, but before I'm even to the parking lot, my phone is dinging its text message sound. It's Beck. Smith-Latin must get out at the same time as Greenough Girls'. *Ding-ding.* Beck again, and then again. I'm about to tackle responding to the first few texts, but my mind (uncontrollable, but somehow ridiculously predictable) zips to thoughts of Austin; and worrying about what to text Beck morphs quickly into worrying that Something Terrible has happened to Austin. Plus I promised myself I could go check on them after school, and it would be a terrible idea to break that promise. And once I'm gripped with that thought, the text message dings from Beck are inconsequential and I just have to *go*. I have to check on Austin.

My car is fully stocked with today's newspaper and my pink notebook with the ugly gold star and the binder from current events class that I have recently stuck a few more articles into. I wish I'd stop carting around the book of Mary Oliver poems from Kurt, too, but I can't seem to let them go. Not the poems, not the notes I have inside about him, and not the very small urge to stop by the ice cream place I know he still probably frequents. I throw the poetry book in the back. I'm not an idiot; I've already gotten into enough trouble with Kurt.

Anyway, there's a half-drunk, mostly cold thermos of hot tea in the car too, and my mother's forty-dollar lip gloss, and cigarettes I bought last night in case Sylvia's out there looking for a smoke.

I think of everything and I'm pretty sure if I could use my organizational skills for something else, like wildlife survival kits or preparing people for nuclear warfare, I'd be a millionaire. Or at the very least actually a useful human being. But as it is, I just have a packed car and a lot of extra shit that makes me look like a sociopath.

I'm dry-mouthed and I don't really want to drive because it seems like the kind of day I might go crazy and run someone over by accident. So I go twenty miles an hour and lean forward to make sure I don't take my eyes off the road, and I stiffen every muscle in my body so there's no chance of relaxing for long enough to do something stupid.

I'm almost at the highway, which I'm going to have to force myself to go thirty or forty miles an hour on.

I hate merging. Let's be honest, it's a cesspool of dangerous possibilities and accidents waiting to happen. Merging should be illegal.

My hands are shaking now, and my phone's still buzzing with text messages until Beck has sent exactly eight. I know 'cause at a stop I see that the last one reads: *Sorry to text so many times. Once I sent 2 I had to send 8. Lucky for you, I'm done now.*

He may be the perfect guy for me but I can't text and drive at the same time and even when I try to smile at the memory of Beck's fingers reaching for mine over ridiculously expensive pasta and awkward glances, I fail. I can't even get the image of his face in my head. In fact, I can't get the image of his *hands* into my head either, but my mental photograph of Austin comes in clear as day. His hair. His stubble. The scuffs on his cowboy boots. The worn elbows on his fitted sweater. His kind eyes and full lips and irrefutably sexy swagger.

When I finally get off the highway almost ninety minutes later, I slow down to fifteen miles an hour but it feels almost excusable since it's a school zone. A girl with pigtails is walking a yellow lab and I'm moving so slowly we're almost at the same pace. It doesn't stop me from slowing down even more, though. I can hear my heart in my ears and I have never been more certain of anything: I am going to run her over. I am used to the thought occurring, but this is the first time it has felt like a prediction and not a fear. I slow down even more until I'm barely moving, but the certainty of what I'm going to accidentally do keeps pounding through my whole body. The gasping, the difficulty breathing, makes it worse. I know if I'm distracted by the need to get a breath in, I'm even *more* likely to lose control of my car. All of that is waving through me and when I finally get past the little girl, she turns onto a side street.

I think.

Then I'm not so sure. She's not in my rearview mirror,

she's not ahead of me, and the more I mull it over the more I am sure, *sure* that I actually did hit her. So I turn around and drive down the side streets until I find her. There she is: skipping now, letting her dog lick her hand, all ignorant innocence and precocious grade-school energy. She's okay. I can continue driving.

But is she okay? Was that the same little girl? Shouldn't I make sure?

Every time I pass her I get an instant of relief followed by a deep nausea at the danger I put her in. And then the need to check on her just that one last time.

By the time I get to Austin and Sylvia's place it's way past five and I've driven so many side roads and made so many nervous loops I'm motion-sick and exhausted. My eyes hurt from the focus of watching so intently. But I'm lucky, 'cause Sylvia's cigarette addiction is seriously hardcore and she's out there smoking within a few minutes of me parking. I guess I hadn't known this was what I was going to do until I got here, but watching her and waiting for Austin to join her or appear in the sixth window up from the ground or walk in with Chinese takeout gets to be too much. I've come this far, it's taken this long, and I need more.

The streets are bustling. I step out and the noise is familiar and disorienting after so long in the car. Kids giggling and throwing tantrums, assholes who don't use headphones letting their music play for everyone, cars shifting gears, amping up, dying down. All the sound is layered on top of a thin layer of icy snow. You'd think the puffy down jackets and wool caps would absorb some of the city sounds, but there's just as much noise in the winter as there is in the summer.

Sylvia's underdressed. Her leather jacket hangs open, a low-cut sweater shows off that perfect boob job, a hat and scarf are maybe keeping her warm, but I shiver just looking at her raw, exposed, practically blue fingers holding the cigarette to her mouth. I'm going to approach her. It's not a decision so much as an imperative, and I wind up next to her without even really realizing it.

"Can I have one?" I say. Her lips are overblown but even that edge of fakeness doesn't obscure the glamour of her beauty. The trueness of it. She is gorgeous by any standard. Her boots are trimmed with fur that I think could be real, and the size and sparkle of her diamond ring hits me hard. I can smell her. I can feel the amount of body heat she has coming off of her; I can see the way her hands shake on the way to her mouth.

"Oh, sure, it'll kill you though," she says. She sounds just like she does behind Dr. Pat's door: brassy and hoarse and opinionated. Everything in me is thrilling at being this close to her.

"That's okay," I say. Sylvia laughs. I don't know if it's 'cause she thinks I'm joking or if she's laughing at the way all teenagers are full of angsty drama. It doesn't really matter, 'cause she gives me a cigarette and lights it and another one for her-self and it seems like maybe she's even in the mood to talk.

"Christ, it's cold," Sylvia says. "You know you're an addict when you'll freeze your fingers off just to get some nicotine in your system."

"You have a no-smoking rule in your apartment?" I say. It's so easy. Just like that I'm asking about her place with Austin. I am moments away from hearing her say his name, from learning more about them, from getting at least a quick glimpse into their lives.

"My husband hates it," she says. And my heartbeat slows. And my hands stop shaking despite the cold, and my head clears up, suddenly ready to function on a normal plane. Sylvia smells like expensive perfume and smoke and some-thing else: men's deodorant. She smells, I think, like Austin must smell, and I could inhale her. But first I need to keep appearing normal.

"Oh yeah?" I take an inhale like I love smoking, but I'm working hard to choke it down without coughing. If I'm going to buddy up with Sylvia I have to be a real smoker. It's like religion: To pull it off you have to be there all the time, not just on holidays.

"He hates a lot of things," Sylvia says. "You know? Some people could make a living from hating stuff." I can do this. I can be Sylvia's smoking buddy. I raise my eyebrows and nod really slowly like we're sharing a real secret.

"But he gave you that ring?" I say. It might be crossing the line, but this is not a puritanical, shy, secret-keeper like the women from my suburb. She is something else and I think I might be on the right track.

"Why do you think I keep him around?" she says with a wink, and we both laugh and take in smoke at almost the same time.

"I'll remember that for when I find a guy," I say, and Sylvia smiles again. "I'm Bea, by the way."

"Sylvia. You new to the building?" There's only one answer, and it's the one that will make it possible for me to share more cigarette breaks with Sylvia. Only one answer that will let me run into Austin on a regular basis without seeming insane.

"Uh-huh." The lie makes me dizzy, but the promise of it bringing me closer to Austin is so strong that I resist the urge to rake it back. I pinch my mouth into a smile and drop my cigarette on the pavement. I rub it out with the scuffed-up edge of my insanely pink snow boots. "But I'm actually heading out. You waiting for the husband to come back?" It's pushing it a little far, trying to figure out when Austin will be back. But if I don't ask I'll end up hiding behind a tree all evening just to make sure, and it's too cold for that right now.

"I have the place to myself tonight," Sylvia says. "When you're my age, you'll know how great that is." She's can't be more than ten years older than me. I remember the last session I overheard. She told Austin she wanted a baby but would never get pregnant if he couldn't "keep it up" for longer than five minutes. I'm itching to reread my notes.

"Thanks for letting me bum one from you," I say, and give her a high-wattage smile. The kind that comes lined in bright red lipstick and is *this*close to a really big belly laugh. Sylvia shrugs and smiles back. I want to say something else, but she does it first.

"I'm sure I'll see you out here again soon." I nod and hope it doesn't look puppy-dog eager.

It takes her going inside for me to realize in a shiny, crystal-clear moment that I have just screwed myself royally. Now she knows what I look like and I'll have to be super-careful at Dr. Pat's not to be seen by them.

'Cause not getting there early to listen in on their sessions isn't an option. You'd think I'd be annoyed at the extra layer of complication I'm adding to my already ridiculous, probably illegal habit. But I look forward to the set of necessary rituals that will come with keeping myself hidden at Dr. Pat's while also convincing Sylvia I am an avid smoker who lives in her apartment building.

More rules to follow. It actually eases the anxiety of having to leave their building now.

I'd like to drive home, but I'm too amped up to be safe on the road, so I walk a few streets over to a coffee shop and call Beck back. Now that I've seen Sylvia, I can picture Beck's face again. The mental image is all cleared up, unfogged. I remember the shape of his eyes. His arms. The ridiculous action-figure way he walks.

"Hi," I say when his voice mail picks up. "It's Bea. Just returning your texts. Which were totally fine, by the way. So, yeah. Don't worry about it. But also, don't call me back right away, 'cause I'll be in the car and driving and stuff. Okay. But call me after. I mean, later. Okay. Bye."

I wish I hadn't left a message at all, but the calm from talking to Sylvia lasts long enough for me to drink a huge mug of mocha in peace and to drive home at an almost reasonable thirty-five miles an hour. I think, not for the first time, that I've had my fill now. That I won't need to do any of that again.

But when I get home, I make a beeline for my room with the notebook to read about their last session. I wrote the notes in such a daze, such an autopilot, zombielike state, that I don't even remember what was in there. So opening the notebook to reread is almost as serious a jolt as the original listening-in.

Sylvia: You must be getting it somewhere.
Austin: I'm not a machine. I'm not some sex machine
   for you.
Sylvia: Most guys—
Austin: You're the one who's gone outside the
   marriage—

Sylvia: ONCE.

Austin: Oh, okay, just once. Then that's fine—

Dr. Pat: Let's all take a moment.

Austin: (mumbles)

Sylvia: I CAN'T HEAR YOU.

Austin: (mumbles)

Sylvia: See, this is the kind of passive-aggressive—

Austin: I said you make me feel like I'm nothing.

Dr. Pat: (something superdeep and meaningful that shuts them both up)

Before I forget, I make a point to write down as much of the conversation I just had with Sylvia as I can remember. I don't let the dinging of text messages coming in on my phone stop me. I write and write until it's all there in print. And when I've read it over once and gotten a little of that peace back, I am ready to look at my phone again.

It's Beck.

He's at the gym and needs a ride.

If I pick him up he'll take me to a movie.

But I can't tell Dr. Pat.

It doesn't have to be a date date, but he'd like it to be a date.

I write back quickly and tell him to not wear a tie or blazer or whatever. Then I add a smiley face so that I don't sound like a huge bitch. He doesn't respond, so I get in the car immediately, before he can change his mind and definitely before I can change my mind, since some of the calm from my time with Sylvia is already evaporating at the thought of being around Beck.

I read an article three weeks ago that said people in relationships are less likely to have homicidal tendencies. I'm not saying that's a motivating factor or whatever, but it made an impression somewhere in my head, and Dr. Pat smiled when I told her about it. She likes anything that encourages me to have things like friendships. If I can fall for Beck, maybe it means I'm not one of those secretly dangerous people. I mean, I bet Reggie didn't have normal crushes on normal girls.

Not that I like Beck because of some sociological study, but it makes the prospect of liking him more manageable, less terrifying. Maybe he'll touch my hand again. Maybe he will put hands on my hips or cup my face. Maybe his mouth will find mine the way it did in the dark, and I'll remember that rhythm we found, that slow pressure and mounting passion from the night of the dance. That's the real reason I go. The hope of losing myself in him for another few moments. The hope of losing myself in anything at all.

He's waiting in the gym parking lot when I pull in. He's changed out of workout gear and into jeans and a wool coat that is, of course, too tight. His hair's wet, hopefully from showering, not from sweat, and there's a woman holding his arm. School ended a while ago and I know from looking at him that he has been at the gym since the second the bell rang at 2:20. The lady gripping his arm is more or less the female version of Beck and hasn't had time to get out of her gym clothes. She is muscular in a bumpy, unreal way that I'm not sure I've seen before on a flesh-and-blood female. Her hair's back in a long, sweaty ponytail and she is so solid I could probably drive my car right over her and not harm her at all.

She would be the perfect friend for me. Unbreakable. Just like the guys I usually like.

Beck's leaning away from her a little, probably 'cause of the unclean hair or the fact that she doesn't use baby wipes after every few lifting sets.

"Hey," I call out, and the woman lets go a whimper of relief at my coming toward them. *Taking care of Beck was not on her schedule for today,* I think.

"Oh, good!" she says. She pats Beck on the arm before beelining for me, and he follows behind at a much slower pace. I notice him wipe off his hands ineffectually with his jacket. Then he uses the sleeves to wipe at an exposed part of his neck and his forehead, too.

"Is he okay?" I say. He is gray-faced and sleepy and she looks exhausted.

"He said he'd call his girlfriend to pick him up," she says without actually answering the question. I can't decide what's most distressing right now: the fact that he's called me his girlfriend or the smell of baby powder deodorant seeping through the woman's skin and clothes. It's an intense, childish sweetness but it effectively obscures the look of her body so that she is two totally conflicting things at once: a little girl and a powerhouse bodybuilder.

"I'm not his girl—" I start. I'm usually the worst with strangers when it comes to oversharing. My throat basically fills with words and thoughts and things I'd like to scream at the top of my lungs the second I meet someone new.

"Bea. Thanks for coming." Beck interrupts before this girl has a chance to hear what I have to say. "Penny was just walking me out. . . ."

"Don't let him lie to you," Penny says, placing a pair of fingers on Beck's wrist like she's checking for a heartbeat. "He overdid it. I'd rather he go to the doctor, but if you can keep him hydrated and resting, he can wait on it." Beck has a huge, family-size bottle of water in his hands and every time Penny looks his way he gulps some down.

"Oh, sure," I say. Penny's obviously itching to get inside. She holds a wagging finger in Beck's face and tells him to be careful, then sprints back into the gym, leaving me and Beck in the parking lot with a whole bunch of crazy between us.

"What the hell?" I say to start. "Are you okay? You called me your girlfriend? You look weird. Are you sick? Is she a doctor or anything? She seemed pretty serious. Did you fall or something? I don't know anything about, like, gym injuries; I've never even been to a gym. I swear to God." I spill out every thought I can until I really let myself look Beck in the face, and he looks awful. His face is a pasty, sweaty white and his eyes have a hazy, glassy look to them. His fingers are shaking, and tapping eight times, over and over, one finger at a time, on his thigh.

"You've got to let me wash my hands," Beck says. "Do you have anything with you?" It's like an alternate-universe drug deal. He's itching for some antibacterial soap and will pay good money to get it.

"I don't think I have anything in—" I start. Beck is having another panic attack. And the realization inside himself that he's having one (eyes widening, then tearing up, then focusing only on me) makes the panic even worse. The gym bathroom is probably just yards away, but there must be a reason he didn't already go in there so I take it out of the running as an option. "Gym bag!" I say, and I hold out hope that somehow Beck is freaking out enough to have forgotten about some stash he might have in there. I grab the duffel out of his hand, unzip and dig through it.

It's oversize and full of pressed shirts and notebooks and packets of Muscle Milk and protein powder. No soap. No wipes. Meanwhile, there's sweat coming out of every one of his body parts. Strangers watch, think about helping, go about their business, take the long way around us, take a shortcut to get closer to us, listen in, shut us out.

Finally, I find a Ziploc bag of baby wipes. And hand them

over like a nurse to a surgeon and wait for him to clean off the disease.

He doesn't.

He opens the plastic bag, and then presses it closed again.

"Crap," he says.

He stamps each foot eight times. I can't help blushing. The attraction is still there, but the gesture makes him look more like Jenny or Rudy and less like a hot, mysterious dude I want to kiss. I try not to think: *This is how I look when I pinch my thigh or take notes in Dr. Pat's waiting room or drive like an old lady on the highway.*

"Crap crap crap crap crap crap crap."

"Oh my God, dude, wipe your hands. Don't try to get through it *now*. If you want to fight the urge to clean off, do it on Dr. Pat's time." I barely recognize the chill in my voice. "For now just, you know, compulse the hell out of yourself. Seriously."

"There's only four wipes left," Beck says. I immediately wish I'd hidden my frustration much better. 'Cause now his anxiety is mixing with some serious shame. And between the anxiety attack and the dehydration and who knows what else is going on in that perfect-looking body of his, we're going to end up in the hospital if I don't solve at least one of these issues right now.

"We will get more. But use four for now. There's a pharmacy nearby." Beck kind of nods but he can't get his hands

unshaken enough to actually do any of the compulsive cleaning. I take the bag out of his hands and before I know it the
baby wipes are in my hand and I'm cleaning him, washing his
hands carefully, one wipe at a time. It's a familiar smell, the
sweet cleanness mixed with a twinge of acid and alcohol.

I used to know a lot about changing babies' diapers. I was
a really good babysitter, actually, until I saw a Lifetime movie
about a sweet nanny who went crazy and hurt the kids she
was caring for. It got me so freaked out that I fired myself and
gave all the families to Lisha and pretended she needed the
money more than me. I think of calling Lisha now, but I'm
sure Beck would hate that. It's bad enough that *I'm* seeing
him like this, I'm sure. I try to do what Lisha would do for me,
though. Speak in a quiet voice, rub his back, act like I do this
kind of thing all the time.

Beck's hands aren't nearly as soft as the dimpled thighs of
a newborn, but it's okay. That's okay. I'm just happy to feel the
rate of his heart start to drop, the rhythm of his breathing still
fast but more functional. I uncap his water bottle and hold it
up to his mouth to have him drink more.

I want the color back in his face.

Water spills down his chin as he drinks. It's a sloppy thing,
turning from careful to desperate.

I've got to get him more wipes before the panic comes
back at an even higher, more intense pitch.

 11.

I WOULDN'T EXACTLY CALL OUR SECOND DATE A "date" either. I'm still the same amount of disheveled as I was the first time: uncombed hair and a sweater my mother knit from pale yellow yarn back when she thought she might be good at knitting. She wasn't. I have on argyle socks with ballet flats, and the oversize glasses I wear to school. Pink skinny jeans. The kind of outfit that screams *I go to an all-girls school.*

And Beck is zoning out from taking a Xanax that Dr. Pat recently prescribed. He's still sweaty and gray like he was when I picked him up from the gym an hour ago. But I guess it qualifies as a date because we're thigh-against-thigh on the couch in my TV room and I am playing nurse to Beck's worn-out self. It doesn't classify as a date in the traditional sense, but then what *would* you call this?

"I'm sorry. I'm so sorry. Thank you. Seriously," Beck keeps saying. It's an endless loop, but not in his usual compulsive eight-times way. This is just a regular run-of-the-mill apology. It's also unnecessary.

"I know how it is," I say. I'm stirring protein powder into a huge mug of skim milk, per Beck's request. It seems like an okay concession to make, since at least the shake will help his body recover from whatever craziness he put it through at the gym. The smell is horrible: a curdling, breast-milk sourness that is so thick in odor I can practically taste it through my nose. It's thick, stirring it is basically like churning butter, and it cannot possibly qualify as food.

And as eager as Beck is for me to make the concoction, his face contorts as he chugs it down without coming up for air. There is nothing comfortable in watching someone torture himself so deliberately. I can hear the clicking sound of forced swallowing, and when the mug is emptied he emerges with a milk and protein powder mustache that needs cleaning up immediately so that I don't vomit right here.

"Sorry, sorry," he says again. He just can't get enough apologies in. The TV drones in the background, some movie I've half-seen a dozen times, but Beck is stuck in his own head. "I know how gross that is. How gross I . . . am."

"Seriously. I get it. I mean, I'm like you. Except without the resulting hot body. But you know, this isn't weird to me."

"But you don't get like this," Beck says. "Not really. You don't have disgusting habits. You're not like the rest of us. I didn't think I was like those other people in group—but look at me. I am. I'm not better than Jenny or Rudy. But you're . . . you're fine. You just have a couple little quirks."

He will not think I am "just quirky" if I turn randomly violent one day, or if I have to start hiding all sharp objects, from scissors to tweezers to toothpicks. He will not think it's cute when being around me is as high-security as going to the airport.

My mind flashes to the bruised part of my flesh. I keep pinching the same spot over and over and it's funny how quickly the skin responds to the repetition.

"Funny" is probably the wrong word.

"I *will* say your protein crap is borderline grotesque. But come on. You know you're cute." Beck basically winces at the word. His eyes are even more beautiful than usual: watery and blue and unfocused. It's sexy—the compromised, drugged-out state he's in.

I like how safe and broad and sturdy he is, but I guess I like the hint of weakness, too. He could crush me with one arm but he's distracted easily by shiny objects and errant germs. He's impenetrable and scared in the same breath. He is that perfect amount of fucked up. I touch his cheek like a test and he smiles. It's lazy, it's Xanax-induced, but it's right there on his lips, and then his dimples appear and I have to kiss him.

He gives in easily. It's not passion or desperation but that's okay because we both have enough of those things. It's easy and sweet and sort of milky-soft. Which isn't to say it's not the kind of kiss you can get lost in. I'm absolutely lost in it. His mouth seems to already know mine, his lips take their time, and there's a heat coming off of him that I have to press right up against. I have been cold for ages, and I can finally warm up.

Those hands—the ones that aren't smooth or well kept or soft—they are strong and big enough to grab a lot of me at once. And they do. They're everywhere. His hands hold me on top of him and they wander my body, but without a goal, without an endpoint, and I can sink into the kissing without wondering what will come next.

It's possible we are kissing like that for an hour or two. *Love Story* was on TV when we started and by the time we've ended it's got to be at least halfway through *Psycho*. The familiar vamping soundtrack has been rising and falling and sort of haunting the whole make-out session, but when we break apart, it's way too much, so I turn it on mute.

I don't think I could ever just turn *Psycho* off. It's too high on the list of awesome movies. Lisha and I used to beg my mother to rent us the scariest films. She'd usually comply, if we promised not to tell Lisha's parents that we were spending our Saturday nights with *The Exorcist* and *Scream* and *The Shining*.

I don't want to have to turn the movie off, but I also know I shouldn't be watching it. I miss those Saturday nights and they weren't even that long ago.

"I'll be right back," Beck says. It's him who stopped the

kissing. Not abruptly, not in a way that would be totally obvious to someone less hyperaware than me. But he sort of eased me off of him, and then slowed down the whole pace, and then turned the make-out into just kissing and the kissing into looking each other in the eyes, and the gazing into sitting side by side on the couch. Beck gets up and starts toward different corners, different doors, but he's never been here before and he seems to remember that at the most awkward moment, when he's already left me on the couch and tried to make a swift, temporary exit.

"Sorry," he says. "Bathroom?" I point him in the right direction.

Five, ten, fifteen minutes pass. The faucet runs and runs and then the shower, and then the faucet again. I'm getting washed off of him.

Half an hour passes.

In any other circumstance I'd knock on the door, but I know what's going on in there and anything I do will just slow the whole thing down. Also: The possibility occurs to me that if I went near that door I would break it down and shove him under the water and drown him. Part of me knows that's obviously not going to happen, but I stay back anyway. Sit on my hands. Avoid the possibility of danger. There's the scene from *Psycho* that we didn't see because we were too busy making out to worry about the screaming blonde on screen. But I know the movie well enough to play that over and over in my head. The knife, the blood, the implicit violence of a shower.

Forty-five minutes pass.

I try Dr. Pat's breathing exercises but they're not working because my entire mind is focused on keeping myself glued to the couch. I don't want to move any closer to the bathroom just in case. But I hate myself for the thought. I know it's not right or normal. I know I'm not simply some cute quirky girl like Beck says, and every moment I can't get off the couch is a moment that makes me one level crazier. That heavy, pre-crying feeling floods my sinuses and I drop my head from the weight of it. Cover my face with my hands for long enough to get out a quiet cry or two. Because there is nothing, *nothing* worse than not being able to undo the crazy thoughts. I ask them to leave, but they won't. I try to ignore them, but the only thing that works is giving in to them.

Torture: knowing something makes no sense, doing it anyway.

An hour has gone by. I have been working so hard not to do anything horrible that I didn't realize I'd been biting the inside of my palm. It's worse than the pinching. More barbaric. More evidence that I'm capable of terrible and unpredictable things.

It's not bleeding. There's no broken skin. It's just the impression of my teeth in the soft skin.

I've got to get Beck to leave. Who knows what I'll do next.

Psycho has turned to *Ocean's Eleven*, which should not

be on the classic movie channel because it's the new one with George Clooney and not the actual classic, so I try to focus all my irritation on that instead of Beck's disappearance.

When Beck finally comes out of the bathroom, he's found a towel and it's wrapped around his middle. The rest of him is all muscle and aggravated patches of scrubbed skin. It's not just that the body-builder physique is hot. It's also totally safe. From me, I mean. I'm not worried about being protected or whatever. But with him so strong, I can't hurt him. Or it would be really hard to do.

"That was . . . a long shower," I say. I assume my face has the telltale splotches of someone who had a quick cry and didn't get to wash her face, but he's not looking at me with anything but apology and shame.

"Yeah. Eighty-eight minutes exactly."

"Eighty-eight," I repeat, emphasis on the *eight*. "Do you do that every day? Or sometimes can you just take, you know, an eight-minute shower?" I do not ask why eight. That's a question for group therapy, not for our second date.

Obviously, there aren't accidents or coincidences with OCD. Or at least, not many. Not with someone as under control as Beck. Every minute that passes for him is careful, purposeful.

"I tried to just do eight. But, um, I sort of lost track of time for a second. You're a distracting thought, you know?" He smiles sheepishly. Shirtless Beck is flirting with me.

The eighty-eight minute shower was weird, but *I'm* weird, right?

"I'm distracting?" I say. I wipe under my eyes in case errant tears have clung to my eyelashes.

"You are. But, I guess . . . I wasn't ready for that," he says. "With you. All the . . . touching. I mean, it was great. You're great. But now I feel . . ."

He wants to say *dirty*. He wants to say he feels dirty. He's too polite to let the word out, so we just stand in the space where the word isn't.

"Can you put your clothes on?" I say. "I don't want to have this talk when you're like a glistening half-naked Adonis in my living room, you know?"

"Right, sorry," Beck says, but he doesn't laugh even though I think I meant to lighten the mood with that.

"I mean, you can also stay like that, but not if you want to break up with me. Not that we're together. You know what I mean. Don't freak out and then dump me when you're half-naked, okay?"

Beck does smile then. Dimples and all.

"Someday you're going to have to be the messed-up one, and I'm going to get to be the normal one, Bea" is his reply.

I'm exhausted and grinning and feeling myself vanish into something scary. I pinch my leg to shake myself out of it as much as possible. Feelings are like blankets, covering you up so you can't see clearly. Or like mazes you can too easily get lost inside. I am terrified of getting lost.

"Clothes. Seriously," I say.

"Will you drive me back to the gym?" he says. I laugh at the thought. He's taken a sedative, fought dehydration, taken the world's longest shower, and spent hours lost in a totally blissed-out make-out session. It's nearing midnight. A gym's not even in the realm of possibility.

But he's not laughing.

"I didn't finish my workout," he says.

"Yeah. 'Cause you got ill. From working out." I keep a smile on. I badly want to keep it light, to say good-bye to him at the door to his parents' house and know that we had a Good Time.

"Right. And now I'm fine." Beck stomps to the bathroom with his gym bag and apparently there's a whole change of clothes in there. (For just this purpose? Just in case he gets some girl's sexy make-out germs all over him?)

"You should really rest. I'll drive you home. Or you could even stay here—my parents wouldn't mind if you slept in the guest room. Or we could drive around for a while if you want and you can decide later? But don't be a total idiot." It's the last part, I'm sure, that makes him bristle the most. But the words tickled my throat too much so I spat them out.

So, okay, I'm not really making progress either.

"I'll just walk home," Beck says. "Thanks, though."

"Walk home? You don't live anywhere near here—" Beck

glares. Shakes his head. Blushes. Holy crap, that's a lot of feelings and reactions at once. "Oh," I say. "You want to walk home. You don't want me—"

"I want the exercise," Beck says. "I'm telling you that so you don't think I am trying to get away from you. I'd love for you to drive me to the gym. I'm not mad or upset or anything. And I could lie and say I want to be alone. I could do that so that you don't judge me or try to stop me from getting my workout. But I don't want you to feel that way—"

"Okay," I say. Because he's said exactly the right thing. Because in my book that kind of sacrifice is full-on romance. That risk. Most of all, more than (or maybe just as much as) he wants to protect his ability to go to the gym, he wants to protect me.

I sort of hate how weak I am, and I definitely hate that I give in so easily.

I drive him there. To the gym. We pick up a gallon of water and I lecture him on what I googled earlier about dehydration and the health risks of excess exercise. But I let him go in there. I watch him relax at the OPEN 24 HOURS sign. He relaxes enough that before he gets out he gives me a kiss on the lips. Not a lingering, wandering marathon kiss like before, but lips held against lips and his hand on my neck and another kiss behind my ear.

"Thank you," he says. He's beaming. I guess I am too.

♡ 12.

A FEW DAYS OF CAUTIOUS DAYDREAMING ABOUT
Beck and taking Latin quizzes and avoiding the dangerous
science lab later, I'm officially desperate for a good dose of
therapy.

Not for me, but for Sylvia and Austin.

It's Wednesday, so they have the appointment before
mine. I get there at my usual superearly time and bring the
notebook and three pens in case something happens and I
lose one or one is faulty or running out of ink or something. I
have to get enough from this session to last me another week,
since I'm only seeing Dr. Pat for private sessions once a week
now.

I'll let them walk in before getting out of my car. And
I'll go to the bathroom when their hour with Dr. Pat is up.
I'm not messing around, and if I'm going to do stuff like take
cigarette breaks with Sylvia, I definitely have to watch myself.
Good thing I have OCD, because that makes me totally anal
enough to cover my tracks.

That's a little OCD humor. Dr. Pat encouraged all of us in group to find some lightness instead of only seeing the diagnosis as, like, the worst thing ever.

Austin and Sylvia are right on time. Separate cars pulling in at the same moment. I make a note of it. I wonder if their session will be even worse than usual, if their new means of arrival is a bad sign. She's in an SUV and he's in something that looks fancy. I'm not into cars, so I let those details slide. Besides, I don't exactly need their plate numbers or whatever. That would be stalkery.

Sylvia's got on the kind of boots that look like a rabbit died on their behalf. Like, yesterday. And Austin's rocking a leather jacket and a bright blue plaid scarf and a cold-weather flush to his cheeks. It's so many kinds of fabulous it almost distracts me from all the other things I need to record about them. I would photograph them for my Costume Ideas folder that I have in my desk at home like a total nerd, but I don't think I can get away with it.

I take what feels like my first full breath of the day upon seeing him. They don't hold hands, but he touches her shoulder and they smile just enough to make it seem like they're not totally doomed.

I tear my eyes away from them for just long enough to write down what they're wearing and what the look on his face was when he touched her shoulder (wistful meets desperate). I count to one hundred after they get inside, long enough for the coast to be clear, and I let myself into the waiting room after peeking through the glass door.

From the outside this place looks like a totally cozy house, but there's a plaque on the side of the building that says NEW BEGINNINGS THERAPY PRACTICES and lists five other therapists. There's no doorman or bell to ring. There aren't even trashy magazines in the waiting room. Only one other girl is waiting for her appointment and she's so lost in her phone's screen that I doubt she notices I come in. So we wouldn't have to interact at all. Except she's in my chair. The only chair that lets me hear what I need to hear.

So I guess I could just give up on the little fix I'm wanting. I guess maybe a few months, or even weeks, ago that's what I would have done. But. If they are in there I *have* to listen. It's not a choice anymore and I don't know when exactly it stopped being a funny thing I chose to do and became a matter of life or death, but it's pretty far on that side of things now. If I don't listen in, Austin could basically drop dead. Or I could. Some people wear the same underwear for every baseball game or have little preperformance rituals like listening to a favorite song or jumping up and down seven times before stepping on stage. What I'm doing is the same thing. Except there's no game or performance, just my life and my desire to be able to deal with it.

I sit in a different chair for a minute. I tap my foot and strain to hear something coming through the walls.

There's nothing.

Something's probably wrong. With them, I mean. Something's happened in there. I mean, it's been like five minutes now and I haven't heard a single word. I pinch, pinch, pinch my leg and it's enough to make me focus, but not enough to stop the fast rise of anxiety.

I try to breathe through it. But that's useless because I'm about to drop dead and if not me, than one of them, and if not one of them, than maybe the whole world. So it's not worth thinking about how bat-shit crazy it all will sound to the girl sitting in my perfectly situated chair. Because when you're trying to save yourself or the world, there's not really anything else worth your time.

"That's my chair," I say to the girl. She has headphones on, which I hadn't noticed, so there's no response. Which means I have to actually walk up to her and then stand there, hovering over her. I don't think I should touch her, just in case she's like, homicidal or something. The hovering works. My shadow must finally register on her radar, and she looks up to find me staring at her. I push my mouth into a little smile because I don't want her to actually think I'm insane, just serious. "Sorry," I say when she pulls one of her earbuds out so that she can hear me. "I have to sit there. It's kind of important." The girl looks to the room of empty chairs.

And that'd be enough to deter me under normal circumstances. But I am dripping in sweat by now. The little tremors in my hands have turned to a full-body hum of shakes and shivers and the hum is mirrored in my actual brain. A white-noise sound puncturing my actual head.

So screw it. Seriously. It's not totally crazy to think something could happen to them. Superstition exists for a reason, right? And the things we do *matter*. Like that whole butterfly-effect thing. Every movement we make, even the movement of butterflies' wings, matters. That's what that theory is *about*. So yeah, this girl doesn't get why I'm doing what I'm doing, but that doesn't mean it's wrong. I clear my throat with more confidence and grip my right hand in my left to try to stop them both from shaking with anxiety.

"Yeah. Sorry. You have to move. Now. *Now*." I try to say it like maybe I'm an actual authority figure, but from the look on her face I'm not pulling it off. It doesn't matter. She moves. Not just to a different chair but all the way across the room to a cheesily upholstered couch that's trying really hard to make this place look warm and homey. And I settle in to my chair. I'm in so much panic I can't determine if it's more important for me to open my notebook up or if it's more important to focus on the listening before attempting note-taking. I risk doing both at once.

My heart is racing so fervently I worry that it could short out. That it will keep speeding up to new levels until there's nowhere else for it to speed up to and it will burst. I pinch my thigh as hard as I possibly can and lean unabashedly against the wall with my pen poised above the pages of my notebook. The girl is avoiding looking at me so she won't notice and besides, she's already written me off as a total lunatic.

Screw it. I just start scribbling. I don't care how it looks.

> *Austin: We don't have kids. We don't have to stick it out.*
>
> *Sylvia: That's not exactly the vow you took. Those aren't the actual stipulations, you know.*
>
> *Austin: Sometimes I look at you and just think . . . Where's my wife? Where's that woman I—*
>
> *Sylvia: Right here. I'm right here. I can't compete with every little girl you—*
>
> *Dr. Pat: Remember how we talked about not accusing Austin of liking "little girls." We need to talk about that insecurity in some other way.*
>
> *Austin: Men have things on their computers.*
>
> *Sylvia: You think that makes it okay to—*
>
> *Austin: I don't even know that woman.*
>
> *Dr. Pat: I'm sorry, can we clarify? Are we talking about someone specific or about pornographic material in general . . . ?*

There's a long pause where no one says anything. My body's cooled off, which leaves that horrible feeling of sweat gone stale all over. And my heart's slowed down and I'm repulsed, kind of. But I also want to hear every word, to have the whole record of it right in my hands whenever I need it. So when the grumbling of voices starts again, quieter now, I close my eyes to hear it better.

Austin: She's twenty.
Sylvia: She.
Austin: Lei-Lei
Sylvia: . . . nickname . . . for the love of . . .
Austin: . . . focus on the most arbitrary . . .
Sylvia: . . . tell me what to feel . . . and then you
  write songs about other women . . . and I sit
  there singing them for the love of . . .
Dr. Pat: (about five minutes of communication
  lecturing)

I'm smart enough to guess at some of the pieces. He's having an affair, or has a crush, or has some webcam girl named Lei-Lei that he's in love with. And Sylvia's pissed. And apparently he writes songs about all of it and makes her sing them. Or something.

But it's not the guesswork that interests me. It's not the pitter-patter of marital back-and-forth that's so enthralling either. I mean, it's intriguing and scandalous and exciting, but I wouldn't be here if that's all it was. It's not interest, it's *necessity.*

And the real mystery here isn't whether or not Austin is sleeping with some twenty-year-old or what kinds of communication methods are best for their marriage. Those aren't the big questions that I am working so hard to answer. What I want to know is: *Why am I so focused on them?* When I was superfocused on Kurt it was because I really, truly loved him, and when I get all amped up about Jeff it's because he was my first kiss and because he turned out to be kind of scary. And Reggie was practically infamous and all over the papers and knew my mother. But with Austin and Sylvia I can't point to love or fear or trauma to explain the obsession. Aside from Austin being hot and looking a little like an all-grown-up version of Jeff, and Sylvia being basically a hipster glamorama life-size Barbie doll, there's no real reason for me to latch on to them.

I have pages and pages of notes by the time their session is over. Some of them are well laid out in full sentences and some of them are chicken scratch, but it's all there, semideipherable and then tucked away into my huge purse so that Dr. Pat doesn't see when it's my turn to sit on her couch. There's the shuffling of feet and pleasantries that mean they're done with their session. I planned on going to the bathroom and hiding out so they don't catch sight of me, but I can't bring myself to get out of the chair. I want one more glimpse of them. So I hide my face in my scarf and then tuck myself away behind a book. And the safest thing to do would be to bury myself there, in the pages, chin all the way to my chest, eyes all the way down.

I can't.

They're talking casually to each other when they open the door, and I have to catch sight of them. Because if I just look this one last time I'll be fine; I'll remember what they look like; I'll let it go.

That's not what happens.

"I gotta pee," Sylvia says. "Wait here a second?" Austin nods and sits down near me. It is the closest I've been to him and nothing can break the spell because Dr. Pat is on her fifteen minutes of unwinding time and Sylvia can't recognize me if she's in the bathroom, and there's this euphoria at the idea that it's all going to work out in some magical jigsaw-puzzle way.

The girl who was in my chair earlier has obviously been in her own appointment for a while now; she didn't show up an hour early like me. So with Sylvia in the bathroom, it's just me and Austin in the waiting room. I can smell him: woodsy and strong, like cologne made for guys who don't wear cologne. Maybe deodorant. It's a thick smell. His sneakers are soaked through from the snowy mix outside and I'd like to take my time raising my gaze from his feet all the way up to his face but there *is* no time, so I make myself just look right at him.

My throat's on fire with words. I am the worst kind of outgoing.

"I have the appointment after yours," I say. Not that he was asking. Not that he was even looking at me, or knowing in any vague way that a person was next to him. And now my cheeks are burning up: "little apples," my dad calls them, since the combination of cheek bones and baby fat and light pink blush highlight that line of my face more than anything else. Some girls are all eyes or all boobs. I am all cheeks.

It's not the worst thing in the world. I'm cute and fresh faced. I'm wholesome.

"Oh, okay," Austin says with a half smile. I hadn't noticed how many tattoos he has. Of course I'd taken note of them, but I'm going to need to make a whole list of them now. I'll make it in my head first, and then hopefully I'll remember them all later in my car.

> *Sylvia's name on his wrist and around his ring*
> *finger.*
> *Chinese symbols checkered up and down his*
> *forearms.*
> *An angel crawling up his neck.*
> *The word ECLIPSE right above the neckline of his*
> *T-shirt.*

"You have so many tattoos," I say.

"Ha, yeah," Austin says. "You got any?" I practically fall out of my chair at the fact that Austin has asked me a question, because this signifies, beyond a shadow of a doubt, that he is having a real conversation with me now.

"My mom would kill me if I showed up with tattoos."

"That's no excuse," Austin says with a wink. He's the kind of guy who can pull off winks and high fives with a sophisticated, tongue-in-cheek irony. Austin takes out a phone, and I should take that as a signal that the conversation is over, but I can't. I dig my thumbnail into my thigh but it doesn't matter; the words are going to come spilling out anyway.

"'Eclipse.' What does that mean?" I point to his neck and smile. But I'm an idiot because Sylvia will be back any second and Dr. Pat hasn't come to the waiting room to get me yet.

"Long story. I'll tell it to you sometime." Then there's another wink and then Sylvia's pushing open the waiting room door to get Austin. I pull my scarf up a little more but it's useless. I don't have one of those faces that people confuse with their sister's best friend or their mortal enemy from grade school. I don't remind people of anyone but me. Sylvia's not going to struggle with how to place me or where I am in her index of names and faces that she, like the rest of the world, spends every day building upon.

She'll know exactly where she's seen me before. I go red again.

Sylvia has reapplied whatever makeup got cried off during her session. She's twisted her hair into a loose bun and her lips are now a dark, expensive, purple shade. She doesn't say anything though. Doesn't wave or smile or ask what the hell I'm doing here. But the recognition registers on her face, followed by a moment of total chaos in her head, and then nothing.

"You ready?" she says to Austin. And maybe it seems like everything's fine, but I can see her tucking the moment with me away until later.

"Sure I am," Austin says. "Have fun in there," he adds, head cocked in my direction. Sylvia does another set of calculations in her head, I think, and then they're off and Dr. Pat's calling me in and I've just crossed one more line.

"I need to tell you a little more about what to expect," Dr. Pat says when I've settled into the corner of the couch closest to the door in her office. I have a theory that she judges you based on where you sit, because she always gestures vaguely to the couch and the two armchairs, and doesn't sit down until I have chosen a place to park myself. I always choose the couch.

"Expect?"

"In group," Dr. Pat says. "I think you saw a little of my system with Jenny the other day, and I wondered how you were feeling about it."

"Like, you not letting Jenny pull out all her hair? I think that's a good idea," I say, adjusting the pillow behind my back so that I can lean into it more easily. There's nothing I hate more than Dr. Pat thinking I look all awkward and uncomfortable during therapy. I like to at least give the illusion of ease.

Fat chance.

"That's right. Not letting Jenny compulse. I'm sure you saw how difficult that was for her," Dr. Pat says. It's all so pointed, but I'm not sure why. I do not pull my hair or pick my face, so I don't know quite what she's getting at. But Jenny was sweating and groaning by the middle of group last time. The urge to pull her hair was so strong I thought she might vomit from the force of it.

Which would not actually be funny, but the idea of someone projectile vomiting in a room full of hypochondriacs and germaphobes makes me smile anyway. Dr. Pat says my healthy sense of humor will save me. Here's hoping.

"Seemed tough," I say.

"Next week we will be doing something similar with Rudy and his compulsions. Eventually we will do that with everyone. Put you each in a situation that exacerbates your anxiety, and prevent you from compulsing. How does that sound?"

Uh, terrible?

"Okay . . . ," I say. By the end of the session with Jenny, her moans and sweat and shaking eventually subsided a little. She didn't suddenly become a zen monk or anything, but the panic attack turned into what looked like total exhaustion, and her hands folded in her lap looked less like they were tearing at each other and more like they were just resting.

"It's called exposure therapy, and it's scary but really effective."

"I'm not really sure I need that," I say. It's not like I think Dr. Pat's going to actually tell me I don't have OCD, but I want her to at least admit I'm less severe than the rest of them. She's doesn't.

"I see—and why's that?" she says instead. Picks up her pen, hovers it above the notebook.

"I just . . . what would you expose me to?"

"I think we still have a lot to uncover about what your triggers and compulsions really are, don't you? But certainly we would expose you to driving without stopping to check, driving at a normal speed, taking fewer notes. Things like that. Some of it would just be you and I, some would be with the whole group. Everyone's different."

"Ah." There is a world of difference between someone who pulls hairs out of her scalp one at a time and someone who is cautious on the road, I think. And taking notes about people and situations isn't exactly ruining my life. There's no way to say that to Dr. Pat, but she seems to sense it anyway. Sometimes I think she can hear my thoughts. Like she's not just a therapist but also a psychic or something.

"Is Jenny okay?" I say at last. Sometimes the silence extends for too long and the discomfort drives me to blurt out random thoughts and I guess this is one of those moments.

"How do you think she did?"

"Looked . . . hard," I say. Dr. Pat glances behind my head where the clock is. I can't ever check the time without craning my neck, but I always notice when she does.

"Yes?" Another tactic to make me keep talking. She knows I hate the empty space where conversation stalls or halts completely. She knows I'll be driven to fill it, with total crap if I have to.

"I mean, it's kinda like, maybe Jenny's happier being able to do whatever she wants to do. I don't know. Not that she wants to be bald, obviously. But it seems like doing her, um, compulsions or whatever, helps her and that maybe it's not so nice to take that away from her, right?"

"Interesting."

"I mean, I don't know. I guess, like, I always feel bad for those little kids whose parents take away their blankies when they turn seven or whatever. Like, what's the harm in making yourself feel better?" Dr. Pat nods and I don't even really know what I'm saying. It's not exactly something I've given much thought to, but I'm creating a whole theory about this stuff on the fly. "I mean, when my parents stopped letting me sleep in their bedroom after that Jeff thing, I thought it was really mean, you know? Like, sleeping on a mattress in their room really helped my nightmares and stuff, and then they just took it away from me, and I don't know, that seems kind of wrong, right?"

I'm surprised to hear Jeff's name come out of my mouth. Dr. Pat knows all about him, but only from my mother, never from me. I don't think about Jeff, or my parents sleeping in my room for a while when I was fourteen, or any of that stuff, but suddenly I'm all weepy and Dr. Pat is reminding me that there are tissues on the coffee table if I need them, and I'm insisting I'm fine, fine, fine.

"Good work today, Bea," Dr. Pat says when the clock has told her it's time for me to go. She says "Good work" every time I cry. Leaving the office, I wish Austin and Sylvia had the appointment after mine and not before, because with my head aching from the tears and my heart pounding from having mentioned Jeff and hearing way too much about exposure therapy, I could really use a distraction.

No such luck. I'm gonna have to get through it on my own. Sort of like my very own exposure therapy. Except, of course, I have my notebook. I flip through it in the bathroom before heading out to my car. Then I can breathe again.

♡ 13.

I'M SO TIRED AFTER MY SESSION WITH DR. PAT
that I decide I can't possibly drive. It wouldn't be safe. For a
split second I consider calling Beck, who definitely owes me
a ride anyway, but I can't make my fingers press the buttons,
and I call Lisha instead.

"Please tell me you are inviting me over to drink a bottle
of wine in your walk-in closet, because I am having the shit-
tiest day," she says instead of hello. It is so rare that Lisha
is upset and needs me to comfort her that I forget what to
say for a few beats. *"Hello?"* she practically screams into the
phone.

"Hi! We can drink in the closet! Or even in the TV room;
my mom and dad are doing a date night tonight," I say. Sometimes we celebrate our boring lives with a red wine from a
good year and act out the idea of being stately and mature.
Lisha knows about "good years" because her parents have
made a point to teach her about things like that. So she'll feel
comfortable at Harvard.

I don't think they know much about what Harvard's going to be like.

On these nights I hijack my mother's pearls and we buy a half pound of brie and take over my basement or my walk-in closet if circumstances dictate it, and we make a crappy day suck less.

"Okay, I'll be right over. Oh my God, thank you so much, I can't even tell you. I'm ready to kill Cooter and my parents," she says. I hate that she has used the word "kill," but I let it go with just a pinch on my thigh and the knowledge that while I am a loose cannon, Lish is just fine.

"You're welcome, but you have to pick me up at Dr. Pat's. I'm not home."

"Pick you up? Where's your car?"

I pace to the side of the building. I don't want to even look at my car right now, truth be told.

"It's here, but I can't drive it, okay?"

"Oh," Lisha says. It doesn't even sound like her voice. I've made her bad mood even worse with my totally incompetent self.

"I know. I'm sorry. You're amazing. The rest of the night is all about you," I say. And I mean it. I can pull it together for an evening of wine and reality TV and popcorn with cheddar cheese grated on top and whatever else Lisha wants.

"It's fine. I'll be there in fifteen."

"Seriously, I love you," I say.

"Well, duh." Lisha smooches into the phone and the sound hits my ear with a loud *smack*. I am the luckiest person on the face of the earth.

For fifteen minutes I watch my car from a distance. It's a sturdy, boxy thing and shouldn't terrify anyone. I light a cigarette. At first I just needed an excuse to be near Sylvia, and I still hate the taste, but it's moved from novelty to habit pretty quickly. I feel powerful, sucking in the smoke, imitating the graceful movements I remember Sylvia making, the pretty shape her lips make on the exhale. I'm not smoking a pack a day or anything, but the urge is there, and growing. Especially when I'm stressed.

I'm stressed.

I think I see a scratch on the front of the car and maybe a tiny dent on one side, but I can't tell from here and I don't want to get any closer; standing a dozen yards away feels safest.

But it does look like a dent, if it's not just the pattern the sun is making as it hits the passenger door. And if there's a dent it could mean I hit something. Someone. Maybe that time I looked at Beck at the stoplight, the moment I got distracted by the shadows his eyelashes made over his ultrablue eyes. It is for that reason and so many more that boys should not have ridiculously long eyelashes.

Lisha pulls up just as I am taking a few cautious steps toward the car, to see if the sun shifting as afternoon turns to night makes the vision of the dent go away. It does not. Crap.

"Come on, get in here!" she calls out. I take a half step, but nothing more. "Bea, seriously, come on."

I manage to look her way, and she's got raccoon eyes from melted mascara and splotchy cried-on cheeks. Lisha doesn't cry.

"Can you check out my car?" I say. I do not want to say it. I know Lisha will be pissed at me for saying it. But I say it anyway.

"Is it broken down or something?"

"I feel like it's dented."

"You *feel* like it's dented?" Lisha does not put her car in park. She doesn't smile or giggle or look me in the eye.

"I don't know . . ." I'm blushing a mean red, and the blush is so hard it gives me a headache, makes me dizzy. If she can just check the car, we can go drink the cabernet I know she's got zipped into her tote bag and talk about her bad day and annoying brother.

"Can we please do this later?" Lisha says after rubbing her eyes with the palm of her hand and spreading the mascara runs even farther.

"Yeah, I mean, of course. But maybe you can, like, look out your window?" I say, and the blush that could not get any redder or hotter gets both redder and hotter. "I'm so sorry. I promise if you just look—"

Lisha looks out her window, cranes her neck to get a good angle, and shakes her head.

"No dent, Bea," she says. Her eyes are flooding with tears because I have pushed her one extra step too far. I want to cry too, with relief and with shame, but I hold back so that Lisha can have one second of feelings of her very own.

"I . . . thank you," I sputter out, and I feel the blush recede the tiniest bit. I'd still like to check the car one more time and maybe drive by that stoplight that Beck and I stopped at the other night, and a few other tasks that would make me calm. But the urge has subsided enough for me to get into Lisha's car, give her a sideways, one-armed hug, and listen to her sniffle back a sob. "I'm sorry your day is sucking."

"Let's just get out of here. I want to get some good drinking in before your parents are back. I'm sleeping over, too. I brought clothes for school tomorrow, obviously."

"Obviously," I say, and squeeze her shoulder. We don't speak much on the drive to my house. I'm pretty sure if Lisha even breathes too deeply she'll start weeping, and I don't trust myself to say noncrazy things yet. I close my eyes and make a wish that I'll stop having OCD so that I can be a decent friend again. If I want it badly enough, hopefully it will come true.

In the basement TV room Lish and I do a sloppy job opening the wine, and the cork floats in the bottle, probably poisoning the cabernet, but I am not afraid of accidental poisoning, thank God. We drink from mugs and tune in to a world of bad accents, massive breasts, and fake laughter on

MTV. Lisha takes one end of the couch and I take the other and our feet meet in the middle.

She doesn't want to talk about what made her day so terrible, so instead we discuss what I should text Beck and what I should wear if we go out again.

"If I can't get a date, you need to at least do something fun with the cute Smith-Latin guy," she says.

"He washes his hands eight times every time he uses the bathroom. *Eight*," I say. I do not want her thinking I have lucked out with some superstar love interest when really we are two ridiculously awkward people who seem to like kissing.

"Just text him. Whatever, so he's a weirdo," Lisha says. She does not say: *You are too*, which is especially nice given the fact that she had to pick me up from *therapy* because I couldn't drive my own car ten minutes down a one-lane country road. So I text him and tell him to meet me in Harvard Square on Friday after school, and Lisha smiles in a way I totally do not at all deserve.

"You wanna come with us?" I say. I want to include her somehow, let her know how much I love her. Besides, I can totally see the three of us getting ice cream at J. P. Licks and picking out used CDs and making fun of the poser punk kids who hang out in the center of the square.

"I don't think I'm ready for all the . . . compulsion stuff just yet," Lisha says very carefully. "I mean, I'm used to *you*, but—" I shake my head 'cause I don't want her to finish the sentence, no matter how delicately she phrases it. "Sorry," she whispers after a moment of both of us staring at the TV screen and avoiding eye contact. I work my face into a smile and refuse to believe there's something between us that we can't talk about. A big swallow of wine goes down kinda rocky, and I practically choke it back up. It sort of dribbles out of my mouth, a bit of red spit.

"Classy," Lish says, tapping my foot with hers, and I try to hold back a giggle, but it comes anyway, with a little more wine dribbling out of my mouth, and she kicks a bit harder with both of her feet until we are laughing and kicking and nearly spilling our mugs of cabernet. Soon I have to wipe tears from my eyes: I'm a girl who cries when she laughs, and Lisha snorts, so the combination is total chaos. After a breathless few minutes we settle back into our seats and throw out snarky comments about the leopard-print bikinis and overprocessed hair extensions MTV can't seem to get enough of. I am proud of myself for the first time in months, thinking I've cheered her up and done something legitimately useful.

"Cooter told my parents he doesn't think we can afford Harvard," Lisha whispers, her voice almost hidden under the relentlessly annoying paper towel jingle playing on the commercial break.

"Huh?"

"Since he's at, like, state school, he thinks it's stupid for me to go to, like, the most expensive school ever," she says, a little louder and angrier.

"Ex*cuse* me?"

"I don't know. He's on a kick. Read some article about private universities, and I think he was sort of just being confrontational at first but then, I don't know, he sort of started talking himself and them into it." Lisha's voice cracks and then sobs heave out in huge crashes. I move to her side of the couch and put an arm around her. Pray to be normal for long enough to comfort her.

"That's completely fucked up," I say. Cooter gets on soapboxes from time to time. He once made their family go vegan for a few weeks. Another time he protested in front of the Catholic church a bunch of Sundays in a row. When Jeff was on trial, he wrote about a million letters to the editor about his best friend, even though Jeff's family had asked everyone to please not talk to the press.

"My parents actually listened to him! My dad said, 'He has a point. Harvard is very expensive and Lisha won't qualify for financial aid.' I mean he literally said that. Like, as if underachiever, live-at-home loser Cooter had a *point!*"

"Ok, try to breathe. They are not going to take away Harvard. Or if they try, you'll just take out a loan on your own or something. You will figure it out."

"Harvard's all I have," Lisha says, and the crying worsens.

"Okay, now that's not true. You have a million amazing

things, including Harvard," I say, rubbing her shoulder and turning down the TV so that our conversation is not conducted to the soundtrack of whiny sorority girls playing drinking games.

"You don't get it. You have, like, nice parents and your whole costume designing thing and boyfriends and everything. If I don't go to Harvard I'm basically a waste of space."

I've never heard Lisha talk this way, and the shift in our natural roles is unnerving. I keep squeezing her shoulder and saying *shhhh*, and when that fails, I refill her wine glass and watch her guzzle it down. Her mouth turns purple almost on contact, her teeth tinged red, and combined with her streaky, splotchy, teary face, it's an overwhelming effect of messiness. Soon she's hiccupping and moving her head in slow motion, side to side. I'm barely even tipsy. I drink just enough to help the anxiety so I can be there for her in the way she always, always is for me.

"You've got so much," I say, sure she won't even remember tomorrow morning. "Harvard, ballet, me."

"I feel like no one is more pathetic than me."

It hurts my ears, the ridiculousness of someone normal like Lisha hating herself. All her limbs are loose and floppy from alcohol, and she's sad but for a real reason. There's no tapping or pinching or note-taking or, God forbid, hair pulling. Just Lish and some tears and the ability to sleep it off and feel better in the morning.

Meanwhile, people like me and Beck are haunted.

"Want me to tell you more about Austin and Sylvia?" I offer. I hope it doesn't sound like what it so obviously is: something that will help *me* feel better, not her. I want to read through my notes, just once before we both fall asleep. I wouldn't mind checking the news, too, but I can probably pull that off by changing the channel while Lish is in the bathroom.

"Depends. How pathetic are they?"

"Not so much pathetic, but totally screwed up and destined to, like, never be happy," I say. I think it might be true: They're magnetic and fabulous, but everything I overhear in their sessions tells me they're miserable. So does the slow deliberation with which Sylvia smokes a cigarette. Like it's the best part of her day. Like it's her only escape.

"Okay," Lisha says, and leans her head back so it rests on the back of the couch and she can stare at the ceiling.

"Lemme get my notebook."

Lisha lifts her head from the couch and sighs. Mushes her mouth around like she needs to chew the words before they come all the way out, but even after a moment of staring at me and chewing, she doesn't spit it out.

"What?"

"You need your notebook?" she says at last.

"I just thought—"

"Yeah, okay. Go get it." I wonder if maybe she'll forget

this part of the conversation by morning too. Her eyes are glassy again, ready to let out a few more tears, and she bites her lips to stop them from coming. For a second I feel my defenses rising, but just as quickly they subside. Because she's going to let me get my notebook. She's going to let me read to her about Austin and Sylvia, even though she knows it's for me and not her. She's even going to let me pretend that I'm being a good friend by doing it.

"It's pretty entertaining, I swear," I say, smiling away the tension.

Lish smiles back but it looks like it hurts. "Yeah, sounds good."

"Hey, you're going to Harvard. Cooter's an idiot."

"Yeah."

"And I do *not* have a boyfriend." That makes Lisha laugh, at last. A quick burst of a giggle and a shake of her head. The sloppy, drunken kind, but still.

"Just get your notebook. I'm good." She doesn't look good, all sprawled out and red-faced on my couch, but I do what she says, because I am too exhausted to have an anxiety attack right now.

When I get back downstairs and curl myself back into the couch with the pink starred notebook, Lisha's almost completely passed out, but she smiles and nods while I read out loud, lets out an occasional huff of laughter. Humors me, really.

"So then they talked about Sylvia's eating habits. Austin wants Sylvia to buy more 'normal food' and Sylvia says she's taking care of his health. And then Austin said men need to eat meat, and Sylvia said if that will help him feel like a man, who's she to argue, and then Dr. Pat asked what the word 'man' meant to both of them, and why it was the focus of so many arguments."

"Mmmm," Lisha says. I should drag her up to the guest room so she can get a good night's sleep and look presentable for school in the morning, but by the time I've done all the reading and reviewing and remembering I need to do, she's fully asleep, and with her being a head taller than me, there will be no getting her up the stairs.

Not to mention I could lose my shit and drop her. I could get a violent burst and break her neck. The thought gives me chills, so I dig my fingernail into the palm of my hand, grip the notebook to my chest, and vow not to touch my best friend in the world.

You know, just in case.

I get a sleeping bag and sleep on the floor, though, so she won't wake up alone and confused and aching. And when I go to turn off my phone so that we can both be guaranteed a semirestful sleep without interruptions, I see that Beck has texted back to my asking him to go to Harvard Square with me on Friday. A string of eight perfect yesses.

♡14.

IN HARVARD SQUARE IT'S IMPOSSIBLE NOT TO
think of my first kiss, when I was twelve. Everything happens
in Harvard Square: my first kiss with Jeff, my first time saying "I love you" with Kurt, and now my first time going on a
totally purposeful date with Beck. It's something about the
brick crosswalks and double-lanterned lampposts that brings
out the sea change in me.

It occurs to me as I walk past centuries-old brick build-
ings that I should never have asked Beck to meet me where
memories are so impossible to fight. My stomach stirs when a
skater dude rolls by and I have to remember more about Jeff.

I pinch my thigh to push the thought down, but it rises
like bile: uncomfortable and unstoppable.

"I wanna kiss you," Jeff had said on the sidewalk in front
of a stately academic building.

"Now? In public?" I'd asked. Cooter and Lisha had run
into Starbucks to go to the bathroom but it still wasn't an
ideal circumstance. Jeff and I had been eyeing each other

for months and accidentally-on-purpose bumping elbows and knees and hips while we played H-O-R-S-E or sat on the couch or ran around the kitchen finding the perfect combination of snacks to devour.

"This isn't public. We could start a wildfire here and no one would notice. Safest place in the world to kiss you," he'd said, and then he plunged in and we were gripped in a kiss for maybe a minute. It was wetter than I had imagined a first kiss being. I played it over in my head for weeks afterward. He was fourteen and I was only twelve, and it seemed scandalous and strange and secret. I wrote in my journal at the time that it was the best day of my life. But thinking back on it now I can't even really picture his face. I think we used to have long talks when Lish and Cooter were having brother-sister spats, but for the life of me I couldn't tell you what we talked about or what his voice sounded like.

The great thing about Cambridge is that it's chock-full of kids with lots of piercings, and middle-aged academics who want to seem cool with whatever, and prissy Harvard students who are so busy taking notes on Faulkner that they don't pay much attention to anything weird I'm doing. It's a relief because the strain of not remembering and remembering all at once makes my breath catch and my head spin. It is not the first time I have had to fight the rush of memory and forgetting, but knowing Beck is going to appear at any moment intensifies the waves I thought I was accustomed to.

I go every week to Newbury Comics, the best music store ever, because I'm terrified that it will go out of business like every other music store I've ever loved. I've invited Beck along to see who he is outside the comfort zone circuit of gym and shower and therapy.

(Truth: Jeff introduced me to Newbury Comics, too. Right after he introduced me to kissing.)

(Truth: This is the most amount of times I have thought about Jeff in a year.)

I took the T into town to eliminate the stress of the car. And the good news is that there's nothing to be afraid of at Newbury Comics (aside from memories, I guess. But with a few deep breaths and a look in my notebook, I scare those off). But otherwise, it's a sharp-object-free-zone and that's extra appealing today. I had a mini-incident with a bread knife back home in the kitchen before school this morning, and though I'm sure there will be scissors behind the counter and the regular cashier with the lip ring, and the tattoo of a demon on his neck might be carrying a knife or something, all things considered, everyone's safe.

Beck's waiting outside for me when I get there, and there's a loaded two seconds before we decide to hug. I feel the shiver of resistance in his spine when my hand touches it, but then he takes a deep inhale-exhale and smiles at me. *Shines* on me.

"Don't be mad," he starts off. I roll my eyes and take a

step back because I am for sure a worst-case scenario kind of girl.

"That is a terrible way to start a date," I say.

"I told Dr. Pat. About us."

"Noooo," I say, even though this definitely isn't the worst thing he could have said. "Why?"

"Private session today," Beck says. "I just couldn't keep it in." And even though he's gotta know I'm pissed, he's grinning stupidly at me. Which means I can't really be mad. It's actually sort of a genius strategy. "But here's where I say something nice, okay?"

"Okay."

"I told her about us because I want to get better now," he says. No one has ever smiled this big for this long. Not ever. "Dr. Pat called it a breakthrough."

"I don't get it," I say. I'm itching to get inside the CD store, truth be told. It's distracting out on the street with the skateboarders and the errant bits of cell phone conversations as people pass by. And though I can't get enough of Beck's dimpled grin and the fact that he hasn't sanitized his hands after our hug, I don't know that I want him getting better. I don't know that I want him grinning and ebullient and full of charming, casual energy. Not really. Because while he's having breakthroughs and working through his shit, I'm getting worse because I'm using therapy to check in with Austin and Sylvia instead of working on my shit.

Not to mention this morning when I had to rip a chunk off my favorite sourdough loaf with my bare hands instead of cutting the thing like a normal person. My dad sat with his coffee and looked at me like I was a caveman. Not understanding that I did it for him, to save him from me.

Beck's talking about getting better and I'm only just now realizing how big the crazy in me has gotten. A few weeks ago I was a girl who was a little squeamish about driving and liked listening in on some sordid therapy sessions. Now I'm an OCD freak who can't cut her own food and is officially a stalker.

And that's the truth. Which means I want to confess it right now to Beck's shining, hopeful face.

I swallow that down, or try to, but I have to say something honest or I'll explode. "I like you messed up" is what I end up saying. "Maybe I won't think you're as cute if you're all stable and stuff." Then I nod toward the store like what I've said doesn't warrant any more conversation.

Beck shrugs like maybe I'm joking. And as we're crossing the threshold into the retro wonder that is Newbury Comics, he leans forward and kisses my cheek.

"Did Dr. Pat tell you to do that?" I say. Then I shake my head because I hear myself and I have too much attitude. "I mean, you told Dr. Pat about us and what'd she say? Or, actually, what'd you tell her?"

"Just that I like you," Beck says.

"Oh!" I say. The front of the store has a few racks of records so I start flipping through those. I bubble a little inside from the impact of the words "I like you," but I don't say them back and I only give him the littlest twinge of a smile.

"Dr. Pat said hanging out with you might be a good opportunity to push myself. So I told her I'd try to wash my hands no more than five times with you today. I mean, I'll probably do the extra three after I get home, but that's the plan, okay?"

"Okay," I say with a big, conversation-ending nod.

"I told her you're an inspiration. How well you're doing, I mean. How together you are."

I jut out my chin a little and let my fingers fall to my thigh for a pinch. It was necessary and I let go of a big burst of breath with that little release. My chest collapses, that pebble of tension slipping just enough to let me breathe.

"So what's up with this place?" Beck says. "It's pretty cool. Look at these records! Classic. You have a record player? Or a CD player for that matter?"

It's lonely to be the one with secrets. It's why I never had them before, I think. But he wants this to resemble some kind of normal date, so I am going to do my best to give that to him.

"I don't know. I must have one somewhere. Is it lame that CDs are retro now? It feels lame."

"It's lame," he says. And I put a hand on his neck because I can. Because if he's not going to be a freak with me, then at least I can let my fingers linger on the hard lines of his body. "Come here." I take his hand and lead him into the back of the store, to the country music section that no one in Cambridge visits anyway, and certainly no one who is cool enough to be at Newbury Comics. And in the back of the store, with Garth Brooks and Blake Shelton and the Dixie Chicks looking on, I press myself against Beck and get a good kiss out of him.

"So, seriously, you're not mad I told her?" Beck says. I'm tired of Dr. Pat being on this date with us, so I try to leave him hanging, but then the finger that's on my forearm taps it eight times and I know that under the bravado of coming out of a solid therapy session he's still the mess I met the other week.

"Little mad," I say, a bit of tension evaporating at the two words of truth. "But I like that you like me." And then more of the anxiety expels itself from my body and Beck's got the grin back.

"I think I made Dr. Pat lose her neutrality for half a second," Beck says. "It was all in the eyebrows. They jumped." He imitates.

This is what a good date feels like. This is teasing and flirting and the strain of brand-new intimacy.

I grab for Beck's hand. He must be unprepared, because he pulls it away like we've reached our limit. Post–Dr. Pat ecstasy only lasts for a few minutes. I know that as well as anyone.

"Sorry," he says. "They got a bathroom? I mean, I'm sure it's pretty awful, but they have one, right?" I point him in the direction of what will definitely be the worst bathroom he's ever been in.

You know how when you learn a new vocabulary word you then suddenly notice it everywhere? Like, when I was studying for the SATs and I learned *"viscous"* and then every book I read, every conversation I had, *"viscous"* was there, front and center. I would have sworn I'd never seen the word before in my life, but then the second I knew it existed it was following me. *"Viscous."*

Austin is that SAT word.

Dr. Pat would insist that life just has coincidences, and that my thoughts do not have any power. Dr. Pat says that multiple times a session: "Your thoughts do not have power. You are trying to control something that is beyond your control."

Regardless: I'm almost positive it's Austin's face on the bulletin board near the electronic/dance CD section, so I take a harder look and it *is* his face, and Sylvia's face right next to his, and in the same instant it makes all the sense in the world and no sense at all.

COME SEE INDIE POWER COUPLE TRYST

AT CLUB PASSIM

TUESDAY, MARCH 13.

Then, under the text, their faces: hers crowded with makeup, his rough with stubble, both looking at each other with that intense, vacant look of love that seems somehow quintessentially indie-rock. They are some kind of singing duo and they call themselves Tryst. Leave it to me to accidentally fall for a musician. I take down the poster (is that allowed?) with as much certainty as I can muster, like I'm meant to be here doing that.

No one notices. The Newbury Comics employees are a pierced, stoner bunch and I have on an A-line skirt and wool tights and librarian glasses, so I can get away with anything in this setting.

Almost.

"What you got there?" Beck says, coming in from behind me. Not touching me, but swooping in sort of close to my neck so I can feel the breath and vibration of his words without ruining his meticulous cleaning rituals.

"Oh! Band I like."

"Lemme see."

"You won't know them or whatever. They're all, you know, hipster and stuff."

"I could be hipster. You're making terrible assumptions just 'cause I go to Smith-Latin and like the gym." Beck takes the poster out of my hands and I can't really resist without getting him suspicious, so I try to look like what I imagine is sex-kitten cute and let him check out the poster.

"Well, we have to go see them, then!" he says. "Let me get us tickets." Huge Beck smile. Quick surge of *ohmygod, he really likes me*, followed immediately by the realization of the mess this is all becoming.

"No, I don't want you to, I said that already" is what comes out from the panic going on in my head. There's something about the way Beck is on top of the world after therapy today that is unsettling and making "us" decidedly not *us*. Like what worked about us, or what I liked about him, was the distance between us, the awkward competing obsessions and compulsions, the way we both darted in and out of unhappiness. This Beck, the one full of hope and recovery and willingness isn't so easy to sidestep. Like availability is in and of itself something unlikeable.

Not unlikeable. Terrifying. But as luck would have it, my totally awkward refusal of his really sweet offer to buy us tickets to their concert brings him right back to his vulnerable state.

"'Kay," Beck says.

Then he taps eight times.

"Don't watch me do this, okay?" he says. "It's embarrassing."

I turn my head, but my peripheral gaze catches him tapping another eight times. He starts touching things. Counting CDs. There are rows and rows of CDs so it's going to be a losing battle, but he's counting them in groups of eight.

Then he's reorganizing them. I stop watching from the

corner of my eye and face him full on. *Flip, flip, flip, flip, flip, flip, flip, flip.* Then a stop. Leaving a space in the racks, and then grouping the next set of eight.

"I'm sorry, that was bitchy. I had a late night. I didn't sleep much. Going to the concert would be great. That's sweet."

Eight more CDs set into a little group.

Eight more.

Then he starts counting them out loud. It's under his breath, but audible. *"Onetwothreefourfivesixseveneight,"* a long and strange whisper of a sound. Odd enough for people to notice, cock their heads, and tap their friends on the shoulders to point him out. I want to cover his mouth with my hand, lead him out, and find somewhere safe and hidden for us to coexist.

The cashiers are starting to look at us funny. Newbury Comics isn't exactly a Friday night hotspot, so there's no crowd to hide behind. It's just a couple of punked-out kids, some young hip mom, me and Beck, and a few old-timers looking for jazz records.

"Hey," I say. I don't touch him. But I get in close, like he'd just done. So my breath is there, the friction of my body is right up next to him but not ever quite breaking the wall between us. In grade school we used to play a game called Red Light, Green Light, and dating Beck is kinda like that. We are playing the longest, most tiring high-stakes version of Red Light, Green Light ever. When we are just normal teenagers temporarily unencumbered by our own lunacy, we rush at each other. Then the consequences happen and we halt. Midsentence sometimes. Midkiss. Midflirtation. Red Light. Green Light.

"Would you call this our third date?" Beck says. He doesn't look blissed-out and energized anymore. He looks just like Beck. I feel terrible and turned on all at once. I feel on safer ground with this damaged Beck.

"Yeah, third date. Sure. Why?"

"Just wondering," Beck says, and for a split second I think it's adorable, like he's celebrating minianniversaries or something, and I look over at him to glow in his general direction, but he's tapping *eight, eight, eight* with his finger on his thigh, and with something like a gasp it hits me that he's counting. Not just randomly, on his thigh, not just how many times he's washed his hands or turned on and off the lights. He's counting me. We're moving toward eight dates. And if his mind is anything like mine, we are hurtling toward the eighth date at an unstoppable speed. And we're in trouble when we get there.

♡ 15.

I HAVEN'T LISTENED TO THE TRYST CD YET.

"Just listen to it already. I wanna hear," Lish says when we hole up in my room googling the shit out of Tryst the next night. I use an entire ink cartridge printing out articles, reviews, random tweets about the band. I look at their website and take note of all the musicians they list as "influences." Then I google all of *those* musicians and Lisha sits by just watching, and occasionally trying to distract me from the whole event with two bottles of wine that she managed to sneak out of her parents' huge wine cellar. I am not easily distracted, since this very second I am glue-sticking an interview Austin did with some lame music blog last month into my pink shooting star notebook, and that takes up most of my mental power. That, and the anxiety and desire to do more, know more, check on them more.

"Pour me another glass?" I say. I'm too busy typing and printing and glue-sticking to do it myself.

"I'm giving up on glasses. Drink from the bottle," Lisha

says. Neither of us holds our liquor well, but Lish gets particularly messy. She still has a crick in her neck from passing out on my couch last night.

"I gotta get over there. Austin's. Are you good to drive? Am I good to drive?" I say.

Shit. Didn't think this through. This is exactly why I don't party. In the battle between safe driving and checking on Austin and Sylvia, I have no idea what will ultimately win out. Maybe if I drive even more slowly than usual it will be okay. Or maybe I could hitchhike. Or I could call Beck and ask him to take me.

It is a bad sign that I am even considering that.

"But aren't we checking on them right now?" Lisha says, gesturing vaguely to the computer and the collection of papers growing in towering piles on the floor, the table, the bed.

"It's not the same," I say. I spill a little wine on the computer keyboard. I'm starting to panic with the knowledge that neither of us should be getting behind the wheel.

"Here's a question," Lish says. She's an aggressive drunk. I've noticed this about people: Drinking gives them permission to be the person they've always wanted to be instead of the person they actually are. "You make up all your own rules, right? So, like, why can't the new rule of stalking them be that two hours of internet trolling is equally as valid as driving by their apartment building?"

When Lish is drinking she has trouble hiding just how

little she actually understands about why I do what I do. She's better at faking it sober, but after a glass or two of wine she's wrinkling her nose and cocking her head and making all the gestures and movements of a person who simply does not get it. When things were bad before, we didn't have wine to bring out the honesty, so I never knew what she thought of the mistakes I made.

It's lonely.

"I don't make up the rules, Lish. Seriously, can you drive? Do I seem sober enough to drive?" I'm giving myself an impromptu sobriety test, which is probably the least useful thing I've ever done. I go cross-eyed watching my finger try to meet my nose.

"I thought you wanted another drink." She's taking another swig, and another. Now she's doing it just to be difficult, just to get me riled up, just to prove that she *can* and that she's not going to drive me to see Austin and Sylvia. Little beads of sweat prickle on my spine. I can feel each individual drop as it's forming. I hate it: waiting for it to fully form and then drop down. A sickening kind of torture designed to make me hate myself even more.

"Maybe I can call them," I say. "Maybe I can check on them that way since neither of us can drive." I'm really only proving Lisha right, that in some weird way I'm making up the rules as I go along, but it doesn't feel that way. "I mean, I just need to know they're okay for the night, and then I'll see them at therapy Wednesday. Right? Do you think that's okay? I mean, if they're answering their phone, then that means everything's cool. And I've, like, done my duty."

Lisha shrugs.

I decide Dr. Pat would approve of the slight shift in my routine. If she knew I had a stalker routine. It's kinda the same thing as Beck washing his hands five times instead of eight: not a solution exactly, not a sign of sanity, but a step in the right direction.

"This is good. Okay," I say. Lisha bites her lips and drinks from the bottle with a few deep swallows. She's all bones and knobby knees and uneaten sandwiches and it's impossible not to wonder if the wine is maybe the first nourishment of her day. So, you know, her judging me doesn't have the hugest impact. Harvard or no, she's not perfect either.

It doesn't take much effort to find Austin and Sylvia's home phone number. Things get easy when you know someone's address and last name and profession, and before long I'm listening to the phone ring and letting my stomach drop more with each unanswered trill. Their voice mail picks up so I hang up and call again.

"They're not home," Lish says.

"They will be," I say.

"This night blows, Bea. No offense."

"Maybe your brother could drive us by there," I say.

"Jesus, no."

"I could call Beck—"

"*Bea,*" Lisha says, loud and sudden like a shot. It goes through me like a shot too. I pinch my thigh. "Please don't be like you were with Kurt, okay? Please?"

I don't say anything.

"I mean, he's cute and a musician and stuff but—please. I'm exhausted."

I don't say anything. I dial Austin and Sylvia's number again, listen to the voice mail, hang up with a sigh.

We polish off the fancy wine.

"Remember Cooter's friend Jeff?" Lisha says in a sleepy drunk voice.

"Hm?"

"Jeff. You had that huge crush on him?"

"I know who Jeff is. What about him?" It's hard to have any kind of conversation right now. I drank an extra half bottle when I realized I couldn't drive to Austin's. I figured if I wasn't going to check on Sylvia and Austin I would do my absolute best to quiet down my mind.

I'm not even really listening to Lish by now because I want to drunk-dial Beck. I want to drunk-dial Beck and have him come over and take me out and try again to be two normal people liking each other. I mean, first I want him to take me to Austin's to make sure everything's cool there, but *then* I want to go be normal. Lisha's voice is basically just a distraction from that desire at this point. Little thoughts ride around a carousel in my mind: Austin, Beck, knives, cars, and then once in a while whatever it is Lisha is saying.

I call Sylvia and Austin again. They could definitely be home by now. Meanwhile, Lish is still chattering on about Jeff, the least relevant person ever.

"Not like Cooter's friends with him *now*, obviously. But did your mom tell you Jeff's in prison again?" Lisha says, her voice finally coming around again on the carousel of thoughts.

At first I don't register the meaning of the words and then I think I heard her wrong, because I'm dialing Austin and Sylvia's place again and finally someone has picked up (Austin, I assume), out of breath, like he ran in the door and sprinted to catch my call. I'm really distracted by a million things so nothing she's saying is penetrating.

Then, just like that, there's a feeling of *zoom* deep in my chest and I can actually listen and breathe and focus on Lisha's face for the first time in a few hours. That is how the carousel of thoughts works.

I hang up the phone.

"Wait, why are we talking about Jeff?" I say.

"I was thinking about all your men. Don't you ever think about him?"

Weird that Jeff is coming up right now. Suddenly he's everywhere. Even when I'm at Newbury Comics, usually it's *my* space now, not his. I have a whole sea of memories of Harvard Square that has nothing to do with Jeff. Three years' worth. But lately he's staining everything I do.

"What do you mean *back* in prison? Jeff was in prison before?" It's been so long since I've even thought of the guy that it's like I've forgotten everything about him and have to start from scratch. I half know everything about him. It's all fog where his face and biography should be.

Sometimes I remember little blips of information, like shooting hoops in Lisha's driveway or the way his face is shaped like Austin's, but mostly he is a blur that I try not to look too closely at.

I lick my lips.

I had just relaxed at the sound of Austin's voice answering his phone. That was only an instant ago, but already I'm gripping my fingers to my thigh. I do not want to think about Jeff and I can't really figure out why.

"Um, hello?" Lisha says. She sighs, a monstrous sound. "Can you stop being such a weirdo? You know all about Jeff having been in prison, or juvenile detention or whatever a while back . . . ?"

I like Lisha better sober.

"Right. I guess I forgot?" I say. Some things get buried deep and finding them again is a fucking excavation. I guess this is one of those things. It's better when I'm in control of these thoughts and memories. I shudder with the recognition of a forgotten piece of information. Something always known but never, ever looked at.

"Can't believe your mom didn't tell you he's back in there. She's the one who told *my* mom about it."

But my mom doesn't tell me any of that stuff anymore. She learned her lesson. She's seen my growing scrapbook of crazy violent delinquents and DUIs. She's noticed glue sticks disappearing because, yeah, okay, I'm following those stories a bit more lately. Maybe she knew I'd find out on my own, and that's why she asked if I was talking to Dr. Pat about Jeff. Maybe that was a hint that something was going on with him.

Lisha falls asleep before she gets much else out. And then it's just me and the dark and the thought of Cooter and his old friend Jeff and the detention center and Lisha and the knowledge of normal people doing terrible things. I try to wake Lisha up because some combination of wine and hearing Austin's breathless voice on the phone before I hung up on him, and the insistent longing for Beck over everything else, is clarifying something that's been stuck in my head for a long long time. Like when you have a kaleidoscope as a kid and things are mostly chaos and blurriness and then for an instant there's some mysterious *click* in the toy and you see a totally vibrant, cohesive pattern.

I see that pattern right now, and I need to show someone.

"Lisha, hey," I try.

"Mmmm?"

"Lisha, wake up. Hey. What happened with Jeff? What'd

he do? And remind me why he was in jail before? How long ago was that?" But she's passed out now and has the almost curdled smell on her breath of wine and sleep mixing together. I try to join her on the bed and in sleep but I have the spins and a really active mind, and my accidental cigarette addiction (courtesy of Sylvia) is sort of keeping me awake too, so I head to the porch with a pack of cigarettes. My parents are asleep, I don't have any compulsions to take care of, and it's too late to call Beck.

Three o'clock drags in and my mind is a crowded closet of crap, but if you shift and shake a few parts, the missing sneaker, earring, mitten will come into view eventually, right where you left it, right where you knew it always was. Like the kaleidoscope. Emerging patterns and memories and pretty pictures and the unexpected shapes you never knew you'd find in there.

So I just have to shake the whole messy thing and remember.

"Boys fight," my mother had said a few years ago when the whole thing was over. That's the first thing I remember when I'm reaching in for the memory.

Then the rest of it.

My dad and I coming by the detention center my mom had been working at. We waited for my mother in the parking lot by her work, a grim place with disintegrating picnic tables and broken bottles and grumpy security guards on their smoking breaks.

A kid ran out of the building: a brick block of a place decorated with wire fencing and superstrong floodlights sticking out of its side. I remember because the sound of the shaking fence collided with the flash of lights turning on and the guard on his break stumping out a cigarette.

The kid ran straight into the guard. The guard said something low and calm, and the kid shouted in response.

Then the kid picked up a broken bottle from the ground and stuck it quick and hard into the guard's beer belly. It was about one million times worse than the worst thing I'd ever read about in the newspaper.

It all happened so fast, but I saw everything.

There was blood.

Then I saw the kid's face. He had freckles and a skinny frame and light brown hair that looked like feathers flopping around his face.

"*Jeff!*" I called out. His name hurt my throat, all edges and jagged noise on its way out. "That's *Jeff!*" I'd said to my father, who was reaching his arm around my shoulder to turn me away from the scene.

Jeff, who had kissed me only a few months earlier in Harvard Square. Jeff with the pretty mouth and wet kiss and pointy elbows that always accidentally-on-purpose brushed against mine.

The Jeff I knew wouldn't do that. The Jeff I knew kissed softly and flirted under his breath and smiled when I laughed and smelled like Hershey's dark chocolate, which he ate voraciously. Someone so sweet and so kind and so gentle was suddenly capable of doing something gruesome and violent and bloody.

I threw up on my father's shoes. And again in the car.

I started having nightmares, when I could sleep at all. I'd wake up sweaty and out of breath. Then I'd cry and not be able to stop. It was humiliating. My mother and father let me sleep in their room for months after.

Thinking about it now, it's a wonder I ever slept again. It's a wonder, really, that I ever forgot. I worked hard to bury that memory.

I fall asleep on the couch downstairs instead of going back to my bedroom, and tell myself it's because of how thickly I smell of smoke and how I don't want to wake up Lisha, but there's something else, too. Maybe if I sleep down here, a comfortable distance between me and Lish, maybe I'll be able to forget again. Put that tightly packed closet back together. Hide this bit in the back again, and put everything back where it belongs.

 16.

I PRETEND TO HAVE AN APPOINTMENT BEFORE school on Monday morning. Crack of dawn kind of thing. I told my mother I was having a bad week and needed the extra session, but really I overheard Austin scheduling the appointment with Dr. Pat after his last meeting. If Austin and Sylvia are going to be there, I want to be there too.

"Oh, that's wonderful you're taking initiative, honey," Mom said with a closed-mouth smile and a look over my head at my father like: *Hey, it's going to be okay.* "I've noticed you've been having some trouble lately. With the knives and stuff." She opened her eyes wide to tell me she's available to talk more if I want, but I do *not* want.

"Yeah," I said.

"Do you think you feel any improvements though?" She went on when the silence threatened to puncture her enthusiasm. "You know, with the OCD things. Do you think you're getting all that OCD stuff, um, cleared up?" I didn't even know how to answer, since she was basically implying OCD was more like an acne breakout and less like a total prison in my head. I shrugged. I don't even like the way the letters sound coming out of my mom or dad.

"I just really want the extra appointment," I said, and they both fluttered around congratulating me for taking care of myself, and holding hands like teenagers without OCD.

I'm almost depressed at how easy it was.

To cheer myself up I take the Tryst CD with me and decide this is the moment to listen to it at last. I hit play before I get on the road. I know there will be the distraction of release when the first notes come out and I want to get that immediate sense of ease clicking into place before I start driving. Maybe I'll even be able to get there in a reasonable amount of time.

It's a little sexual, the way the first notes hit my body and the rush that comes on strong and hard and then turns to sweet calm moments later. For one second I am a normal girl, because the excitement and romantic first notes and blossom of release make me think of Beck, the guy I should be thinking of. Not for long, not in any way that would stop me from needing to be near Austin and Sylvia. But enough to let me know there's something in me that isn't quite so deranged. Something that has the look and feel and general shape of a teenage girl falling in love.

Beck told me I was a good-luck charm in helping him get better.

He held my hand for a few minutes, and only spent five minutes washing it off later.

It seems like I could show him my bruised thigh and he would maybe kiss it instead of shrinking away from its raw reality.

I could love the way he's mostly mouse-quiet with just the occasional burst of joy or terror. I could love the terrain of his moods.

Then it's gone before I have a chance to really enjoy it. Because I could hurt him if I loved him. I mean, some of the most violent crimes are crimes of passion committed by people with zero history of aggression. If human beings are unpredictable in general, they are total loose cannons when they fall in love. I decide to stop thinking of the possibility of falling in love with Beck, which is maybe a sign of me loving him even more. I lock all the nice thoughts and feelings about him away, for his own good. Try to forget the spinning in my stomach when we make wordless eye contact for more than three seconds.

I start the drive to therapy at fifteen miles an hour. The last snow of the year is still a few inches deep on the lawns, the remainder of a depressing March snowstorm. I keep the music on very, very low, so I can hear its general shape but not be distracted by it. I'll turn it up once I make it to the highway. A mother and her kid are making snow angels on their front yard so I slow down in case the little girl runs in front of the car. People should have fences. I am a huge thumping heart as I drive past and I think it went okay, but I don't know for sure so I circle around. There they are again, windshield wiper motions with their limbs and red, wind-burned faces.

And I really, really think it was fine, they stayed on the lawn and I stayed on the road, but I have terrible depth perception and just . . . you never know. I drive by again. The mother takes notice. A five-second pause while she watches my car crawl by her house, then she takes the hand of her daughter and drags her inside.

It's humiliating, but safe at least.

I move on at last by turning the Tryst CD up a half level and letting the loveliness of acoustic guitar and a pretty piano solo calm me down. Their voices fill the car: hers throaty and hot, his a choir-boy's attempt at rebellion. He's got a clear tenor voice that he's working hard to dirty up. They sound good. They sing about love. There's the hint of a fight in their lyrics, in the back and forth friction of the duet.

I like it, and I like the easy access I now have to their voices in my ear.

It's no substitute, though, for the real thing. Listening to the album is nice, but it does nothing for the *need*, the pressing, concrete nature of necessity. And Austin's voice last night on the phone wasn't enough either. Nothing's ever enough, I guess.

Huh. Minor epiphany happening right now.

The drive to Dr. Pat's and the length of the album are almost exactly the same. I arrive a few minutes after Sylvia and Austin's session is supposed to start, but practically tiptoe in anyway, my body reflexively scared of being seen or heard by Sylvia or Dr. Pat. Still, I am expecting an empty waiting room, and beeline for my chair before seeing him. Austin. Magazine in hand, stubble out in full force, a quiet hum barely brushing his lips, a noise so small it almost blends in with the white noise of the heater. And, most notably, no sign of Sylvia.

Holy. Crap.

Austin's always been the focus, and Sylvia the secondary way to get to him. I knew that, but I know it even more clearly now. My anxiety slips away seeing just Austin. No worry about Sylvia being here, no concern about what it means about her safety or mine, no thought that I have to hear what's going on in her head this morning. Austin's got a thermos and a purposefully ugly trucker hat, and I notice (how did I ever miss it? A reminder that I need to be more diligent) a tattoo crawling from his ear to the top of his shoulder that says TRYST. The word settles into me. It's right there in everyone's view and he's semifamous-ish and it's like now that I've seen it on his body and listened to him in my car I feel a sentence forming in my mouth that is going to have to come out.

I swallow. Maybe I can fight it.

Nope, I'm going to say something really lame. I mean, I have to. The words are there, he's there, and as much as I tighten my jaw and bite my lips, I know without a shadow of a doubt that if I don't say it *right now* I'm asking for trouble. For me. For him. I'm going to feel like an absolute idiot, but it's the lesser of two evils.

"I love your band," I say. I know there's a giggle in there and I just sound so much like a teenager. Austin looks up from his phone and smiles. Cocks his head. Remembers the other lame conversation I had with him the other day.

Awesome.

"Hey, thanks," he says. He winks. An impossibly perfect gesture.

"You guys have a gig coming up, right?" I push some hair behind my shoulder. Bouncing curls that won't stay put, and bear not even a passing resemblance to the sunny, honey blond silky straightness on his wife's head. I might as well be ten.

"Yeah, yeah," he says. He's got this goofy grin that doesn't make much sense on his face. There's no irony in it. And he's not leaning away from me or looking for the quickest way to get out of the conversation. His eyes are on me. First my face, but then the rest of me too.

Maybe I don't look ten after all.

His eyes linger on the curviest parts of me. I look right back at him, focusing all my attention on his tattoos. He is covered in symbols and dates and names, like his body is some calendar or scrapbook where he records the most important things that have happened to him.

"Last place you'd think to meet someone, right?" he says, gesturing around the office. There's a fish tank with sad blue fish and a rack of pamphlets on different disorders.

"Oh yeah. Sorry. I don't usually talk to people in the therapist's office." I shake my head, like that will somehow help make my point. It's a lot to take with his eyes right on me and the waiting room empty except for the two of us.

"I'm glad you made an exception for me," he says. Whereas Sylvia always has that movie-star, over-the-top, aggressive perfection, Austin's the other thing: a little grimy, a little unkempt, like maybe he slept in his clothes last night but maybe you don't care. He kinda jerks his head like I'm supposed to come sit by him. He pats the chair. So I sit by him and he leans in and I can smell sleep on him and something else too: maybe whiskey or maybe coffee or maybe just whatever it is that grown men use after shaving.

I don't know. I've never been so close to an actual *man* aside from my father, who only ever smells like Dove soap. Kurt liked cologne and Jeff smelled like cigarettes and cough drops and the dirt under his fingernails.

"You like musicians?" Austin says.

"I'm a music nerd," I say. My mind is spinning through conversations I've heard between him and Sylvia. Therapy moments. I know almost everything and almost nothing about Austin at the same time.

"I hear that," he says.

I am talking to Austin. Austin is flirting with me. Which isn't really what I care about, the flirting. I mean, he's hot, and I have some kind of crush, but not like I do with Beck. With Austin I am eager for relief. I am *compelled* by him.

It's not the same thing as love. But the way I watch him, the way I have to say his name when he's in my presence, I'm sure it looks a whole lot like something groupies do, like I'm some love-struck teenager.

Which I am.

But not for him.

"I think my therapist is late," Austin says when no one seems to be coming out to usher him into the familiar room.

"That's so weird, Dr. Pat's never late!" I say before I have a chance to censor myself. There are a few therapists in the building, and only a crazy person would know which one he goes to.

"You go to Dr. Pat?" he says, tilting his head like shifting the angle might help him make sense of this lapse in logic.

"Yeah. Yes. You too, right? I think I've seen you go in before, maybe. What time's your appointment?" My cheeks are burning. There is no reasonable way to explain my being here right now, and he's already shifting in his seat with the knowledge that I've noticed him before. My heart pounds and my hands shake, so I scoot them under my thighs to gain some control. I take a huge inhale. I probably seem even more unstable now. But I can't let him know I don't have an appointment. I can't let him know I'm here to see him. That he is my appointment.

"Eight," he says. "You?"

"Oh. I thought, um, mine was at eight. She must have double-booked herself." I move my hand from under my thigh to the top of it and give a hard pinch, the only remedy I can think of for the massive lie I just told. My voice is shaking. He must be able to hear the strange vibration of the words, the way they leave my mouth with a tremble.

He shrugs and half chuckles. Like it's no big deal.

"Late and double-booked, huh? Dr. Pat's losing her touch." There's that laugh again. It's part air, part grumble. A deep, untethered, kind sound.

"God, that's so not like her." It's a funny thing, joking around about your shared therapist. For all she knows about both of us, we have limited ways to make judgments about her. Just the upholstery of her furniture and the routinized way she handles her appointments with us. But we both nod and smile like this somehow says everything there is to say about her.

One of the other therapists emerges from the back.

"You Dr. Pat's patients?" We nod. "She's out sick. She apologizes." She has that same neutral demeanor that I thought maybe Dr. Pat invented, but one look at this woman in her oversize suit and thin wire-frame glasses says these therapists are all the same, all have the same set of expressions and gestures and semicomforting words.

"Lucky us—let me buy you a coffee. It's early as shit, right? You got school today?"

"Yeah, but it's senior spring," I squeak out. "Coffee sounds great."

All this before 9:00 a.m.

"How do you like Dr. Pat?" Austin asks when we've both settled into standard-issue Starbucks green armchairs. I officially do not care if I don't make it to school today. We are out of place in Starbucks, too. It's all businessmen on their way to work and mothers waiting to drop their toddlers off at daycare, and then me and Austin. I'm wishing I had worn something other than my school-appropriate but totally ugly olive khakis. I take off the cashmere sweater my mother lent me and at least then I am edgy in a weather-inappropriate, almost-see-through camisole and a black-and-blue-striped handmade scarf.

"She's . . . good," I say, still thinking about the way I look to him.

I could be in an off-Broadway play about romance and poverty and runaway youth. I could be in *Rent*. I do this sometimes, when I'm hating the way I look. I think of a play to put myself in, a costume that I could be wearing, and then

I delight in the perfection of my outfit in that context instead of the way the khakis are too stiff and fall awkwardly, bunching around my ankles.

I can't stop squirming, so I give myself a hard pinch when Austin goes to get sugar.

"Usually I see you with your wife," I say when he gets back to the table, like the complete and total psycho I am.

"Aha," he says.

"And she's your partner, too, right? In Tryst? Which came first?"

"Fell in love first. We were doing our own things musically. Then we joined forces."

I nod and sip my chai and miss the rightness of being with Beck. I wonder if sitting here with Austin is curing my OCD. Maybe if I just talk to him for an hour I'll get it all out of my system: The impulse to check on him, to know him deeply and worry about him, will disappear.

"She's pretty."

"She is." He nods, all serious, and I think with a flutter that maybe he's going to tell me *I'm* pretty. I swallow and he swallows and I don't want what's about to happen, but then maybe I *do* want it, just the teeny-tiniest bit. Etta James is on the shitty Starbucks stereo and chai is burning my mouth and Austin is getting stares from the soccer moms and business douches. I give a closed-mouth smile.

"Very pretty," I say again, in some sort of throaty voice.

"So, speaking of my wife, she mentioned you've been to our building."

Bam.

I remember that look on her face when she saw me at Dr. Pat's. I'm turning red and hot and teary-eyed now. What I thought was intrigue and flirtation and maybe even perversion in Austin's face and actions is actually sad concern. Something a lot like pity.

This goddamn armchair is basically swallowing me whole. I don't know what kind of person sits comfortably in these things. Austin sits at the very edge of his, but I made the mistake of leaning back into mine and now I'm stuck in the plush ugly green monstrosity. Austin looks older than he did a few moments ago. Like a father. Like someone embarrassed to be here with me in my see-through shirt and ridiculous breasts.

"You seem very sweet. And I thought this might be a good opportunity. Serendipity, sort of, to just let you know how we feel, so we don't have to talk to Dr. Pat about it."

"Oh. Thanks," I muster up. I bite my lip really hard and I think I taste blood. I need to get out of here.

"And maybe you're just a fan of Tryst? Which is great. Hey, when I was your age I wrote about a hundred letters to the lead singer of the Foo Fighters. Who you have probably never even heard of. But there you go. I mean, listen, if I can be someone's Foo Fighters, that's just awesome."

I've heard of the Foo Fighters before, I guess, and I think I should know who they are if I'm going to be hanging at record stores and wearing thrift store clothes, so I make a note to look them up when I get home.

"Yeah. I'm a fan of Tryst. Really huge fan. I'm sorry." Maybe my OCD is getting better, because I am about to let fly on a huge lie. "I recognized you when you came out of Dr. Pat's once . . . and you're just my favorite band. So I sort of freaked out. I listen to you guys all the time."

It doesn't feel good, the words coming out all silky smooth and *false*, and I have to pinch myself to make it okay.

It is still not okay.

"*Totally* get it," Austin says. His face has stopped scrunching into awkward positions and he leans into the side of the armchair like now that that's all out in the open we can just chat it up.

"Sorry," I say.

"Nah, we didn't mind. I mean, we thought we'd ask Dr. Pat if we should be concerned, but look at you. I can tell the scary-obsessed from the cool-obsessed. Sylvia used to go to every single Green Day concert. You know, when they were cool. She thought if she went enough times they'd pick her out of the crowd."

"Did they?"

"Sylvia didn't used to be such a knockout. I mean, she was cute. But she puts the work in now."

"Huh," I say. It seems like a mean way to put it. It seems like decidedly not the way I'd want to be loved.

"So, no reason to feel weird, okay? We are fellow music fans, right?"

"Right." The word barely comes out. My eyes are glued to the pattern on the linoleum floor and my whole body screams with heat. I am almost certainly fire-engine red from the part in my hair all the way down to my toes.

"I've embarrassed you," Austin says. "I'm so sorry. If the Foo Fighters had talked to me about my superfandom I would have been embarrassed too. Hey. *Hey.* Look at me." I do. "It's totally cool. I told Sylvia I'd check in about it, and now I have, and I'm psyched we have such a cool fan chick. I mean, how lucky are we to have you, right? You're, like, exactly who we want to be singing to and about and for. So, please don't look like that."

Austin has probably not talked to a sixteen-year-old girl in years, but he recognizes the change in my breath, knows it's about to turn from shaky inhales to actual tears, and no adult man can handle that.

"You know what I'd love?" he says, patting my shoulder with a timid hand. "For you to be our special guest at our show next week. It would mean the world to me. And just so you know, there's no weirdness, we're totally cool. We're happy that we have a real fan."

"Yeah, I mean, I was planning on going," I say. My voice

is still not my own, but my body temperature drops a little and the sweat rolling down my back seems to have slowed, chilled, and changed into goosebumps. Sweet.

"We'll hook you up," Austin says. "With tickets I mean." Then he pats my knee, and I'm still stuck wondering if there was actually some sexual charge earlier, or if this was only ever pity and concern about the crazy teenage stalker girl.

Probably the latter.

"Being in high school sucks, huh?" he says. Patronizing smile.

I shrug and try to smile and look like a harmless troubled teenager, which shouldn't be too hard because I *am* a troubled teenager. And according to Dr. Pat and my mom and Lisha and all the literature I've read on OCD, I'm allegedly harmless.

"So, you won't tell Dr. Pat that I, like, got all creepy with you, right?" I say, like it's a joke. Austin grins and I know exactly what this is now. I am a charity case. I am there to make Austin and Sylvia feel like in the midst of their completely bat-shit crazy marriage, they can help a troubled teenage fan who is lonely and desperate and pathetic.

There are celebrity stalkers who end up killing their celebrity fixations. I can't think of a specific example right now, but stalking has a kind of violent implication, and I wonder if all the time I've spent worrying about hurting people and about Austin and Sylvia's safety are actually related. Maybe I am the real threat against them.

I survey Starbucks. Plastic knives, but they're behind the counter. I can't do much harm with napkins and soy milk and tiny wooden stirrers. We're all safe for the moment.

And that realization makes me a zen princess of calm, despite the embarrassment.

"Let's get you to school, right?" Austin says. "Can't have you skipping classes to hang out with rock stars." Wink. Pause. Wink again.

We walk back across the street to Dr. Pat's office together. Austin pats the top of my car, which is only a little bit less demeaning than him patting the top of my head.

"Hang in there, Bea," he says. I let him drive away first, so he doesn't see what kind of driver I am.

And for four hours afterward I'm an unwavering line of coolness and calm and I don't feel the need to do anything other than take notes on *The Great Gatsby* for English class and think about admiration and obsession and how Austin is every bit as flawed and beautiful and unattainable and incorrect as Gatsby is. When the teacher assigns a paper on the book, I'm almost excited to tackle the subject. I know exactly what to write about. I know exactly how to feel about Gatsby and Nick and the world we're never quite a part of, no matter how hard we try.

♡ 17.

BY MY FIRST ENGLISH CLASS THE NEXT DAY (YEP, I take two English classes, prep school at its finest), I have written down the conversation with Austin no less than five times. I try to explain it all to Lisha again, but I keep losing details, and the mounting certainty that I'm not getting it quite right starts to press on my chest. Soon it feels like a whole Austin-size person is sitting on my chest, collapsing my rib cage, and I have to try again to write it down *just right*.

Lisha shrugs. "Yeah, I mean, I think I've got the basics," she says, and tries to smile, but it comes out more like a grimace.

It's funny how badly I want to tell Beck that I finally spoke to Austin, that I spoke to one of the patients I told him I listen in on, but he's starting to have too much information. If he tried hard he'd be able to connect the dots and make a constellation of my craziness and I can't have that. So I've ignored eight texts and eight missed calls and I know that will be it for a little while at least.

Lucky for me, we're just droning through advanced vocabulary today. I'm a vocab machine, so I don't need to use any extra parts of my brain.

"'Ineptitude,'" Ms. Peters says. She's giving each of us a word to define aloud, one by one. "'Clemency.' 'Mendacious.'" That last one's me, lately: given to lying. "'Flout.'" Reject. Also totally relevant at this moment. "'Venerate,'" she says. I know that one too. To worship. I venerate Austin. It's like a fucking vocabulary test of my life right now. "'Punctilious,'" she says when she gets to me, and for the love of God, of course I know this one.

"Paying attention to small details," I say, not able to stop the flush from rising in my cheeks.

I miss Beck, if it's possible to miss someone you've been actively avoiding all day long.

I sort of knew it would happen this way, that opening that little window of information about me would make things harder, not easier with Beck and me. That if I told him even one little thing about me, I'd want to tell him everything. It's not itching in my throat, I'm not tapping it out into a text message or melting down with the trapped words. It's not OCD that's making me want to share; not this time. It's the look of his face and the shape of his hands and the way we are when we kiss. It's that he told Dr. Pat he likes me.

I know what's going to happen: He'll ask me to tell him one more thing about myself and I'll have no choice but to let it out in a blizzard of words and thoughts and feelings and crazy.

"'Esoteric,'" Ms. Peters says. "Can you use it in a sentence, Bea?"

"I'd like to remain esoteric, because being mysterious is best," I say. There are giggles and Ms. Peters smirks and shrugs her shoulders.

"Sure," she says. "Okay."

Well. At least I'm going to kick some serious ass on our vocab quiz.

When Beck phones my cell during lunch period he calls me "babe" and says he's been listening to the Tryst album we both bought at Newbury Comics, and thinking about me.

"What the hell? Don't you guys do schoolwork? Or do Smith-Latin guys just sit around listening to their iPods?" I say, but he's not looking to tease.

"You know the song 'Blue-Eyed Danger Lover'?" he asks. "I like that one. The title makes me laugh, but it also . . . I don't know. I love their lyrics. He's kinda Dylan-y right? And she sounds like some old-school jazz singer. Oh! And the song 'Ask'? That's great too."

I don't say much. Not because I'm not into the sweetness of his voice. Sometimes getting what I want gets me choked up, and I think I've always wanted to be spoken to in just this way, so I'm sort of swallowing back tears while eating a cheese sandwich in the cafeteria with Lisha. "Am I being way too intense?" Beck asks. "I'm sorry. Maybe it's the drugs Dr. Pat's got me on. I usually play things a little cooler, I swear."

"You're cute," I say. Lisha rolls her eyes and leaves me alone at the table so that she can go get an order of french fries that she'll probably never eat. I'm off the phone by the time she's back; she nibbles at one single salty fry.

"Does he know you're, like, in love with another guy?" Lisha says. "Does he know you had a little Starbucks date yesterday with a rock star? I mean, save some men for the rest of us, lady." This is the way we've always spoken to each other: verbal elbowing and big smiles. But today Lisha's eyes are in little slits and there's a new crease in her forehead. Her legs are crossed very tightly, her thighs and knees squeezing together. I bite into my cheese sandwich and try to laugh it off.

My biggest fear, bigger than cars or knives or going crazy, is that our friendship will change. But of course, the more I fear it, the more it comes true.

"I think you're confused about what *dating* is. And I told you. I'm not into Austin," I say. We are straining to keep it light.

"Oh, I know. It's just your OCD." Then lunch is over before Lisha even really has a minute to roll her eyes.

We finished discussing *The Great Gatsby* yesterday in my advanced literature class, so today we're reading the short story "The Lottery" out loud, and I think it's going to be fine until I realize it's a story about stoning someone to death.

I have never before thought about the possibility of stoning someone to death. But now the thought exists and I know I'm going to do it someday because stones are *everywhere* and I can't possibly avoid them with the same reliability with which I can avoid sharp objects.

Crap. I do not want to be one of those people who can't leave the house.

I pinch my thigh as hard as I can. I cannot have a meltdown in the middle of class. It's not like I have some great reputation here but I have not yet been deemed a total lunatic. I'm okay looking. Popular girls compliment me on my accessories sometimes. I get the occasional party invite, so Lisha and I have the grudging acceptance of the prettier, richer, much more athletic girls. But at Greenough you can't get anywhere without being an athlete. And even the girls who hang out in the library loft have been giving me funny looks lately.

Like right now, for instance. Kim and Lacey are whispering about something in the back row and I think it's me.

Don't think about it, I say to myself. *Forget about the stoning. Don't listen. Think about Beck's forearms.*

I want that to be enough. I know for other girls it *is* enough. That falling for someone is enough to make even the worst, most gruesome thoughts bearable. I thought, when I was kissing Beck the other day, that I would be able to return to the memory of his mouth on mine over and over and that just that thought would make me somehow magically normal.

I was wrong.

So I go back to what works: the pinch on my thigh and some serious note-taking. I list every household object that could potentially be used to kill someone. Then I list school utensils that should be kept locked away instead of out in the open for anyone to grab and attack with.

Sudden, very serious concern: How can I be a costume designer if I am afraid of scissors?

Saying I hate myself right now would be an understatement. Lisha has to poke me when class ends to remind me to get up. And maybe we're on edge with each other, but she is still a lighthouse for me, still something to give me hope in the midst of all the crap.

"You're sweaty, Bea," she says, and pulls me into the bathroom where she hands me a bunch of cold, wet paper towels.

"Come on. We're skipping history class," she says when we're done dabbing me off.

"Hm?"

"You can't make it through a short story about sacrifice and farming, you're certainly not going to get through a class about gas chambers and human suffering."

"I'm fine."

"Bea. You're not fooling me. You weren't taking notes

during class, you were drilling holes in paper. That's what it looks like when you go all hyperfocused and weird. It's not like you're hiding it well or something. Seriously. You think people don't notice that kind of thing?"

I hold my notebook closer to my body. She's not saying it to be mean, but it still hurts.

"Do you really think it's okay to have a bunch of unstable *kids* read about stoning their *parents*?" I say. I think if I emphasize the right words, Lisha will finally get it. That I'm not crazy for being vigilant. Maybe I'm just mature.

But Lish shakes her head and gives a laugh that is more an exhale than anything else.

"Bea," she says. It's a tone of voice I'm getting used to. Part exasperation, part condescension. I miss the way it was just a few months earlier: me telling her what sex feels like and how to wear her hair and what fabulous thing I have been up to all evening. "You need to skip last period. I'm gonna go get ready for my recital. You go do what you need to do beforehand, okay? I really want you there."

"I don't have to *do* anything. I'm totally fine," I say, but we both hear the lie in it. She's going to rehearse for the world's most boring dance recital and I'm going to drive slowly to Austin's but make it back in time to hand her some roses and pretend she could actually be a Harvard-educated ballerina. (She won't be. If Lisha can be honest about my OCD, I can be honest about her future as a ballerina.)

Lisha drives off and I've gotta get out of the parking lot before a teacher catches me. The end of the school day is still an hour away but there's nothing safe to learn about in there. They're pushing violence down our throats like Columbine never happened, like it's Canada or something and schools are safe.

They're not.

I know if I get in my car, it will drive itself to Austin and Sylvia's place and I'll be able to breathe normally but I'll be right back at square one. Dr. Pat encourages us to find ways to resist compulsing when we can. "Challenge yourself," is how she puts it. Like not performing the rituals that keep me and my friends and the strangers of the world alive is some kind of worthy goal instead of a death wish.

But I do what she says. I challenge myself.

New plan. I want to love something normal; I want to want something that other girls want. A cute guy with muscles and a kissable mouth and an interest in indie rock.

Smith-Latin's not far from here. And I wore my old-school hiking boots ironically over my dress-code-appropriate khaki pants, and I've got a very serious winter coat, so it's not a completely insane walk to be taking. If I text him first he could say no, so I just go for it. One foot in front of the other. I have to believe Dr. Pat would be proud.

I walk back roads and the being alone is bliss. I can pass boulder-size rocks or dangerously broken, splintered tree branches and it doesn't matter because there's no one for me to hurt. I totally *get* Thoreau or Salinger or whatever famous writers shacked up in the woods for decades on end. Maybe they weren't hermits. Maybe they didn't hate people. Maybe they just were looking out for the rest of the world.

By the time I get to the Smith-Latin campus I've moved from chilly and windswept to full-on sweaty and hot.

I swear to God, someday I will hang out with Beck when I resemble a normal human being with glossy hair and clean hands (but not OCD clean), but I guess today isn't that day. I don't know where to find him so I do the only thing I can think of, which is staking out a couple of the bathrooms and hoping I'll catch him on his way in. The day must be almost over, so he's either in his last class or getting ready for sports, but either way he's not going anywhere until he's washed his hands.

Sudden terrifying/gratifying realization: I'm not stalking Beck because I have to; I'm stalking Beck because I want to be around him. There's no higher purpose. He is not some OCD creation. He's like Lisha—just a person I actually like.

I find him outside the bathroom right off the main hallway. He's suited up in Smith-Latin dress code: collared shirt and a tie and shoes without laces. His are so shiny they remind me of the shoe-polishing kit my dad used to keep in the kitchen and use every day before work when he was still at a big corporation. I liked the early-morning ritual and the way the box got shifted around to become the foot stand, and then folded back on itself to become a box again.

The thought of that small pleasure isn't enough to distract me from the rush of words pounding in my throat and then spilling out so they don't singe the delicate inside of my mouth.

"I decided to go for a walk and I ended up here. I look like crap because it's actually a really long walk. And I promise I will wash up first, but will you go to a dance recital with me? Is that the weirdest thing I've ever asked you?"

"Yes," Beck says. But then: "How long will it be for? How many dances will there be?"

"I'm not staying there for eight dances," I say. "You have no idea how boring it's going to be. We are talking some seriously lame choreography and some seriously uncoordinated little girls. The only thing I like about it is the ridiculous costumes, but you're probably not going to be into that either."

"Are you trying to convince me to come or to not come?"

"I want you to come," I say. "Eighth row? Eight minutes? What are the rules of your eight thing?" Beck gives a sheepish smile and shrugs. Classes are letting out all over the building and I'm suddenly the center of attention in the hallway of the all-boys' school. I've never been as desirable as I seem to be for these few moments. The standards of beauty change quite a bit when there's no one to compete with.

I don't need to pinch my thigh or anything: I am *here*. I am holding everyone's attention and if there's anything I know for sure, it's that at this moment, even in fluorescent lighting and the ugliest boots I own and my hair in a pile on top of my head, I *exist*.

"Kind of a big deal, meeting the infamous Lisha," Beck says at last. He's moved in a little closer to me since the boys started pouring out of every classroom. But he's still not close enough to touch and he's still keeping a steady eye on the bathroom and the good clean soapiness it promises.

"Famous. Not infamous. They teach you guys anything at this fancy school of yours?"

"Ok, smarty. Famous Lisha. You said she's the person who knows you best," he says.

"I did?" I'm not remembering any of this. I experience group therapy amnesia, I think. I'm working so hard to not talk about Austin and so hard to not wrestle Rudy's Swiss Army knife out of his hands that it's impossible to actually take much note of the little bits and pieces of my daily life I *do* divulge. I kinda think I have no idea what I have actually talked to Beck about, I only know what I've managed to hide from him.

"Well, you seem to have crawled all the way out here just to ask me out, so it's a date," Beck says. I go to give him a playful shove, a flirtatious bit of contact with his shoulder or the solid mass of his arm or whatever but he sidesteps it on autopilot. "Meet me outside, okay?" He hides his hands in his pockets and bows his head and pushes his side into the bathroom door to open it before he even hears my response.

If Austin lived an even remotely walkable distance from here, I'd skip out on everything and head to his place, where he's safer, and I'm safer, and Sylvia's safer, and maybe the whole world is actually safer.

I make my way to the far side of the Smith-Latin campus, a soccer field near the parking lot where I think I recognize Beck's car. I sit on the ground without thinking through the potential for getting my pants soaked with snow or muddy from the patches where it's melted away. Sometimes I wish more than anything that I had an entirely different kind of OCD that would keep me clean and pretty and presentable. I'm going to need Beck to drive me by my place or the mall or something to get another pair of pants. I have passed into the Unacceptable, even for me.

It doesn't take him an hour this time, at least. Beck cleans up quickly and finds me like we are magnetically drawn to each other, and I make an apologetic half smile at my now completely disastrous outfit. Ironic dirt-caked boots. Wet, loose-fitting khakis. For someone who hates dirt as much as Beck, he's certainly tolerant of me.

"You have to drive me home," I say. "I'm like a five-year-old boy. I cannot stay clean to save my life."

Beck doesn't reply, but we get into the car and he's driving and it seems like it's in the direction of my house until he makes a swift turn and pulls onto some bumpy unfinished road.

"Do you hike?" Beck says.

"I wasn't kidding. I legitimately have to go to this ballet recital . . ."

"I know. Answer the question."

"I've hiked before."

"Me too. I used to really like hiking," he says. "Your boots reminded me. And the mud on your pants. And your hair. Your hairline. It's sort of frizzing and it's just like my sister's used to do when we were on a family hike." The car's still running, so I guess we're not getting out, but we have a view of what should never qualify as a mountain. Hiking trails twist up its sides in lamely named paths. CLEAR CREEK TRAIL. BEAR MOUNTAIN PASS. WHITE WATERFALL WONDERLAND.

I don't even have to hold my tongue. I'm not fighting the overshare or any other impulse. It's pretty here, the way the sun hits the snow and the trees shake off little showers of flakes every few seconds. And Beck is beautiful here, his eyes half shut and blurrily focused, his fingers totally still.

"Sorry," he says after a few moments of breathing in time and watching the wind.

"No. Why? No," I say.

"You want to try on the jeans I keep in the back? Is that

an insult? I know girls don't like to have the same size waist as their—" I cut him off at the word "boyfriend." Not because I don't want it to be true, but because I can only take so much in one day.

Dr. Pat says for some people even good news is anxiety inducing.

"Your jeans would be great."

Beck is all broad shoulders but has a tiny waist and undersize legs, and he's the kind of guy who spends money on things like jeans, so the ones he hands me are neatly folded up and dark denim and probably more expensive than anything I own.

"Should I . . . ?" I point to the backseat and Beck pops to attention.

"Oh yeah, of course. I didn't mean you had to, like, strip in front of me. I'm sorry. I'm doing this all wrong. I'll close my eyes."

I'm sure there are girls who wouldn't find a beat-up Jeep in winter romantic. Girls who don't see any kind of sexiness in the smell of dried mud or the clunking sounds of an old car or the idea that you can do the least expected thing and just see what happens.

I'm sure there are girls my age who haven't had sex and are waiting on some kind of sign from above or a romantic gesture or at the very least for an aggressive guy prodding them along in order to give it up. But that's just not me. I've had sex. It was pretty fun. I wouldn't mind trying it again.

"Help me out of this stuff?" I say. My heart's going hard: *pound, pound, pound.*

I think it's his fear of physical touching that makes me want it more. Kind of like a challenge, but kind of like a validation, too. If I can get him to love me like this (dirty, undone, brazen, unabashedly myself) then maybe this is something real.

Beck keeps his eyes open but he doesn't rush at me. It's an even sweeter thing that way. I'm goosebumped from the waiting and he's giving a half smile, and then he hooks the palm of his hand around my neck and pulls me in to kiss me.

He doesn't help me out of my pants or even my shirt, but there's that lost-time, lost-location kissing again. My lips cling to his; I don't want to let them slip from mine for a moment. The bottom half of my body leans toward his and I tighten my arms around his neck. A little sigh escapes from my mouth to his.

Then he slows down, like last time. He busies himself with his baby wipes when we pull away, and I change in the backseat.

"Hey, it's okay," I say to his face in the rearview mirror. He's on his tenth wipe. "I don't mind the cleaning-off thing. So, just, let's not feel bad about it, you know? Can we make a promise not to feel bad about the weird shit we do?" When I'm saying it I think it's a perfect, selfless kind of moment: accepting someone for who they are. But as I crawl into the front seat again, I realize I said it so that he won't hate me when he finds out all the things I haven't told him yet.

Beck's jeans fit loosely, falling off my hips in a way that I hope has an easy comfortable cuteness, but the jeep doesn't exactly have a full-length mirror so I can't know for sure. I've got a chunky sweater and a thick scarf and the whole look is maybe hanging off me just right.

Dr. Pat's always amazed at my inherent optimism.

"So. Dance recital?" Beck says. Now that he's clean and I'm at least in clean clothes, he's all smiles. I sit on my hands so that I won't grab his hand on impulse. I know he wouldn't mind, but I felt the dry patches of his palm when he wrapped his hand around the back of my neck, and I don't want to do anything that will make him scrub the poor, peeling parts of his body any harder.

"Dance recital," I say. I'm grinning too.

For a few minutes.

It keeps seeming like the magic of falling for him will last longer, but the surge of goodness is always followed by even worse panic than I started with.

Beck's driving all easily, and I don't know if it's the same for him, this part of things. I think he's fine with the feelings as long as he's clean and properly body-built. I'm his mirror opposite. Everything is footloose and fancy-free until I feel something good.

"I like that you're a good friend," Beck says. He nods

along with his own words like they're a favorite melody. He's proud of the compliment, of the adult way it slides off his tongue.

"Oh. No. Lish is the good friend. This is just the kind of thing I do because I'm so crazy high maintenance. It's, like, the only way I can think of to give back at all."

We don't get there until close to the end, which is fine since that's when the oldest girls, the ones hanging on to the idea of being ballerinas even though it's never going to happen, have their big dance. It's a relief to miss most of the younger groups, the ones so toddler-ish they can barely walk, let alone dance; the ones battling awkward weight and height gains who should not have to be subjected to things like leotards and tutus in their preadolescent states.

One year I offered to do costuming for the show. I thought it would look good for college and, honestly, I thought I could do something magnificent. Or at least a little meaningful. And in my opinion it *was* magnificent, but I guess the result was lacking in sequins and puffy sleeves, and ultimately people want that in a dance recital, so ultimately my costumes got nixed.

Lisha told me I did an awesome job, and that our stupid small town wasn't smart enough to appreciate the way I was transgressing the medium.

I actually think she meant it. She even wore the costume I made her to Homecoming that fall. A tiny silver dress with the kind of skirt that flies out like a parachute when you spin. We spent that dance splitting a bottle of peach vodka with Kim and Lacey and spinning so much we got dizzy. I hadn't met Kurt yet, hadn't done anything too nuts yet. I was a whole different Bea. A better Bea. I miss that Bea.

Beck likes the story. He grins at the way I giggle through the telling of it. I like having him right there next to me, still blushing from the kiss in the car and then the filled silence that followed and the chemistry that comes from avoiding instead of giving in to touch.

We don't hold hands at the recital. His body keeps moving next to mine, the muscles in his arms and legs flexing and releasing like he's getting a little miniworkout in right here, right now.

He keeps checking his watch. We've got eight minutes and then he'll have his Cinderella moment and vanish.

Two minutes in and the beginning chords of "Tiny Dancer" ring out over the crappy speakers and I know it's Lisha's turn and everything's fine.

The three oldest dancers, Lish and two girls she's been dancing with for years, are in the palest of blue leotards. So pale I'm scared I'm going to catch sight of dark nipples. They are all so skinny and flat-chested that they go braless, and it lends itself to worrying about unforeseen costume mishaps. (See? They *needed* someone like me helping them). After the cheap, puffy, bedazzled costumes of the dancers before them, the elegance of the long tulle and pale silhouette is actually kind of totally beautiful. Not unique, not genre-bending, but delicate and lovely. I've never seen Lisha like this.

But after the first few leaps and twirls, I don't watch any of it. I watch Beck checking his watch. I worry about his worrying. And then because the dance is short, it ends long before the eight-minute limit is up and we have to stay in the auditorium while everyone else trips past us. We stay in silence, and the empty stage is covered in a layer of glitter and condensation, and it is not entirely unlike the view from earlier today with the shining trees and the melting snow.

Beck stares at his watch, waiting to reach the magical eight-minute mark. He keeps telling me I can go, I can look for Lisha, he's fine. But I wait it out, even though the moment the eight minutes are up, he's off to the bathroom anyway.

When Lisha comes out, she's covered in slippery foundation and dusted with glittery eye shadow and she's sweating under her arms, but she's about as happy as I've ever seen anyone. I have a bouquet of roses Beck and I remembered to buy at the grocery store on the drive over, and a big smile, and a really strong urge to immediately tell her everything about what happened with Beck this afternoon, but she doesn't even let me start.

"You brought someone," Lisha says. "I mean, thank you for coming, but I did not say it was okay for you to *bring someone.*" She says all of this directly into my ear while we're still locked in a hug and her bobby pins are sticking out of her hair and poking me in the neck.

"I thought you'd want to meet Beck," I say.

"Yeah, I figured that was him. Some of the other dancers saw, you know? Saw you guys sitting there after the curtain call while he sweated it out or whatever. He looks like . . . like . . . Arnold Schwarzenegger or whatever," Lisha says. "I mean, he's *huge*. And kinda sweaty." She's scooting me toward the exit, ushering me out while keeping her arms around me.

"Whoa, what? He doesn't . . . *what*?"

"I didn't say it was okay for you to bring him! This is my world, my place where I'm not a huge freak, and you brought . . . I mean, come on, Bea! It's not okay. I'm sorry, maybe it's bitchy, but he seems weird. People are definitely weirded out."

"What are you talking about?" I'm getting close to screaming now. I can't keep the words in, can't keep the volume down.

"Oh my God, *shhh*." Lisha practically spits in my ear. "Look, just—I can meet you later at the diner or something. Just—why don't you guys go and I'll meet you later and we'll talk about it." Lisha is biting the lipstick right off her lips. I get that I can't be superpicky about friends when I'm this much of a weirdo. And I get that Lish is really good to me and usually pretty fun and like 110 percent not full of shit. I mean, I probably don't deserve her.

But.

This is one big, powerful punch because what I've been worrying about is actually true: The tables have turned. I'm the crazy friend and Lisha is doing me a favor by sticking by me. She's right there, whispering into my ear and pressing up against me while she force-walks me to the exit. And she's looking around nervously for Beck like one moment in his presence could ruin everything. Like he's the worst thing she can imagine.

Thought I don't want to be thinking: The bobby pins in Lisha's hair are maybe pointy enough, maybe strong enough to break skin. Her. Skin.

I take a few steps back from her.

I don't want to hurt her. This is not a big deal. But then Beck emerges from the bathroom really quickly, which must mean he rushed his rituals to get out here and meet Lish. And that kills me in a total, heart-squashing way. He's trying to be just that littlest bit more normal, and meanwhile I'm blowing it all apart with my bitchy friend and, let's face it, my secret stalker identity.

This whole evening is turning so quickly from twinkling brand-new bliss to disaster.

Carrying all of these thoughts is downright *heavy.* I know I should take Beck's hand right this second and walk him out of the danger zone and try to just be good and understanding of everyone, of both these people who have been so good to me. Beck can see, I think, what's happening. Lisha's ballerina friends are flitting around and some almost attractive guy I think she likes is approaching us and her parents are waving at us and I can see her nose wrinkling at Beck, at the way his skin is dry and flaky, at the strange proportions of his body, at every funny little movement he makes.

I don't like seeing him through her eyes. I don't like seeing *me* though her eyes. She grips my elbow, her nails pinching the thin skin at the joint. I can feel her flush through her hands to my skin, it's that strong. Beck and I are that embarrassing.

"Oh my God, get him out of here please," Lisha says in a stage whisper that definitely reaches Beck's ears. And I should hug him and get him safe. I should even maybe slap Lisha or yell at her or apologize on her behalf. If I were a good person, a person capable of making her own decisions, I would do one of those things. But I am not that person, and all I can think in the midst of this humiliation is that I haven't done enough checking today. Something terrible is going to happen.

I meet Beck's eyes for just long enough to give him a strained, face-twisting grimace.

And then I run out of there.

 18.

I KEPT IT CALM FOR SO LONG AROUND BECK, but in this moment, the one where he's supposed to meet my friend and he needs me as a buffer and he's tried to curb the very compulsions that make him who he is . . . this is when I leave. I hike up Beck's pants so I don't trip over them on my spastic run out the door.

All these hours I've been spending going totally gooey and sweet over Beck I should have been paying attention to the important things. I need to check my notes on Austin and Sylvia. I should be sequestering myself in a room full of soft blankets and no knives. Every moment I spent kissing Beck in his car and pushing close to him were moments I should have been spending on my other tasks.

Dr. Pat says you can only repress things for so long, and I think this is what she meant.

I get right out of there and run back to school and get in my car. When two insane compulsions are battling each other out, you never know which one is going to win. I very badly need to see Austin and make sure he's okay, and I very badly do *not* want to drive that car and wreak havoc on the streets of suburban Boston.

Fuck it. Austin wins this time.

I take back roads and get out of my car no less than four times to make sure nothing is wrong with the engine, the wheels, the windshield wipers. I walk in circles around the stupid Volvo, looking for scratches or blood or smoke. I'm sweaty from the run, weepy from the terrible decisions I'm making, and so angry with Lisha and myself and Dr. Pat that a few times I just let out a scream in the confines of my car. It is a harrowing, two-hour trip.

The three-hundred-pound Anxiety Man is sitting on my chest again, compressing my lungs and making it hard to breathe.

The drizzle doesn't start until the moment I park my car in the lot near Austin's. For a half second this seems like a miracle of enormous proportions, proof that I am meant to be here, checking on them. But the relief is painfully brief; I realize I'll eventually have to get home, and even if it stops raining by the time I'm ready to leave, the roads will be slick with the remnants of the drizzle.

And this time I can't call Lisha to pick me up.

There isn't room in my raging brain to really feel the sadness of that fact.

I lean against the building, smoking. This obsession with

Sylvia and Austin is doing a number on my lungs. I can feel my body craving the smoke, the inhales, the give in my head and my body when it gets a hit of nicotine. The doorman eyes me a little. I'd forgotten about what I'm wearing, and the simple, obvious fact that nothing about the farmer-meets-prep-school-meets-asexual-hobo look is helping me blend in here. The bottom of Beck's pants are wet with rainwater now, and my chunky sweater has a hole in the sleeve that I hadn't noticed before, and a stain on the collar. My ringlets are turning to frizz in the rain; I haven't bothered with an umbrella or even a hoodie.

I take just a few drags of the first cigarette before squashing it under my foot and starting over. The only part of smoking I actually like is that first burst of light and the moment before the inhale. I like the certainty of that beginning, saying to the world, *I will be standing out here calming myself down for the next five minutes and I don't care if you know it.*

When I've snuffed out a second and third one too, I know I'm looking even more suspicious. It's not like there's some NO LOITERING sign or anything, but I guess the rule is implied, because as my fingers turn blue and freezing from the cold, the doorman saunters right up to me and raises his eyebrows. It's the look someone gives you when they're taking pity.

He's not much older than me, with short, gelled hair and a wrinkled uniform. I try a bright smile for about half a second before I decide I'm too tired to flirt. With the last cigarette rubbed into the pavement I revert right back into a ball of nerves.

Since my talk with Austin it's even sketchier than usual for me to be hanging around his building. I definitely should not, under any circumstances, be here.

"I'm hoping that's your last cigarette," the doorman says.

"Gross habit, right?" I say, gesturing to the pile of butts at my feet.

"You waiting for someone?" he says. There's no smile, no apologetic undertone. I must look really bad right now. I mean, worse than I thought.

"Yeah."

"Someone in the building?"

"Uh-huh." I decide to don an attitude. It's a tactic I got from my mom. I once asked her how she earns the respect of all the seriously tough dudes she's in charge of. And she said she just acts like she belongs, acts like she came from some city way tougher than they did, and then they give her respect.

Normally, I'd go for that effect with a quick costume change: leather, studded belt, dark eyeliner. But I don't have that option right now. I stand up a little straighter and try to imagine how I'd feel if I were wearing that fabulous, vintage, black leather jacket I saw in the window of the best store ever, All Used Up. I cross my arms over my chest.

"I'm going to have to ask who you're waiting for," the doorman says. The whole conversation is taking way too long for him.

"Sylvia, up on the sixth floor."

"She's not home."

"Yeah."

I hoped saying as little as possible might either buy me time or get him to offer up information on his own, but instead he tilts his head down like I'm even smaller than I actually am, and stares at me until I speak again.

"I, um, left my keys? To my house? At their apartment. By accident." I clear my throat and shift my hips to give off more certainty. With lying being so one hundred percent new to me, I don't think I'm doing *so* terribly.

"Uh-huh," he says, not budging.

"I know, I'm a total idiot, but I really need to get them. Can I just run up and—"

"You understand my job is to keep people *out*, right? Not to help people get in?" he says, crossing his arms over his large chest.

"Right. Yeah," I say. I just need some sign of them, some way to check on them. I'm obviously not getting in, so I try something else.

"They said they'd be around today . . . do you know when they'll be back?" I bat my eyes. "Or maybe you know where they went . . . ?" God. Now I wish I were wearing a nice Greenough Girls' Academy sweatshirt and one of those lame ribbons lacrosse players wear in their hair. Something to give me that casual innocence people respond so well to.

"What's your game? You trying to distract me? You think I don't know these games?" He's getting testy, bristling and letting his muscles bulge, letting his size intimidate me. Of course I like his size, his imposing body. Makes him seem safer, harder for me to harm. "Don't play me," he says.

"Maybe I could go find them if they're in the neighborhood . . ."

I used to think of people with OCD as so organized, so anal, that they couldn't possibly be spontaneous. But the worse my disorder gets, the more likely I am to fly by the seat of my pants.

When you get down to it, it's all about priorities. And it is obviously not my priority to be normal, right now. I've completely lost this guy and he's stepping in closer to me. He's about to get pissed for real.

"They won't be back tonight. I don't like whatever it is you're trying to pull here. I'm going to have to ask you to leave."

I swallow. It's a particular kind of brick wall in the conversation that I'm coming up against. One more idea.

"I'm sorry, of course. But I can't . . . I am not in a good state to drive. I need to call someone. I'm underage. If I could just sit in the lobby . . . You could keep an eye on me . . . ?" If I'm not going to see Sylvia and Austin and I'm not going to see their apartment, I need to at least get a good look at the lush lobby of their building. If I do that, maybe it will be enough to sustain me for a few days. I need *something*. I let my eyes tear up a little.

"Aw, man, don't do that," the huge guy says, and unwinds his arms from the pretzel they've been in. I wipe away a tear, and he's done for. It's the biggest cliché ever, but he softens. With a huge sigh he nods and points to an armchair right in his eyesight.

"Make the call. Then skedaddle," he says. I try hard not to laugh at the word "skedaddle." Then I scan the room for information and make a mental list that as soon as I'm back in my car I'll transfer into a written list:

Antique chandeliers
One dark purple wall
Cheesy/cheap black-and-white photography
Mirrored coffee table
The fleur-de-lis armchair I'm sitting in.

I need a notebook in a really intense way.

"You call your ride yet?" the doorman says. He sees the crazy in me. A total stranger and he sees the part of me I've been working so, so hard to cover up. I feel practically naked. He's got a hand on his belt and I see it's covering some kind of pager, like he's poised to call 911 or something. There's a horrible sickening feeling at being this exposed. At a stranger seeing up close and personal how messy I am.

I nod but he's not taking his eyes off me.

"I didn't see you even take out a phone. We're not a waiting room, okay? I don't want to have to kick you out or make you feel bad, but it's time to make your call and move on."

Then, tears. Real ones. Dripping not just from my eyes but seemingly from my nose as well, until my whole face is a sopping wet faucet.

"P-p-please . . ." I don't have anything else to say but that one word. I can't leave without seeing Sylvia and Austin. If I could, I would. I'd love to spend this cold, rainy evening making myself from-the-box tacos and watching Netflix and living the normal life I used to at least be able to sort of enjoy.

But I can't. There're too many other things I have to do.

"Let me do it for you, okay?" the guard says. Softened up a little again. Or maybe just desperate and trying a new tactic. "I'm not trying to be mean. I gotta do my job. Let's get someone to pick you up. Phone?"

And I hand it to him, just like that. I mumble the name Beck, then melt back into the chair and wait for the rest of my life to fall to pieces.

When he shows up forty minutes later, Beck doesn't ask questions. He's brought an extra sweater and some mittens and a hot chocolate and his nice, quiet, steadiness. It smells a little like the gym in his car. It looks a lot like forgiveness or understanding or somehow miraculously getting that the worse a situation is the more likely I am to vanish.

It's the best kind of silence all the way home.

♡19.

DR. PAT'S ASKED US TO MEET HER AT A HIKING
trail outside of town. She says it's Beck's big day, which means
it's Beck's horrible day, and he knows it. I'd take his place if
I could, but Dr. Pat says I'm not ready for exposure therapy
quite yet. I'd do anything for Beck in this moment. His silence
the other night was so kind and unwavering it became full-on
sexy. Hot, beautiful silence. I bet I could stay calm, I could be
OCD-less, if I could just live in Beck's car with the radio on
low and Beck not speaking and maybe his arm against mine
and his hand within reach of mine.

These are the kinds of things I can't say to him, but I hope
my body next to his, steady and inching ever closer, commu-
nicates everything I've left unsaid.

I wanted to call Lisha and get her advice on the best possible outfit for a group hiking exercise. Outdoor activities are
the worst, because you have to look both cute and low maintenance. I kept putting my finger to her name in my phone,
but not pressing the screen. I'm not ready.

On my own I put together what I decided was a hiking ensemble: light jeans and my mother's winter boots, a navy turtleneck, and an oversize down vest. No one looks like themselves out here. Fawn is in pressed pants and a fleece jacket. Beck's clothes are actually loose for once, like he's wearing borrowed clothing, and he's piled it on in layers: a long-sleeved shirt underneath a short-sleeved one and a hoodie on top of it all, a knit cap covering his hair. Rudy and Jenny look like they've hiked up a mountain or two before and have the thick-soled shoes and backpacks to prove it. There's something like a smile on Jenny's face and she's got deeper dimples than even Beck, and a more striking face by far than me. She's blissed out and almost pretty except for the lack of eyebrows and the sad not-ponytail she's worked her few strands of hair into.

"So valuable to get out of that ugly room, huh, guys?" Dr. Pat says. I'm liking her less and less lately. I have a theory that she gets off on pushing us so hard out of our comfort zones. I stick near Beck. She hasn't brought it up in session with me, but knows about us, I guess, and he needs me. He's worked himself up into a mini–panic attack. It's a funny thing because I associate the panic with meeting him, so it makes this mirrored experience almost romantic. I don't hold his hand because I won't break the rules, but I stand as close as I can without touching and we wait for Dr. Pat to tell us what to do.

"It's so pretty out," she starts. "We're going to hike up the mountain and have a picnic at the top. Beck, Fawn, no hand towels, no antibacterial soap, nothing. We'll hike, eat, and then come back down." Fawn looks ill but I try to focus all my energy on Beck and the way he's looking at the mountain like it's threatening him.

It's the same mountain we were looking at the other day. The one he said reminds him of his sister. His sister who likes hiking. *Used to like hiking.*

I am the most self-obsessed person in the world because I am just now putting this together. I mean, either his sister stopped liking hiking at some point, or she's gone. From the haunted look in his eyes and the way he keeps counting to eight under his breath, I have to assume it's the latter.

"Your sister . . . ," I say.

"Yeah. Later, okay?"

"Okay."

Lish is the only person I've ever had that kind of short-hand with, and it makes me want to run away to Austin's. Just that tiny bit of intimacy and knowing of each other and I'm singing Tryst lyrics in my head, and then under my breath, and then I guess loud enough that Beck hears them.

"Tryst!" he says. We're on the easy part of the trail. The part where it's just a field and some dirt leading into the woody uphill climb.

"Yeah."

"I've been listening to them a lot." Beck beams and it's

so light and beautiful on his face I forget why we're here. We walk in time with each other, like it's something we've done before. But the moment lasts only a few short seconds and then he's breathing deep and tapping eight eight eight. His middle finger moves in quick little rhythms as it hits his forehead.

I let him do it, but Rudy sees it and glares at me and I remember Beck's not allowed to compulse right now.

"What's he doing?" Rudy says, all accusatory like it's my fault that Beck's freaking out. Rudy calls up to Dr. Pat. "Beck's compulsing! Bea's letting him do it!" Dr. Pat was apace with Jenny and Fawn but she comes back to where we are on the path and asks Beck, gently, to take his hand away from his forehead.

"Bea saw. She's letting him do it," Rudy says again. His scowl is so deep it's a gorge, a valley, and Dr. Pat nods with that stoic expression and puts her hands on my shoulders to move me aside so it can be her next to Beck, not me. Rudy runs up ahead to be with the other girls and I'm left on the outside of everything.

I just wanted him to be comfortable. And Dr. Pat is systematically stripping us of everything we need and want.

I try to be okay for a few minutes, notice that it's finally warming up a little, and I guess if you're the hiking type this is probably a good day to go hiking. There's sun and the last few days have been warm, so all the snow has melted and the ground has dried out. There's a satisfying crunch every few moments when I step on a twig, and I get why people do this. I get why Beck's sister used to like this.

Some of the branches on the ground are thick and have pointed tips, kinda like swords or something. I shove my hands in my pockets when Rudy and Jenny pick up walking sticks. If I keep my hands in my pockets all afternoon I should be just fine. Anyway, this isn't my day to be working through shit, so I try really hard to keep it to myself. I go on singing Tryst songs under my breath and pinch the inside of my forearm, which is less impactful than my thigh, but easier to get away with right now. I try not to look at my feet where the dangerous branches are.

Fawn's doing well, heading up the trail at a fast pace with Rudy and Jenny. They're keeping Fawn in line, I guess, because I don't see any of her weird statue-stillness moments and she's definitely not washing her hands. A few steps behind me, Beck keeps whispering anxiety level numbers to Dr. Pat, and they're zooming up sky high.

"I'd like you to reach over and touch this tree," she says.

"That's going to make it worse," he says. She nods and asks him again to please touch a tree.

"For eight seconds?" he says.

"No. Let's try for five seconds," she replies. She's so calm she's barely human. I hate it. Meanwhile Beck's so huge next to her little frame; he's so huge next to anyone's little frame, that it seems ridiculous for him to be listening to a word she says.

"I can't . . ." His voice is so small on its way out of that lumbering body, it seems impossible for it to be his.

"Yes, you can. What's your level?" Dr. Pat says. She's leading him to a small tree, but I know she's got her eye on the piles of dirt, the brown swampy rivulets over to the left. She has it in for him.

Bitch.

"Eight and a half . . . ," Beck says.

"Come on. I'll do it with you," Dr. Pat says. And I've finally got an in.

"I'll do it with you too!" I say. Dr. Pat looks over and I'm still definitely in the doghouse with her, but she nods.

"What do you say?" she says to Beck. We've all stopped at the tree and are hovering around it like it's some holy shrine.

Beck's tearing up and his breathing is so heavy I'm afraid he'll pass out. Dr. Pat puts her hands on the tree and motions at me to do the same.

"Is he okay? Beck, do you need a break?" I say, but Dr. Pat just glares and says he's fine and invites him, again, to grab the trunk.

His chest is heaving and he's making a terrible honking noise as he cries, and finally Fawn, Rudy, and Jenny seem to have heard. They turn back around but keep their distance.

"It's fine," I say to Beck. "It's nothing. It's a tree. You've done way worse." I try to say it with a little attitude, a little sass, so he knows what I mean.

We get locked in a seriously extended eye contact and it's like he's sucking in all my encouragement. Like he's taking what he needs from me, and it's feeding him. He takes a big last gasp that's full of drama, then thrusts himself on the tree. His arms wrap around it, his whole body leans into it. He's making a guttural, animal noise as he does it. Fawn, Rudy, and Jenny's shoulders jump in surprise and Dr. Pat counts slowly to five and you can see he wants to hang on for those three more seconds but she puts a hand on one shoulder and I put a hand on the other and he disengages with the same throaty noise.

It's all drama and fanfare and I grin at him as he sort of half sobs into his hands.

And it's like we've conquered the world, the five of us fucked-up kids. We're applauding and slapping high fives that never actually make contact (no-touching rule).

"All this 'cause I touched a tree," Beck says, and then it all shifts to the most delicious stream of laughter. Even Rudy is rocking back and forth from the force of the ridiculousness of it all, wiping his eyes with his sleeve.

And I'm laughing too, so hard it's hurting my stomach, so hard I have to sit on the ground. And they all join me there, collapsing. Even Beck sits in the dirt, and stays there. And it's fine. For that moment it is hilarious and fine.

• • •

Dr. Pat doesn't therapy us for the rest of the hike. We pull ourselves up off the ground and it's a quick forty-five minutes to the summit, where we can look out on a view that is really just more trees: New England pines that rise up green and familiar and crowded in the woods. We eat. There are sandwiches and cookies that Fawn picks at halfheartedly, and Beck says he's not hungry, but Dr. Pat tells him she knows that's really because he wants to wash his hands before eating. He sets his mouth in a straight, unanswering line, and bows his head. He takes a large inhale before every bite; with his huge shoulders and always-at-attention biceps, it is this, a turkey sandwich on rye, that threatens him most.

"We did this together," Beck says. We've all been staring out at the way the sun hits the trees, the way the birds burrow in the branches and then reappear, over and over again. "My sister and I. My sister who, you know, died. She loved being outside. We'd bring food up here. Hike and picnic. Just like this." As a group we hold our breath. Beck has never talked about a dead sister before.

"You've mentioned that to me," Dr. Pat says in her even tone as she bites into an apple with gusto. She's funny outside of her sweater sets and swinging bob. She's all bundled up in fleece everything and a ridiculous neon hat she says her niece knitted for her.

It's the one and only time I've heard her say anything about her own life, her own family.

"I didn't know, man," Rudy says. "How old was she?"

I know the answer before he says it.

"She was eight."

I mean, of course. Eight. We may all be crazy, but there's logic behind even the craziest things we do.

"She was eight and I was fourteen," Beck says, his voice a little dreamy but not cracking with grief.

"How?" Fawn asks, leaning in toward him.

"Drowned. I couldn't get to her in time. Not a strong enough swimmer. Or I wasn't back then. I probably am, you know, now."

Not strong enough. Beck grabs his own arms; it's awkward the way they fit, crossing his Superman-style chest. Everything is too built up, out of proportion. I want to hug him. I want to nestle into him and let him know he doesn't have to be that strong.

Even though that's part of what makes me like him.

Maybe more. Maybe love him.

He tears up. It's so beautiful in those blue eyes, I'm out of breath just looking at him. I'm not thinking of anything else but how badly I want to let him know it's okay.

"Violet. Her name was Violet," he says at last. We all nod and I break the rules and wrap myself around him. Dr. Pat looks away, like if she doesn't see it, it doesn't count. The rest of them look away too.

Beck's lips hit the space where my neck meets my shoulder. And I know he's getting better. I know he's doing something big and real.

And I know that I'm somewhere far behind.

What comes next is the fifth date.

We stay on the mountain after therapy is over. Fawn, Rudy, Jenny, and Dr. Pat climb down when the ninety minutes are up, but Beck asks me to stay with him. Dr. Pat lets us hang on to her picnic blanket and we both lie down on it, side by side. I think, from the flash I catch of Dr. Pat's face before she leads the rest of the pack down the mountain, that she is a romantic at heart. Under the oversize glasses and probing questions, she's still someone who likes seeing two people fall in love.

I know that's what we're doing as soon as we're alone and Beck takes my hand and pulls me into him so that I can find a space for my head on his chest.

"Violet's a pretty name," I say. I've never known someone with a dead sister. I've never known someone who's drowned. It's not the kind of thing I'm interested in researching. Drowning isn't usually something a person does to another person. Drowning is a different kind of accident and it's not part of my OCD repertoire. So there's nothing to distract me from listening to him talk about her. I don't compulse, thinking about how sad it is. I just let it be sad.

My heart's banging around my chest, but not with the

worry about accidental drowning. And there's nothing sexy about this kind of tragedy, but that doesn't stop Beck from pulling me on top of him. The kissing is profound. Deep and unrestrained in a way it never has been with him before.

And the touching.

He's not pulling back from me. Something about hugging that tree and laughing it out and speaking aloud his sister's name seems to have changed him. Or at least has made him want me more. Because in a moment his hands are sliding down, underneath my pants, and we're taking our clothes off, and maybe someone could come by at any minute, but I don't think we care.

Which is saying a lot. We have OCD. We care about *everything*.

I don't know that I'd ever wanted to have sex before Beck. Not that I hadn't said yes to other guys, because I had, but it had always been a passive choice. A kind of giving in to something, or a not needing to make a big deal about something. But with Beck right now, on the picnic blanket with the threat of random dog-walking or outdoors-loving strangers hiking by, I want him. And what we do there is a little bit illicit, it being outside and all, but mostly it's just sweet and good and surprisingly real.

Beck strokes my hair afterward. Twirls it in his fingers. Sighs out a single syllable "wow."

"I think I love you," he says. "I don't know much about you. But you make me feel calm. You make me feel like it's okay."

"Like what's okay?"

"Pretty much everything," he says. "Is that weird? Is that okay?"

"Yes to both," I say, and lift my head to kiss him.

We hold hands the whole walk back down the trail. Now that late afternoon is hitting, normal March temperatures seem to be taking over and I think by tonight it will be almost winter again. Like what happened up there this afternoon was an almost impossibly perfect thing: warm and sun-hit and captured in that one unlikely moment.

♡ 20.

THERE WAS AN INCIDENT LAST YEAR. IT'S NOT like they gave me an official restraining order or anything. There was just some legal jargon and a strong talking-to and some extra sessions with Dr. Pat and an evaluation with another psychiatrist who looked like Mr. Potato Head. A couple lawyers. A few papers. They put me on some extra Zoloft and called it a day, basically. It wasn't some huge thing.

Dr. Pat said I was lucky that Kurt, that guy who dumped me, was keeping the whole thing totally private. She said I was lucky I went to an all girls' school where I couldn't get myself into any real trouble on a regular basis.

I don't think my obsession with Austin is quite as "lucky."

People are starting to know, I think. *Someone's told Dr. Pat everything,* I think. *"Someone" might be Beck,* I think.

Because today Dr. Pat says it's time for me to open up to the group about the things my compulsions have driven me to do.

It pisses me off more than usual because I am supposed to be enjoying my extralong, private-school-size vacation and this is starting to feel like the exact opposite of a holiday. Kim and Lacey and girls like them are in transit, right now, flying to Florida and Mexico with their families, and all I wanted was a morning off from my illness to lie in bed and think about Beck's arms and count the places he's touched me.

But.

I'm still in a love and sex haze from my time outside with Beck, so maybe she's right and maybe it's the perfect day to get this over with. Beck's not in group. Beck has not called me. Neither has Lisha. I texted her to tell her on Saturday about being with Beck on the mountain, hoping it would smooth things over, but all she said was *Omg. Scandal.* I wish we were in school so that she'd have to see me and talk to me, but no such luck. And so far there's been no follow-up phone call or Pancake House date. We're speaking, I guess, so that's good. But just barely.

Between no Beck and no Lisha, it seems everything's come to a screeching halt, and I'm letting it crash and burn. Just like that. The silence in the car Saturday afternoon as Beck drove me home had the blissful decadence of sleeping until noon or eating in bed. It was that comfortable, that delicious. I was so certain in what we had on the mountain and fell asleep the moment I got home

Except: The silence from the car has continued for a few days, and now the silence doesn't feel so sleepy and comfortable and worn in anymore. I'm squirming in it.

If I'm going to speak, it's got to be now, in the safety of his absence. Okay. Caution to the wind or whatever. If Beck's going to get better, I'm going to need to get better too, and according to Dr. Pat, the only way to do that is to be honest.

Historically speaking, I'm all about the honesty, right? So this shouldn't be too hard.

"I get sort of overly invested in certain people," I say to start. I focus on Jenny, who is sporting a turban today. "One of my compulsions is weird . . . it's these people—just strangers mostly—I get scared they'll get hurt or disappear and that if I don't do a certain ritual of checking up on them then a terrible thing will happen." Nods all around. Rudy, Jenny, and Fawn do similar stuff: They check on locked doors and weather reports and the cleanliness of their hands. I just check on people.

"You know when you're a kid and you do those Magic Eye things? You stare at something and see just a big mess, but then you look for a little longer, and a clear, unrelated image pops into view? Those things always really disoriented me. Because that must mean something, right? It's this hidden message and we're all using it for our enjoyment but . . . no. It's not like that. It's more like ink blots? That psychiatrists in old movies have?" I heave out a sigh. Explaining the logic of something I know is crazy to a room full of people I know are crazy is singularly exhausting.

Dr. Pat nods at me to keep going and I shift my focus

mostly to Fawn since she's the most harmless person here. She keeps adjusting her chair to line it up with some invisible blueprint we can't see. But otherwise she's simply listening and looking sad. She has an always-sad kind of face though, so I don't take it personally.

"The inkblots. You see something in them. It pops out at you. And it's something bigger than it was. The fact that I'd see a cloud and Fawn would see a . . . a . . . puppy . . . it matters, right? Anyway, I guess I feel like the whole world is like that for me."

"Prep school asshole," Rudy says. I don't know what that means because I didn't say anything about prep school. And though I upgraded my outfit from Saturday's hiking ensemble, I'm still pretty innocuous in old jeans and a blazer my mom used to wear in the eighties. I have on bright yellow hoop earrings and sweater boots.

"Rudy, we can talk about your feelings later. But Bea is allowed to express herself however she's comfortable," Dr. Pat says with what I think has got to be an internal eye roll.

"I *feel* like Bea is a show-off, and I hate girls that go to Greenough, and I'm not in therapy to get some lecture on inkblots and their deeper meanings." Dr. Pat gives Rudy another glare since the first one obviously wasn't enough. He continues. "I'm just saying it's rude to talk down to us, you know? Sorry we can't all afford fancy private schools or whatever."

"There's a real danger to judging someone based on their

external circumstances. As I think we all know," Dr. Pat says. I hate when she uses "we" when she really means "you crazies."

"That's really all I had to say anyway, Rudy, so chill," I say. I think it's the first time I've spoken directly to him. He stares back. The gruesome scars on his face seem almost purposeful in moments like this. Like he's using them to be aggressive and intimidating. It works. "So, yeah," I conclude. The awkward silence is totally begging for a fight, but I can't muster up much attitude. "Chill out."

"How about you explain what you mean about the inkblots and how they are like life?" Dr. Pat says. I'd hoped we could let go of the inkblots, but I can't think of another great way to explain.

"The people I get . . . obsessed with. They pop out from everyday life. And I don't know why, but it's, like, I see a hundred people a day and then one day, *bam*, I'll see some guy and there's more to him. He's not just an inkblot, he's a cloud or a puppy or whatever, and then I know that the way he pops out at me must mean I am connected to him in some way and then I absolutely have to check on him over and over."

"But it's always guys?" Jenny says. "You always are getting obsessed with random strange guys?"

And that, of course, is when Beck walks in.

Vulnerable isn't the word for it. This is something else. Exposed.

"I guess it's been only guys, yeah," I say. Beck's in clean gym clothes but he looks worn out and winded, like he's coming from some epic workout, which he probably has.

"I lost track of time," he says with his face down. Dr. Pat's mouth stays in a straight line and she nods but doesn't tell him it's okay and doesn't admonish him either. I can't find a way out of finishing this conversation now that he's here. I've waded so far into the crappy shark-infested waters that I can't make my way back out.

"So you're a stalker," Rudy says.

"Excuse me—have you seen yourself?" I say. It's not any sort of planned assault on Rudy. But once I open the door just that little bit, I lose all control. Because he's sitting there with scabs on his face and his arms crossed and making *tick tick tick* noises every time he hears words that begin with the letters *B* or *P*, but he has a look on his face like *I'm* the really crazy one. "I mean, honestly, look in the fucking mirror. Yes, okay? I get a little fixated on stuff. It's a fucking OCD group. What did you expect? But don't throw words around like . . . like . . . 'stalker,' and then expect me not to describe you as an ugly weirdo."

Dr. Pat is squirming. That's new. It sort of takes my breath away: the humanity of the person I've come to think of as unable to be moved in any way. She buries her face in her notebook like she has to hide whatever feelings are most certainly leaping across the edges of her lips, the wrinkles in her forehead, the crinkle of a nose, or the roll of her eyes.

"Bea . . . ," Beck says, mostly under his breath. He looks almost guilty, like he did this.

Dr. Pat breaks in before I have a chance to say anything else terrible. "Well. So. Though I'd urge everyone to get away from words like 'ugly' and 'weird,' I also think Bea is doing some important work here." There is no protocol for this particular moment. It's written all over her face. Dr. Pat is going rogue. She clears her throat. Squirms again. We are all rapt. "So Bea, Rudy, I appreciate you getting in touch with your feelings and I applaud that. And it requires honesty to work on our compulsions together. Excuse me. Your compulsions. Everyone's compulsions. You know, can we take a bathroom break?"

I have undone the one stable person in the room.

And it hits me, the way Rudy has been looking at me, the way they are all looking at me now, the way realization and understanding is dawning on Beck's beautiful face, the reason I haven't wanted to talk about seeing Jeff attack a guard, my little legal issues with Kurt, or my interest in Austin . . . it's me. *I'm* the crazy one.

Beck and Fawn leap up for the bathroom break. Dr. Pat doesn't tell them to sit and work through the anxiety without compulsively washing. She just heads out the door and before it closes behind her I see her shaking a cigarette from a packet and my insides crash.

Then it's just me, Jenny, and Rudy in the room. They're both crossing their legs and turning their bodies distinctly away from me, because that's what you do when you are alone with someone bat-shit crazy. Rudy looks pissed, but he's not yelling or leaving the room, which surprises me.

After a few minutes Beck and Fawn make their way back into the heavy, heavy silence and Beck sits next to me. I'd be falling just that tiniest bit more for him if my mind weren't racing with terrible thoughts right now. If I cared about him I'd tell him to get the hell away from me because I am the most toxic person I know. *I'm the crazy one, I'm the crazy one,* my brain realizes over and over.

"You have your knife?" I ask Rudy. "The Swiss Army key chain thing? Do you have it?"

"Bea?" Beck says. He can't put his hands on me, so he puts one on the back of my chair, and I'd like to lean into it, to have that one moment of private intimacy, but I don't deserve the smoothing-out calm it would give me.

"It's just a question," I say. "He's the one carrying a knife around." I cross my arms over my chest like I used to do when I was two and not getting my way. I just want to know the lay of the land right now. I need to know there's nothing in this room that I could accidentally hurt someone with. I need to know that even if I'm going as crazy as the inside of my head feels, I'm at least not going to turn into a serial killer too.

"I stopped carrying it. Dr. Pat asked me to leave it at

home. For your sake. And I did. It seemed like you needed some help," Rudy says. For the first time ever, he's not sneering or growling. He's being kind, because I'm so unstable.

Anxiety Man sits on my chest. I should be relieved Rudy doesn't have his knife, but instead I'm worried that someone else has something I could use. My mind and stomach spin in perfect panicked unison and the things I'm realizing about how terrible and destructive and cruel I actually am are making it all even spinnier, dizzier.

When Dr. Pat gets back, it's to a room of chilly down-turned faces and the sounds of obsession: Rudy's ticking, Beck's tapping, Jenny rubbing her hands against her jeans to keep them busy enough to not pull her hair. Fawn's chair screeches back and forth against the cheap finish of the floor as she tries to find the perfect position.

I'm dead quiet. My compulsions don't involve noises or movements, they just involve ruining people's lives.

Dr. Pat smells like the cigarette she just smoked, and for the first time I notice the telltale smoker's wrinkles starting to take root around her mouth.

"I have something to say," Beck says at last. It's funny hearing his voice hit the room. He hasn't spoken much in group, I guess, because the way the low, wrecked tones of his voice fill the space sound new to me. "I was late because I worked out for seven hours today. Seven. I got asked to leave before I could get to eight. They said I was making people 'uncomfortable.' I have to find a new gym. I keep getting a little better, and then getting worse." He says it all facing me: eyes right on mine. He's saving me from being the craziest maybe. But he's accusing me too. He's letting me know in front of everyone that I'm making him worse, not better.

It's not a surprise, but a little bit of me shatters anyway.

"I've got to go," I say.

And for the second time this week, I leave him, stranded.

♡ 21.

THIS TIME THE DRIVE TO AUSTIN'S ISN'T HELPING my anxiety at all.

No shock there. Whatever just happened in group has only cemented my certainty that I am dangerous and violent and not to be trusted. And also, scarily destructive to other people's lives. I mean, just look at all the trouble I've caused. Just look what my thoughts and actions and words have done to everyone else. This whole OCD thing seems like a crock. What if Dr. Pat is wrong? What if I'm not suffering from obsessions and compulsions and anxieties? What if I am exactly as dangerous as I think we all have the potential to be? I've been working all this time to deal with my OCD, but I'm terrified that my problem is much, much worse.

Going to Austin's is a terrible idea. I'm probably getting crazier, but I'm definitely getting stupider.

Dr. Pat asks us all the time to rate our anxiety on a level of one to ten. I've been at a solid seven-point-five for the last twenty-four hours and it's not budging. Dr. Pat would say this is physically impossible, but I don't buy it. I can feel every shiver on my skin, every breath not taken, every superspeedy beat of my heart. And it's not diminishing as I drive. It's only escalating. Moments after driving too close to a bicyclist and a jogger, I'm at an eight. By the time I have to get on the highway, it's eight-point-five.

I drive in the breakdown lane at twenty miles an hour. My hazard lights stay securely on, and I'm almost wishing for snow or rain so that I won't stick out so ridiculously in the midst of the confident, speedy sports cars taking up the rest of the highway. No such luck. Outside is all blaring sun and smooth driving conditions, so I put on sunglasses and duck my head a little. I don't want to be the person I am anymore.

I have done this before.

I guess I wasn't totally honest when I said I started seeing Dr. Pat because of a breakup. I more started seeing Dr. Pat because of what happened after the breakup.

Here's what I was going to say in group today: After Kurt stopped returning my calls, I couldn't let the whole thing go. It didn't feel safe. Lisha got the brunt of it.

"I think there's more to it," I'd said to Lisha when she let me cry about Kurt over ice cream. "I need to see him," I said. And also:

"I think he's in trouble."

"I just need to check on him."

"I have a responsibility."

"I know it sounds weird, but I'm terrified that if I don't check on him something terrible will happen and it will be my fault."

"Shouldn't I trust my instincts? Even if my instincts are weird?"

"I'm just going to check on him. Then I'll know and it will be fine."

Lisha shook her head at all of it. But when I wanted to drive by Kurt's place, she wanted to come along for the ride. And when I created a fake Facebook account to check what he was up to, she helped me make it look real. And when I started stopping by the gym to look for him, she wouldn't stay the whole time that I was camping out there, but she'd come by with coffee and an hour or so to chat.

It only became a problem when I started going to his house every day. Lisha stopped coming along, so I'd bring a pack of saltines and a notebook and I'd stay for as long as I could, taking notes of any movement inside or outside his house. I didn't think they saw me. I thought my boring Volvo blended in enough with the pavement that I could just sit there for as long as I wanted, whenever I wanted. Sometimes in the mornings, before school. Sometimes in the middle of the night, after the Pancake House, when I was fueled by hot chocolate and maple syrup. I noted every flap of the curtains, every flicker of the TV through the windows.

It's almost a zen kind of thing. Awareness. Being in the moment.

Nothing else would make the horrible gut-eating feeling of expecting his demise go away. I had to check on him. Nothing else would stop the chest-tightening anxiety. I just needed to check. Just one more time. And then just one more. And then just one more after that.

Until he reported me to the police.

Crap.

I'm not an idiot. I mean, I'm not in denial or something. I know I am drowning in the middle of the exact same situation right now. And I can't make it stop.

But Christ, it's dangerous to think about these things when I'm in my death-machine Volvo. I wonder if pinching my thigh will distract me from the memory.

Nope.

I slow down even more. I turn my hazard lights off and on to keep guaranteeing they're actually on. They must be on, I hear the *click click click* sound and see the light blinking on the dashboard, but it doesn't matter. Now that it's occurred to me that they *could* be broken, I have to get out and check.

Then my phone's ringing over and over again and it gets so distracting I have to get off the highway before making it all the way to Boston. That takes about fifteen minutes of careful maneuvering, and the whole time I'm trying to focus on the expanse of road and not the twinkling ringtone that won't shut the hell up, because I can't turn my phone to silent without taking my hands off the wheel.

I'm pretty sure other people's lives have this same level of casual chaos, but somehow they manage to plow through it.

By the time I've finally pulled over into a Dunkin' Donuts parking lot, I'm a shaking, sobbing mess. It's not pretty, when all my different fears start to collide and snowball into one massive monster of anxiety.

I can't get to Austin's. I had to pull off the highway at a dangerous intersection. I couldn't turn off the unsafe cell phone sounds. I need to check on the tiny red smart car that I might have smashed into on my way getting off the highway.

I'm at a nine for my anxiety level and it's building to a nine-point-five and I'm caught listening to the phone ring over and over, what I assume is probably eight times.

But it's not eight times. It's not Beck calling me after all. It's Dr. Pat. And when I answer the phone with a shaky, squeaky, trying-too-hard "Hello?" Dr. Pat pounces.

"What's your level?" she says. And I can't decide between answering honestly and trying to breathe, so I reach into the backseat where I'd flung my notebook. And I start reading, one finger helping me follow along with the words. I read until I start to chill the hell out. But Dr. Pat notices my sudden silence. "Are you compulsing?" she says to the quiet, chilling-out me. "What are you doing? Don't compulse."

"Don't therapy me right now!" I whine into the phone.

"Where are you?"

"Dunkin' Donuts."

"Somewhere off the highway? Beck thought maybe you might go to Harvard Square?"

"You can't talk to Beck about me. Doctor-patient confidentiality. If he's so sure of where I am, tell him to come get me."

"Bea."

"It's not like you're helping me! It's not like I'm getting better!"

"I'm coming to meet you, you've just got to let me know a little more specifically where you are. You have a sense of what exit I might find you off of?"

It's impossible to read lists and talk to Dr. Pat and pinch my thigh all at the same time so I just keep letting out exasperated sighs that sound like growls. Maybe it's a good thing that Beck's not the one coming to save me this time.

"Is that even allowed?" I say.

"Sure, it's allowed. It's encouraged. We're not doing Freud stuff here. For this kind of therapy to work, I have to be part of your life; you have to let me in. Remember? We talked about this." I guess I read some of this in a pamphlet Dr. Pat gave me about exposure therapy and how it differs from traditional blah, blah, blah. "I'm along for the ride," she says. I think we both shudder at the double meaning. "You know what I mean. This isn't traditional boundary time, okay? I'm doing this *with* you, not *at* you."

And because I can't drive even one foot farther in this compromised state and I can't expect Beck to come pick me up and I can't let Lisha see me like this, I nod my head. Tell her where exactly I am.

"Okay," I say. "It's not pretty."

"I know. I'll be right there."

There is a little bit of hope in all of this. A tiny pocket of possibility that there could be a day when I could do things the way other people do them. I managed to give up the Kurt thing once upon a time. I stopped compulsively following that Reggie kid's story in the newspaper after a while. I have stopped myself before.

My anxiety starts to sink. Eight, seven-point-five, seven.

I'm okay. As long as I can keep Austin and Sylvia safe, I can deal with the rest of it. If I can just keep myself from—

Oh, shit. I let my mind go back to him and it's drowning me again. The Need. I'm desperate to get back on the road. I don't care that Dr. Pat's coming. I have to check.

I have to check.

I have to check.

I take the deepest kind of breath and hold it in hard as I merge back on to the highway. I decide not to blink, just in case, so my eyes start to sting with unblinked tears. I don't get very far before my phone starts ringing again, and I do everything in my power to tune it out. I slow down even further. I adjust my rearview mirror and take mammoth breaths that do nothing but get even more caught in my throat than my normal pathetically little ones do.

I manage to travel one exit farther before I have to pull over again.

"Aghhhhhhhh!" I scream at myself. The sound gets caught in the car with me, its echo reverberating against the windows. The tears are coming again so I dig fingernails into both thighs at the same time and wince from the pinch as I make the bruise worse, still. I let my head collapse against the steering wheel.

And that one-second thrill of screeching away from Dr. Pat seeps out of me as quickly as it seeped in. I'm sweating so hard under my clothes that I have to crack the windows a little. I smell myself, all fear and sweat and unfocused adrenaline, and it's not pretty.

Last year when the whole thing with Kurt came to a head, we ended up in mediation.

"I don't want to embarrass you," he'd said. "I just really don't want you to drive by my house anymore, okay?" I'd nodded and we'd agreed on more therapy, upping my Zoloft, and some kind of unofficial restraining order that would go away when I turned eighteen. "We don't want it to stay with you forever," his mother said, "but we are serious about this. We don't feel comfortable with you around so often. I'm so sorry we had to involve authorities, but I have to protect my family."

Against me, I remember thinking, breathless from the reality of what I'd become.

The mediator referred me to Dr. Pat, and before we all shook hands and said good-bye, she unbuttoned the too-tight button of her suit jacket and cleared her throat and looked me in the eye.

"Surrender," she said, like she cared for some reason that I get my shit together. "That's the most important thing I ever learned. You seem like a nice girl. You're catching a break. *Surrender.*"

I made fun of her to Lisha in my retelling of the event. Some middle-aged former alcoholic, I decided. It made it easy to dismiss her. *Weirdo,* I'd called her.

But now here I am, on the side of the road with bruised thighs and a hoarse voice from all the manic yelling and a list of all the items in some rock star's lobby.

The word comes back to me: The breathy voice of the mediator finally hitting something in me.

Surrender.

The next time the phone rings I pick it up.

"Bea . . . ," Dr. Pat says in a warning tone. She doesn't need to guilt me though. I've done the math and I know full well I'm not making it to Austin's today. I tell her where I am and she's there in five minutes since her dimension of time and space is so vastly different than my tortured navigation of these things. She pulls her little Jetta right up next to my

Volvo and comes around to the passenger side. I let her in with my head bowed.

She settles in.

"What's your level?" she asks. I dip my head even closer to my neck, all of me folding in on myself. It won't work, of course; I'll eventually give in to the growing urge (stronger by the second) to tell her everything. But I try anyway, swallowing as best I can the words I know are going to bubble out.

The windows of my car are fogging up. The highway's white noise of vehicles is on a constant whirr.

Dr. Pat waits. She sits all solid and unspeaking. I don't want to tell her too much and I can't stay silent, so I do the conversational equivalent of driving myself off a cliff.

"Don't ask where I'm going," I say, instead of admitting it straight up, which is what my mind would like me to do. I know that the instant (inevitable, looming) I admit to what's going on, Austin will be taken away from me, so I resist. This means that I have to do something else, so I start jabbering about a stabbing that happened in the Bronx over the weekend.

"It was a girl," I say. "Girls don't usually stab people, but it happens. And actually the rate of girls stabbing people has gone way up. So. There's that. I mean, if ever there was a time to be worried about someone like me stabbing you . . . it'd be now." Dr. Pat nods. It's a move that means she understands this is *emotionally* true for me but that she isn't about to enter into a real-life conversation about it because it's not *realistically* true. Allegedly.

"I want you to drive me home, Bea. Okay?" She buckles her seat belt. *Snap.*

This is not expected. Again something flickers, telling me that this can't possibly be legal. She's crossed some therapy line and she's putting herself at risk. I say as much and pinch my thigh for extra security.

"I'm not concerned," Dr. Pat says. "I know you're a good driver. What's your anxiety level?"

"Six . . . ?" I say.

"Great. Let's just wait until it goes up more, then," Dr. Pat says. "Why don't you tell me how you think Kurt's doing these days." Dr. Pat has her hands folded and her ankles crossed and it all fits so well with the pressed pants and the flouncy blouse and the expensive haircut. She's exactly who she is supposed to be.

"I don't think about it much," I say.

"Mm-hmm. Let's talk about the car accidents that happened on the highway this year, then," she says. I don't think you're supposed to talk about car accidents when you are *in a car.* That's sort of asking for it.

Dr. Pat is sort of asking for it.

"No thanks," I say.

"Bea. Try harder." I give my thigh the hardest pinch yet, and hate the pain. It's a reminder of the bruise there, the part of me that is as ugly as Jenny's bald head or Rudy's scabbed face or the dry and flaking palms of Beck's hands. The pinch both helps and hurts. Like all the other compulsions, I guess.

"I have some articles . . . ," I start. We have never had therapy quite like this.

We have not had therapy even remotely resembling this. Where is Dr. Pat's Laura Ashley floral couch from her office? Where are the metal folding chairs from our group meetings? Where is the box of tissues positioned squarely in the middle of the coffee table every single session: the innocuous, semithreatening presence a reminder of how vulnerable you are supposed to get in that room.

"I bet you have them with you," Dr. Pat says. "The articles? If I know you, you wouldn't get anywhere near this car without your notes."

"I'm like a seven," I say, shoving myself into her cooling-off tone of voice.

"That's what we're going for. We're going to start driving when you're at a nine, okay?"

No. Not okay.

"I can't drive when I'm at a level nine," I say.

"Why don't you just read some of those scary articles. Out loud. Whatever the most recent car accident is." She's done it again. Saying the words "car accident" inside an actual car. I wince and pinch my thigh and this time Dr. Pat catches it. "You're not hiding it well, I hate to tell you," she says. Then she puts a hand on my hand, flattening it against my thigh, and looks right at me the way she does with Jenny. "Just wait." Then she reaches under her feet where I did a terrible job of hiding my crazy-person scrapbook of serial killers and car accidents and things that I have to try to prevent from going wrong. I hold my breath, praying her fingers don't find the Austin and Sylvia star notebook that's also down there. Luckily, her hands emerge with just the accident notebook. She's seen it before, but I think the weight surprises her: the heft of it, the splintered pages, the rough edges, the sloppy glue job, the fact that I have doubled, maybe even tripled, the thickness of your average spiral-bound notebook. "This thing's turning biblical," she says.

Dr. Pat has made me laugh. Not dutifully, not to divert attention away from my nervousness, not in that accidental "time to laugh now" way that I think everyone does a little too often. She makes me laugh because underneath the loose-fitting, pale pink blouse and indeterminate age of her face, she's brassy and a little bit sarcastic and completely not afraid of anything, even me. Even after the disaster of today's session.

She gives me a page to read from and I do. My own notes always calm me down, but the articles terrify me, especially knowing I have to drive. I read the most gruesome details of the article over and over until the shaking and sweating and unbelievable urge to cry and cry and cry get strong enough to scare the absolute shit out of me.

"What level are you at now?" she says when I repeat the part about the unseen ice patch that the car skidded against.

"Eight."

"And now?" she asks in the same steady voice after I read again how the driver thought she'd looked both ways, but must have only looked one way because a bicyclist zoomed right in front of her from the other side.

"Eight."

My voice dips into shaky, baritone territory as I describe the car flying off the road and into a tree, severely injuring the driver, the passenger, and of course the bicyclist. My hands keep trying to make their way to my thighs, but Dr. Pat urges me to not compulse, not compulse, not compulse.

"Time to drive," she says when I declare myself at a nine. And I fight everything in my body that tells me no and I turn onto the road that will lead me to the highway.

"I'm going to hurt you, I'm going to hurt you," I say, begging her to insist I stop driving.

"Stay with that feeling. What are you experiencing physically? Drive and tell me how your body feels as your drive."

"It'll make it worse," I say. I don't want her to know that I'm nauseous and dying to scream and sweating so badly that my shirt is shrinking with the dampness, fitting too tightly around me, suffocating me and making it that much harder to breathe.

"*Bea.* What are you feeling? Talk me through it. Stay with

it. Talk." It's a whole new thing from Dr. Pat: an order. An inarguable, deliberate, military-type order. And the certainty of it shocks me into speaking. I tell her every single thing my body is saying and every single thing I want to do to make it stop: slow down, turn around to look for dead bodies that I might have run over, pinch my thigh. The list goes on and on and I speed up in tiny increments like Dr. Pat orders.

"It's a nine, it's a nine. What if I hurt someone? Was there a school back there? With kids? Can we check?"

"No. Stay with the anxiety. It can't last forever. It's too tiring to stay at a nine for very long."

But in the cloud of the anxiety I can't see even the hint of a way out: not a shadow, not a slit of calm opening up in me, not a crack in the walls. I can't imagine ever leaving this terrible place. But I keep doing what she says.

"Can I just put on this CD?" I say, and press play. Tryst's album comes on quietly and a secret part of me collapses with a bit of relief. Dr. Pat must see my shoulders drop. There is also a silent flicker of recognition behind those tortoiseshell glasses. Like maybe she knows Austin and Sylvia's album. Like she might finally have guessed at the real secret here.

"I know a compulsion when I see one," she says, turning off the music. "Sorry. We need to get through the anxiety the old-fashioned way, okay?"

The panic swirls inside me.

"It's a ten. This is a fucking ten, I swear to *God*," I say.

Seconds pass. They could be months based on how fucking intense and deeply felt they are.

And then:

The road is smooth underneath my car. Cars aren't honking at me to speed up. My level's starting to wane. The heart pounding hasn't flatlined, but I feel it go down just the tiniest decibel.

It feels like giving up.

It feels like falling into bed after an all-night rave.

It feels that right.

It's surrender. It's that thing I have been searching for.

"What's your level?" Dr. Pat asks.

I like the way her voice sounds with hope in it. I like the way she's looking at me: focused but relaxed. She's not gripping the door handle. She's not wincing or holding her hands together in prayer.

"Seven-point-five," I say. And as soon as those numbers come out of my mouth I feel it drop again. "Seven."

"Good. See? It drops away. It lowers. Keep driving. Keep talking."

"I don't want to hurt anyone."

"Okay."

"Six-point-five," I say.

"There you go."

"Six."

"Stay with it. Keep driving. We'll get off up here."

It's funny how short the trip is when you are traveling at the same speed as the rest of the cars. It's funny how I'm already nearing my exit. This is what people mean when they say something is anticlimactic. It's been the longest day of my life and all I'm doing is going home.

"Five," I say as we exit the highway.

"I think that earns you a trip to Friendly's," Dr. Pat says. The Friendly's is right there: red sign, cursive lettering, a kind of home base of everything I like about the suburbs, about the world I've grown up in.

When we are tucked into a booth, I think I could fall asleep on the familiar red vinyl.

Dr. Pat orders us a peanut butter sundae. They bring us the extralong spoons that anyone with a heart would have to fall in love with, and the supersweet overload of vanilla ice cream and fudge sauce and peanut butter topping and airy clouds of whipped cream have never tasted even close to this good.

Fifteen minutes later we are sticky mouthed and staring down at a mountain of used napkins and that perfect, exaggerated nostalgia of an old-fashioned ice cream cup. The kind that looks like a vase and not a bowl. It could be made of crystal in this moment.

It's all made of crystal: all of me. I haven't been so clear in such a long, long time.

♡ 22.

CLARITY DOES NOT MEAN I SUDDENLY MAKE good decisions.

Kinda the opposite. I decide instead that I have earned a night out, after what happened in the car with Dr. Pat.

Three nights later I am armed with the promise of free tickets from Austin and a few bottles of juice spiked with peach schnapps. Lisha's gone full out: An oversize schoolgirl skirt hangs off her hips. On top she's in a corset that would show cleavage if she had any. Instead there's just orange-streaked fake tan skin and the unmistakable shape of her collarbone sticking out more or less where her breasts should be.

It's spring break, so there's no holding back. Besides, Lish is still fighting with her parents about the money for Harvard, so her drinking and her wardrobe have both gotten a little crazier. Her enormous luggage-size purse could hold not only our alcohol supply but also my pink shooting-star notebook.

"Hang on to this?" I say.

"Taking notes tonight?"

"I'm hoping not to, but just in case," I mumble at the ground. It would be impossible to miss her eyes rolling, her minisigh. She takes it though, packs it into that enormous purse, and doesn't say another word about it.

"You look great," Beck says to me, when we meet up outside The Middle East. Lisha: stockingless, cold. Purple eyeshadow and red, red lips. Me: red skinny jeans and a cut-up navy Red Sox tee, which I repurposed using child's scissors. The edges are jagged, but I looped silver ribbons at the shoulders and bedazzled the seam that runs down my torso on each side.

We haven't spoken about what happened at her dance recital, but after our few strained texts about me sleeping with Beck, she said she wanted to come to the concert and she half apologized for her behavior the other night on our drive here. She did not, however, ask me for specifics. We didn't giggle about how it felt or what he did or how many rocks dug into my spine that afternoon. I guess I don't expect much, now that I know how truly insane I actually am. I'm now that person she lies about; I'm that secret friend that every Harvard-bound skinny nerd has to have.

"You made it," Lisha says to Beck, distinctly not as an exclamation.

"Wouldn't miss it," Beck says. I stand by and swallow a lot and hope that Lisha will more or less keep her mouth shut. It's the first time I've ever wished she knew less about me.

I'm wanting (badly, lately) to erase our intimacy. I grab Beck's hand and not hers and try to remember why I said she could come.

We find a table up front and order coffees and don't really speak. When Austin and Sylvia don't get on stage immediately, I remember why I'm making Lisha tag along. So I don't do anything truly stupid. I'm going to be with Austin and Beck in the same room. I have no idea what might happen. She's chaperoning my date. (Sixth date, but who's keeping track?) A whole pile of feelings go right to my chest and nestle in there.

None of us speak. Beck tries to avoid glancing at Lisha's not-chest and I try to access that feeling I had the other night with Dr. Pat, breathing into the anxiety, riding it out until it fades into something silly and small. But I can't seem to make Austin and Sylvia silly and small.

"So," Lisha says at Beck. There's a mean look to her tonight, but maybe it's just the makeup. More likely, it's the booze. Lisha and her unexpected alcohol-induced meanness. "You like Dr. Pat? 'Cause I feel like she's my ally, you know? When Bea talks about her I always feel like . . . someone's finally taking *my* side in all of this."

She can't have had more than half a juice bottle of weak, childish cocktail, but here she is, being the exact opposite of a useful chaperone.

"Lish, can we not?" I try. I don't know what I pictured for

tonight. Some teen movie version of friendship where me, Beck, and Lisha drink tea and lattes and sneak sips of alcohol and manage to not puke up that terrible combination and also manage to laugh at each other's jokes and have the lovely sort of night they have on the Disney channel. For once in my life I want life to be more like the Disney channel.

"I just mean, you know, finally I have this person in authority seeing things my way, you know? I trust that woman, I'll tell you that much. I trust the shit out of her. Have for the last few years. She's going to bring my friend back, you know? You know what I mean, Beck?"

Beck shrugs and gives the weakest kind of smile before excusing himself to go to the bathroom. The goal is only two times on the whole date, so this isn't a good start.

"Are we in a fight? And if we are, shouldn't it be *me* mad at *you*?" I say. "I seem to remember you hiding me and Beck from your stupid ballerina—"

"Small price to pay," Lisha says.

I wonder if she's been like this all along. It seems like she must have been, like this twist in her personality can't possibly be coming on as quickly as it's seeming.

"Seriously, leave if you don't want to be here," I say. I so badly want Beck to come back to the table, but a minute and then two and then three tick by and I think there's no way he's coming out before eight minutes is up.

Which more or less means I'm destroying him. Or me

and Lisha are. Either way, this isn't exactly how I'd envisioned love to be. Ruinous. Destructive and selfish. Four minutes have passed.

"How do you feel about Beck and Austin being in the same room at the same time?" Lisha says.

"I'll let you know."

"Come on, your boyfriend's got what? Another like five minutes until he's coming back out? Spill." It's funny the effect wearing a corset can have on an otherwise totally normal girl. Lish is all attitude. She keeps crossing and recrossing her legs the way people do when they think they're hot shit. I say as much, and Lisha practically stabs me with her eyes.

"This was a terrible idea," I say.

"Agreed."

"What are you even doing here? Are, like, the police coming to raid this place after getting a tip from you? Are you hoping me and Beck get dragged away in straitjackets?" I don't even know where these words are coming from, but Dr. Pat said this might happen.

"When you start letting go of your tightly wound way of life, of the things that keep you feeling safe, new feelings will come up," she told the group when Jenny had gone three whole days without pulling out a single hair but had also written hate e-mails to an ex-boyfriend. Dr. Pat called it a step toward healing.

"I want the exact opposite of that," Lisha says. "I want the exact opposite of you in a straitjacket." And Beck comes out before I can ask what that means.

"Don't worry," Beck says. "Wanted to wait the eight minutes, but I made it out in seven." He winks and kisses the top of my head like we've been doing this forever.

"You're kicking ass," I say.

We missed the opener, so the crowd is gearing up for Tryst and I'm sweating bullets with anticipation.

"Are Sylvia and Austin Dr. Pat's only famous clients?" Lisha says. She looks so strange in her stripper getup. I'm pleased to have a T-shirt and yellow duck rainboots pulled over my skinny jeans. We're not attracting any attention either way. In this crowd—mostly college kids and a few tired-looking thirty-somethings scattered along the edges so they can keep getting their glasses of wine refilled—Lish, Beck, and I pull off a certain kind of normal.

I work hard to look like I'm taking the crowd in while Beck registers the last fucked-up thing Lisha said.

I hope that maybe if I'm quiet and distracted enough the moment will vanish and become something else.

Presto-change-o.

No such luck.

"The people in the band . . . they go to Dr. Pat?" Beck says, like if he turns Lisha's sentence around just a little bit it will mean something different.

Lisha feigns innocence. She makes her eyes wide and

looks from me to Beck and then back to me again.

"Yeah," I say. Because really, what else do you say?

"Your favorite band goes to Dr. Pat?" Beck says. I'm familiar with what he's doing and it's not going to end up well for him: He's trying to make the very basic and obvious facts of the situation not mean what he most fears they mean. He is trying to see any possible scenario aside from the truth. But he's about to get hit with it hard.

"They're not really my favorite band. I mean, I like them, but I only just started listening to—"

The lights shift. On cue, the crowd does too. Kids who were hanging to the sides or in the back rush the stage. Roadies adjust instruments and there's a heated, sweaty smell of anticipation hanging over us. Lisha leaves the table to join the thick of the crowd but I keep Beck away from the densest part of the audience, hovering over the table with me instead. That way I can see Austin better *and* feel like Beck's not going to have some germ-related panic attack.

"Up next: Tryst!" a tech guy yells into the microphone, and there's a shuffle of laughter and discomfort like he's never heard his own voice over the loudspeakers before. There're maybe a hundred people stacked in here, one on top of the other, but it's not too loud yet so I've got to get this conversation over with before the music starts.

"So they're patients. Sylvia and Austin . . . oh my God," Beck says.

I can't leave before they play.

I can't leave without saying hello.

I can't let this conversation with Beck go too long.

"I should have been honest . . ."

Beck's hunched over and no one else would notice, but his thumb and middle finger are tapping against each other in rapid succession: eight times, stop, eight times again. If he could, he'd probably try to bench press the nearest heavy object to stop the cramped breathing and sweaty hands. "I don't understand. I mean, I almost think I understand, but there is no way that when you said you listen in on people's sessions you meant—"

"Yes," I say.

"And in group. What you were saying when I came in. About following guys, about having some weird guy obsession and being a stalker—"

"Yes," I say, but this time it's a growl, because in just those few words I have heard something true and horrible about what he thinks about me. Behind him Austin and Sylvia are walking onstage, grabbing guitars, and starting their half-smiling, half-snarling set. I watch them for a moment without apology.

"So I'm here . . . stalking some guy with you," Beck finishes off. He raises his eyebrows. I think he's going to spit on me, that's how pissed he looks. Sylvia's voice is singing out over Austin's, prettier, more melodic. But Austin is the star and he plays his guitar like it's a woman or a wild animal, and the bar swoons and sings along.

"It's not romantic. Or sexual. It's not sexual," I say. Beck's face has gone into such a severe frown that I let all my attention go to him instead of Austin and Sylvia.

"God, he's hot," I hear Lisha say at that perfectly incorrect moment. She's made her way back out of the crowd and goes into her purse to get some more alcohol.

"Shit show" doesn't even begin to describe what's going on here.

"I can't be a part of this," Beck says. He shakes his head and wraps a hand around his neck like he's feeling for the bulging veins, the oversize muscles, the rock-hard consistency of a body part that isn't supposed to feel so impenetrable.

I expect to feel a desperate sadness, guilt, a rush of regret.

Those are not the feelings that rise in me though.

"Oh, great. That's really great!" I say, my voice now a yell that will get lost under the music. "You spend weeks telling me to open up and I *do* and you just—"

I cut myself off, because he's gone. The loud guitar eats up my words, and Beck is making a beeline for the door. Didn't consider staying for even one extra second, once he saw who I actually am.

The sadness, I'm sure, is on its way, but I finally feel that other thing. That feeling I never, ever feel: anger. For all he let me see, for all I accepted in him, for all I've been hiding this whole time. And here he is, meeting expectations. Becoming without shame a perfect cliché. I run after him. He couldn't hear that first outburst, but I'm not letting him get away with it. I will say this right into his ear.

"You know what's funny?" I say at his earlobe. The words pound in my mouth for an instant before I let them out. The other part of my mind is listening to Austin riff in between songs. Not the specifics, just the general vibration and movement of his voice, but that's enough for the moment. "When I said I was falling for you—when I did what we did the other day—I did it knowing who you are. I mean *knowing*. Sweaty and blistered and scared to touch me and crying, for the love of God, *crying*. But then here we are, and this is me, and you're just going to leave me." I think on some girls falling in love is a kind of weakness, a willingness to give up everything else. But on me, on my shape and body and heart, falling in love is the opposite. It's the strongest thing I've ever done.

Beck stares at me like he's never seen me before.

Lights shift a little, to let us know Sylvia and Austin are going to be switching to a ballad, and I know within a note it's definitely my favorite one, "That Lingering Thing." It's about what happens when someone has left you and all you remember about them five minutes after they're out the door is the way they smell fresh out of the shower.

Something like that. But said in, like, pretty lyrics.

It reminds me of Beck, the shower part. He always smells

like he just got out of the shower because he mostly *did* just get out of the shower. I can smell him now. The clean scent of him rises up from the sea of other smells: tequila and spilled beer and just-smoked cigarettes. I reach for his elbow.

"Can you guys get off each other and just enjoy the show?" Lish says. "We came all the way out here for you, Bea, and all you're doing is staring down your boyfriend or whatever."

"Yeah, you guys stay, enjoy," Beck says. "Don't worry, I'm heading out, Lisha."

"I don't get a chance to explain?" I ask. I give big eyes and feel a hot rush in my sinuses that says I'm going to cry the second he's out the door. I'm going to cry because if he can't understand me, who will?

Beck doesn't leave right away. He pauses, thinking it over. And I know, I *know* I need to focus all my attention right on him and his blue eyes and the perfect shape of his shoulders and ignore everything else. I know if I can do that, if I can hold his gaze, he'll stay. It will be enough, if I can hang on to his stare for this extended instant.

I can't.

There's an instrumental break, Sylvia playing a piano solo, which means I can't hear Austin's voice. I know he's there, but I have to see. I have to look. I have to check. Beck's mouth is relaxing from tight line to slow smile and I wish I could get lost in it but I need one little glance at Austin. And I need it now.

Shit.

When I look back Beck has taken a step toward the door. Then another.

The song's over and Austin's mouth is on the mic. I start saying something to Beck, I open my mouth to call out to him, when Austin's sex-filled voice hits the room.

"My favorite fan is here tonight," he says. "Bea? Where are you?"

No, really. *Shit.*

The crowd rustles and shifts to find me and Lisha bangs her bony body up against me, takes hold of my elbow, and lifts my arm into the air. I don't even fight it. Beck will be out the door before I have a chance to turn back to him.

"She's here!" Lisha screams. You'd never guess she's going to Harvard and hasn't kissed a boy. She's a whole new person tonight, letting go of the million little things she's been holding in all this time.

"There she is! The beautiful Bea!" Austin says with a wave. He plucks a few chords on his guitar and they shake me, not just from the vibrations. They're for me. So is the smile (less quiet than Beck's, more purposeful). He's mine, for just that moment. I don't pinch anything; I don't even worry about someone slipping in the puddle of wine some drunk woman just spilled. It's a glorious moment of not thinking followed immediately by remembering that Sylvia is up on that stage too. The lighting guy has found me with the spotlight. One fake suburban hipster in the crowd of real rockers and lame posers. Me.

Sylvia finds me the moment after the spotlight does. She gives a little smile, a nervous wave, and I know she and Austin have discussed my superfandom, but I'm still not totally normal in her eyes. And I'm young and maybe okay-looking and Austin is beaming, *beaming* at me. And I am beaming back. She bangs the piano and Austin snaps back to his performance with a last wave my way. Lisha giggles and doesn't let go of my elbow. I have to jerk away from her.

"I'm sick," I say, meaning it in every sense of the word.

I throw up in the bathroom.

Lisha does too, but it's not the same thing.

I stay until the end of the concert, not because I want to but because I have to. I stay out of Sylvia's sight lines as best I can and Lisha keeps hanging all over me.

Panic hits me the second my hand hits the car door, like the whole thing is charged with an indisputable electric force. I do a quick calculation on my cell phone to consider whether or not four sips of alcohol two hours ago will affect me at all. It keeps coming up fine, but I still can't start the car. Every way I type in the numbers and the timing and my body weight it comes out the same: four sips two hours ago is basically nothing. So I decide on a speed: twenty-one miles an hour. And drive home while Lisha stays at the club because there's a cute boy and some girls from school she knows that have extra booze. It's not like her to actively seek out other people, but I guess when your best friend turns out to be a psycho, you have to start opening up to other normal people.

I pull into my driveway ninety minutes later and consider it an accomplishment. At least I made it all the way home. Had Dr. Pat been there she would have been crowing in my ear to speed up the whole time, but I am physically unable to press my foot any harder on the gas.

I need the night to figure out who to be most mad at: Lish or Beck or the stupid indie horseshit that is Tryst or (the most likely culprit) me. There are no calls on my phone. I try calling Beck even though it's late. I think his phone's on, and when he doesn't answer the first call, I do seven more, in case the whole OCD goes both ways. I guess it's easier to hope for that than to admit he doesn't want to talk to me.

I play the new Tryst album to help me sleep. It seems to work, because when I wake up it's bright outside and there's a song on repeat, which I must have pressed before I fell asleep. I guess it's been playing all night at a parent-friendly quiet volume.

The song is called "Almost Over but Not Yet." I couldn't make this stuff up.

♡ 23.

I ONLY DRIVE TO THEIR APARTMENT WHEN I CAN'T stand it anymore. Twenty-four hours have passed, and some people would call that progress. I only go back after I've thrown up a slice of pizza and driven in circles for hours trying to resist. I only go back when the threat of what might happen, what kind of trouble I might get into, is completely obscured by the anxiety, covered the way the sun is in a solar eclipse. I'm thinking of those photographs of eclipses. I've been looking at them pretty often since seeing the tattoo on Austin's neck. I like the photographs because there is a halo of light around the moon, but mostly the sun is entirely blocked by the mass of the moon. It's such a precise representation of my OCD, I'm basically mesmerized by image after image online. Normal thinking is the sun, and the moon just keeps crossing in front of it, sometimes only partially blocking normal thoughts, sometimes obscuring them entirely.

I am in a full-on solar eclipse when I light up on the patch of pavement in front of their building. I don't even check to see if the doorman who kicked me out (is it Kevin? I think his name tag said Kevin) is manning the front desk today. I just lean against the building and wait.

And though I'm waiting for Sylvia or Austin or a sign that they are fine and I can leave, it's of course Kevin who finds me.

"I'm Sylvia's friend," I try, like the conversation the other day never happened. Like he won't remember me now that I'm in wool tights and a bomber jacket and a huge floppy purple hat.

"So I've heard. Sylvia's home," he says, not breaking eye contact, not blinking. He crosses his arm and widens his stance, so I won't be able to get by, I guess.

"Oh, great," I say. I stare right back. I have to see her. ". . . with her husband?"

Eyes on me, Kevin takes out a cell, dials, and smiles when someone picks up.

"You have a friend waiting for you down here, Ms. Bannerman," he says, but I will not move. I can do this, I can find some way to make this whole thing okay. I try to brainstorm excuses and reasons for being here and casual ways to convince Sylvia that I'm not whatever it is she thinks I am.

God. I'm in for it. Even superkind Austin will think it's messed up that I'm visiting right now.

Kevin uh-huhs and mm-hmms a dozen times. He is probably (definitely) figuring out how to have me arrested or put in the psych ward. He is probably taking down my vital stats (is that a thing?) and—

"I'll bring her up," he says. There was no announcing my name or what I look like, so I get the distinct impression that they were expecting me.

Kevin hangs in the door of the apartment and it weirds me out for a second. Sylvia's funny too, squirrely and not acting anything like the rock star, plastic-surgery goddess she is. She keeps raising her eyebrows at Kevin, and I could easily get caught up in the weird back and forth of their expressions and nonverbal ticks, but Sylvia says to come on in.

"Take a look around," she says. She stays by the door with Kevin. I think it's weird to just walk around their place like I'm a real, live guest, but with the open invitation and the two of them guarding the door, I don't really see a way to say no.

Here's what I notice right away:

Sylvia and Austin have portraits of themselves in large gold frames. They've signed them, like they might at some point forget their own celebrity. I stall in the living room like any normal person might do, but everything in my body screams at me to explore more, and Sylvia hangs back, not stopping me.

"Um, can I . . ." I gesture to the rest of the apartment and blush. My mother would murder me, being this rude, and in a few hours I'm sure I will relive the awkwardness of the request and want to vanish forever, but my feet move regardless of what my rational mind is telling them to do, and Sylvia nods after a quick glance at Kevin.

The bedroom is worse than the living room. Mirrors. Everywhere. Reflecting on each other. Mirrors reflecting mirrors reflecting mirrors, and the idea of Austin and Sylvia fucking in between.

No matter how far gone they think I am, there's nothing sexy in that. Besides, their inherent lustiness is a sidebar to the main event: my needing to vigilantly watch them and thus somehow protect them.

Sylvia and Kevin hang a few steps back, but follow as I push open different doors and lean into different rooms.

There's no room for anything else here but their perfect faces, the unmistakable lines of their bodies, the way love and success fit them. In their CD rack, which hangs next to an expertly installed stereo system, there's a few embarrassing holiday compilations and a stack of blanks, and then two full rows of their own albums. I recognize it all from my google binge the other night: everything from their self-produced *Boho Love Story Redux* to the most recent *HotDirtyLonely*.

"Cool," I say, making fleeting eye contact with Sylvia. Her smile is tense and her lips are blown up to twice their normal size, but she seems at least a little bit proud to have someone check out her digs.

"I love this place," she says with a shrug, in a way I know she's done probably one hundred times.

There's something inherently and impressively embar-rassing about these details. I want to look away. Which is of course saying a lot. I've made a career lately out of looking more intently, staring down the details of their existence.

In the living room their wedding pictures are in a cluster above the fireplace. None of family or sad hipster bridesmaids or chubby, poorly lit nieces and nephews. Just Sylvia in her vintage lace and rhinestones and Austin in an ironic top hat and their look of devotion, their movie-star kisses, the shape their bodies make when leaning against one another.

In the bathroom: more mirrors with expert lighting and a marble countertop with a department store worthy collection of makeup, organized by color, the rainbow moving from light to dark in a perfect parade. A collection of fake eyelashes, vary-ing in size and shade. Like there's a perfect eyelash length for every possible scenario. I'm a little shocked at the effort it takes to become Sylvia.

That's not all.

Once I start looking I realize the apartment is full of monogrammed *everything*. I make my way back to the living room and notice Sylvia vanished to the kitchen at some point. She emerges with two steaming mugs of tea. The mugs are the same silver color of their self-titled second album, and I wonder if those, too, were once promotional material. The mugs seem decidedly self-satisfied.

I don't see Kevin but I smell his cologne: cheap, heavy, young.

"This is a little something special I've been brewing up just forever," she says, fascinated with herself. "You probably wouldn't think it to look at me, but I know a lot about herbs and tea leaves and, well, this is my signature blend."

It's a sweet kind of Earl Grey that needs milk and then stays coated on your tongue for hours after.

And it hits me: It's not just me obsessed with them. They are ferociously obsessed with themselves and that makes the whole thing immediately simpler and sadder.

"You like the place?" Sylvia says with a big gesture to all of their things. She looks at herself in the mirror above my head, missing my gaze entirely. And there's more: a locket hanging down to her sternum I just know has a picture of her and Austin inside. Not just Austin alone. Never just Austin alone.

Sylvia is the kind of person who has to be in every picture. She's the kind of person who has a photograph of herself tucked into a locket engraved with her initials. And there it is, in her eyes: not fear of me following her around, not a reprimanding sternness or a warning tone. Instead, all over her face, is the thrill at being watched. The desire to see herself through my admiring eyes. The complicit agreement that she and Austin are definitely worth watching. It's on the tip of her tongue, and then it's out of her mouth, excitement poorly hidden.

"Why us? I mean. Is it just the music? It's a little freaky, honey, but a little awesome, too. I mean, it's like full circle, you know? Like, we loved musicians in a really hardcore way and they mattered to us and changed us and . . . it's cool, right? It's cool, you being here. It's cool you going to our therapist. I love that kind of thing. Fate." The words are fine, but the thing underneath them, the tone or whatever, the energy, has the frenetic pace and fear factor of a tiny hummingbird's heartbeat. "Little weird that you pretended to live here, right? I mean, we both know that's a little strange. Cute-ish, though. I mean, don't feel bad."

She's filling space with words. I pinch and pinch and pinch my thigh. There's a block of knives on the kitchen counter. I go over the relative pros and cons of asking her to please put them away. I don't really have a choice, though. Isn't it basic safety? I know they're rock stars and stuff, but it seems irresponsible. Maybe it's not a big deal to ask her to put them in a cabinet. Maybe she meant to put them away and forgot. Maybe she'll be grateful I reminded her.

"So? How's the tea?" she asks. I have not said a word.

"Oh! Great, thank you."

"Seriously, don't feel weird. I mean, after Austin talked to you he explained *everything*. Being a teenager sucks. We get it." These conversations I've been having with Austin and Sylvia keep being completely and absurdly disappointing. Profoundly. Because against all odds, in spite of all my blustering belief about their awesomeness, they're lame. The kind of adults who think it's cool to be "down with" the teenagers, to acknowledge our feelings, to remember their days of acne and driver's permits and awkward losses of virginity, and they think they're doing us a service by being so accepting of our superobvious flaws.

Sylvia sips at her tea mug. It's clearly a discarded party favor from her wedding. It has a date and cheesy silver font: AUSTIN AND SYLVIA: PUNKROCKLOVE. Punk rock seems like something that has no place on wedding favors. It seems like the more aware you are of your own punk-rock-ness, the less it actually exists. They're making me so sad, so utterly let down I want to cry.

"So what brought you to Dr. Pat?" Sylvia says. It's fake-casual, like we're just girlfriends drinking Sylvia's special tea from our branded mugs. I've been doing such an excellent job at lying through my teeth, I think for a minute I'm going to be able to manage it here, too. I'll say something predictable about my horrible parents and my mean friends and the stress of trying to get into college with lame grades and a poor attitude.

But the truth has, of course, found its way from my brain into my mouth and I dig a fingernail into my thigh but with the thick jeans it's not really doing much of anything. The words are burning. If I don't say them something terrible will happen. I can't believe I even considered lying, knowing how dire the consequences are, and now that I've lied a few times to Austin I basically need to make it better by saying even *more* truth. I don't want to. I know how she'll look at me after. But that's nothing compared to the ceiling falling in on us or the words burning a literal hole in my throat or the thousands and thousands of calamities that could possibly occur if I keep all the truth trapped inside me for even one second longer.

"OCD," I say. Not with up-speak. Not like a question or an apology, which is a good way to say it when you don't want to freak someone out. "Anxiety at first. And then OCD. I'm in group therapy too. When I was younger, I saw a guy get stabbed with a broken bottle. Or, well, I mean I saw this guy I really liked stab a guy with a bottle. This guy Jeff? Anyway. I mean, that's what I've learned. I'd forgotten. But I remembered a few days ago. So. Yeah. OCD."

Sylvia swallows and plays with her locket and then musters up a smile so full of effort I'm worried her Botox will somehow crack and I'll be faced with the actual lines of her real face. And neither of us is ready for *that* kind of honesty. Austin comes in just then. Sylvia must have called him, and I can't really blame her for wanting backup.

He's brought cupcakes, because that's what all the kids are eating these days.

"What do you think of the place?" he says with that same swinging arm Sylvia gestured with just a few minutes earlier. The cupcakes have silver frosting. I think that's their signature color. They are without a doubt the kind of couple that would have a signature color.

I've never wanted to eat something silver and I'm not about to start now.

I'm pretty sure I'm never coming back here. I don't know what I'm really doing here in the first place. Whatever I thought I would get from being near them, being in their space, seems to not really exist.

"Really nice," I say.

"So, Bea. Sylvia and I talked after the concert last night," he says. They're both straddling the same few emotions I think. They like how into them I am. They can't help the thrill of fame and *mattering* and being an object of desire. I mean, look at Sylvia's pushed-up breasts and painted mouth and popping-blue eyes that seem almost neon because of all the dark eyeliner surrounding them. They've been noticed, and I don't think they can help liking that at least a little. "And I meant what I said, absolutely, about understanding being a fan and being a teenager and being in this totally awkward life moment."

I wonder if they are practicing to have kids.

I wonder if I am convincing them *not* to have kids.

"You've been great," I say. I'm not even really in this conversation. I mean, it's about me and all, but mostly it's Austin and Sylvia exchanging a really complicated set of glances and and trying hard to be cool and understanding. They're talking to each other, not me.

Like their bedroom, the mirrors reflecting mirrors reflecting mirrors.

I'm in that funhouse with all the mirrors and Austin and Sylvia.

"And of course I'm the one that invited you to the concert, but after what happened with your friend . . . well. I think we're feeling a little less comfortable. I'll be honest, we figured you might stop by today. It seems like you're stopping by a lot. Too much. And we did ask Kevin to look out for you. He said he'd . . . seen you around?"

I nod. This is mortifying.

"And we also put a call in to Dr. Pat," Austin concludes. "And we want this to be safe and calm for all of us. No police, no security. So. Dr. Pat's on her way."

I keep completely misinterpreting the situations I get into with Austin and Sylvia. Which is weird since I'm working so, so hard to take it all in accurately.

"Huh?" is all I muster up. I cling to one little phrase in all he just said, because it lodges in my head and doesn't make sense. "What do you mean 'what happened with my friend?'" It's possible he means my fight with Beck, but that doesn't seem like such a big deal. Did Lisha get wasted and throw herself at Austin or something? Did Austin hear what I told Sylvia about Jeff and the bottle and the guard? My mind's working overtime to try to fit together pieces that aren't quite right.

"I hope you understand. I think you're such a great kid.

But this is our home and we do need to take care of ourselves, too." Now Austin is talking like a therapist. And it's sort of like I've been framed, except I did it all to myself. And they're right, of course they're right, in their cozy Austin-and-Sylvia-themed home. They're right to have called her, they're right to be worried, they're right to see that I am not, and never was, just like them.

It's the worst kind of silent waiting that comes next.

Then Dr. Pat's at the door and she thanks Austin and Sylvia for calling and leads me to the couch in the lobby. Austin's and Sylvia's smiles change from painful to peaceful as soon as I've stepped from their apartment to the threshold of their home. Dr. Pat keeps a hand on my shoulder the whole elevator ride down to the lobby.

"They could have just called my mom," I say. "Or the police. They didn't need to bring you over here."

"You should have told me, Bea," Dr. Pat says. For someone whose job it is to listen, she's plowing right over me. "I can't help you if you're not honest. Do you get that? There are a lot of people who would love to be getting the help you're getting. And I don't mind slipups; I expect them. But it's insulting for you to be spending all this time in group and in one-on-one therapy and to just be lying. How can I help you if you're lying all the time?" The doorman pretends to ignore us while we have some kind of impromptu session right here in Sylvia and Austin's lobby.

How many times can I be blacklisted as full-on insane at the same building?

"I just hadn't gotten to it yet," I say in the weakest voice imaginable. "I'm really fucked up. I had a lot to talk to you about." I'm pissed at Dr. Pat and I know that's not really fair, because I'm the one who keeps messing up. But she's on my turf now. All the little pieces of my life, all the little things I've been keeping separate and manageable . . . she's invading all of it: Beck, Austin and Sylvia, my car, my life, my past, the things I do just to keep myself sane.

She's a thief. That's the best word for the kind of person she is.

"Bea. You have a history of stalking. You knew this would be a priority to me and our work together." She has never used the word "stalking" before. It's an ugly, ugly word.

"I didn't think—"

"You're a smart girl, Bea. We need to get more aggressive with your treatment. And I can't do that when you aren't actually telling me what you're doing. Use Beck as an example. See how that worked for him? He was honest, and that allowed us to really work through his problems and he's made leaps and bounds—"

"I don't want to talk about Beck." There's this horrible edge in my voice that I don't recognize as my own, but I can't stamp it out. It's making me sound like some cliché of a surly teenager. "I get it. Beck's all better and I'm just getting worse. That doesn't exactly help, you know?" I sigh. Not a little breathy sigh, a fully voiced *sigh* that includes crossed arms and a pout.

I hate myself.

There was a time when I could exercise some amount of control over the things I did and said. I mean, it was never my best skill, but it was there a little bit, once upon a time. Now the doorman, Kevin, is raising his eyebrows at me the way you do when a baby is throwing a tantrum on an airplane. An unspoken *hmph* on his face. I hate him too. I'm making a list now. Of people I hate. It's extensive.

"I'm all for you going at your own pace," Dr. Pat says. She's wearing more makeup than usual, and there's cleavage showing in her black shirt, and there's a whole world of things I don't know about this woman. "We need to change your appointment times though."

"Why?"

"You know why, Bea."

And I stare her down for a few long, satisfying moments, but she wins out. She goes into her purse. And pulls out a notebook.

A pink leather notebook.

My pink leather notebook. Shooting star embossed on the cover. The height of ugliness and humiliation.

Certain moments don't make sense.

"Austin said he found this. Do you have an explanation for this? Do you understand the ethical, even the legal . . . ?"

She can't even finish her sentence. I swallow and my fingers crawl toward my thigh and I want to dig in there so hard because I am going to either vanish or do something terrible to Dr. Pat, and it's the only way to stay in control of the rushing, terrible feelings.

There's a vase on the coffee table in front of us. I could break the glass and use a single sharp piece to hurt her, like Jeff.

But she grabs my hand before it makes its way to my thigh, and she holds it still.

"I have to do it!" I scream, and then there's more crying, the kind that makes my eyes sting and my insides feel all squeezed out and overworked. But Dr. Pat doesn't say anything, she just holds that hand still and I let my head drop into her lap and we stay like that until Kevin asks us to please leave because we have worn out our welcome.

Dr. Pat drives me home. I tell her I can do it myself but she says that's not an option. I try to put the notebook away in my purse, but she grabs it and puts it on the dashboard so it's watching us the whole drive back. Heavy and pointed and unavoidable. And no longer mine.

"You looked inside?" I say when we're off the highway and getting close to my house.

"Austin looked inside," Dr. Pat says, which doesn't answer my question but definitely tells me all I really need to know. "You should feel lucky, *very* lucky that they are such kind people. Scared them, seeing this, reading their personal conversations, their most private, vulnerable moments . . . you terrified them." I wonder if this part is therapy or her showing her actual feelings. I'm the kind of dizzy I usually only get after a really serious wine-drinking night with Lish.

"I probably need a new therapist," I say. My mother does this sometimes—she calls it taking the high road—where she makes the horrible decision before someone else can do it for her.

"I still want to help you," Dr. Pat says, but she's rubbing her eyes with one hand and rolling her shoulders like I'm giving her knots in her neck. She says it like she doesn't yet know what's best. "We're going to destroy this." She continues nodding to the notebook. "You and me together. We're getting rid of it. That's the first order of business. Then we'll see."

"Can I have it just one more night?" I ask. But she's smarter than me, she knows I'd copy it all down in another notebook, and I guess it's almost a relief when she shakes her head and takes the notebook off the dashboard and tucks it under her thigh so she's sitting on it. It's a good gesture. Final. Inarguable.

My parents are on the porch when Dr. Pat drops me off. We don't say much and they basically put me to bed. They might as well be tucking me in. I'm not tired. I don't sleep. I am already missing the words in the notebook, the little stabilizing scratches I made in there.

I am running out of things to comfort me.

♡ 24.

SOMETIMES LISHA ROCKS IT OLD-SCHOOL.

By which I mean she prefers a handwritten note to an e-mail, and a bit of embossed stationery to a piece of note-book paper. My mother serves it to me with my breakfast: eggs and cinnamon toast and crappy instant coffee.

"Lisha dropped by with this," she says, and hands me the kind of envelope that costs *money*, that recycled-paper tex-ture. My name in Lish's pretty handwriting on the front. I've been to the mall enough with Lisha to know she can spend some serious time in a stationery store, buying up the pretti-est notecards and embossing materials I can imagine.

Lisha at a stationery store is like me at the Salvation Army.

Every muscle in me shakes, opening that thing.

Dear Bea,
    I keep thinking I'm helping.
    But when I woke up the other morning, I realized that all the things I'm doing are actually fucking you

up even more and I'm not saving you at all. Not even close.

I gave Austin your notebook. I guess I should have just started there, so you know what we're dealing with. Maybe it was wrong, but when I saw Austin and Sylvia up on stage, all real and stuff, it started to make me sick.

Not sick. Scared.

Did you ever see the movie Single White Female? It was on TV the other day, and Cooter sat down while I was watching it and we both got pretty into it. Then out of nowhere Cooter started laughing and goes, "Hey, it's a movie about Bea!" and I didn't yell at him or anything because he was basically right.

I mean, I actually joined him in laughing at you. About you.

Then I backed up and tried defending you: "Yeah, but Bea's got OCD, so she's a different kind of stalker." And Cooter shrugged. There was this bizarre moment where I think we both really heard for the first time ever how insane that sounded. You know, as a legitimate excuse.

So, that happened. And then we were at that concert and yes, I'm drinking, and your stupid notebook is in my purse and I'm about to give it back to you except . . . that makes me some kind of

accessory, you know? And the world sort of clears up
for a second because I can see perfectly that I need to
turn you in, to get everything out into the open.

It's just—I'm going to Harvard, you know? And I
know this sounds paranoid, but how can I be someone
big if I have some sketchy, assisting-a-stalker incident
in my past?

Bea, there was really personal stuff in that
notebook. And I thought about it and there're all
kinds of ethical issues with, like, doctor-patient
confidentiality, and vulnerability and secrets and
a right to privacy . . . that all just popped into my
head when I was watching Austin and Sylvia rocking
out on stage, and once those thoughts were there, I
couldn't unpop them.

I know you know how that feels.

After you left they were signing some CDs and I
went up to Austin and I handed over your notebook.
I didn't say anything, just, "You know that Bea girl?
Here."

He looked inside and turned gray. And red. And
then really, really sad.

I don't know. As weird as Beck is, at least he's just
doing it to himself, you know? Like, okay, he does
that weird counting thing and he goes through a bar
of soap a day, I'm sure, and he looks like he's popping

steroids. That all definitely makes him weird. Weirder
than us, I think. But at the end of the day it's not
illegal to be weird. There's no big ethical conundrum
when it comes to excessive hand-washing.

Do you ever wish your OCD was more like his?
Wouldn't that be better?

You're my best friend and that is exhausting. You
need to know that.

I sort of hope I get to college next year and meet
some nice girl whose biggest problem is getting a B
on her chem final. That's the kind of person I'd like to
meet next.

Even given all of that, I'd give up Harvard if I
thought it would make you better. But it won't, and
that's what sucks. That's what really, really sucks.

Love,
Lish

I'm sweating when I've finished reading. She is either my
biggest enemy or the most amazing best friend ever, and I
could try to figure it out, except I'm having a panic attack at
the breakfast table.

The instant coffee spills and just misses my legs. My mom
hugs me until it's over. Like I'm a kid, but I'm not anymore,
and I think that's more or less what Lisha's note was trying
to say.

Some therapy-ized part of me gets that, but the rest of me hates her and her too-skinny frame and the Harvard-red-striped scarf she's been sporting lately. The fact that ever since she and Cooter and her parents fought, I've mostly only seen her drunk. The impulse is strong to tell her parents all about it.

Then it's even stronger when I think through the reality of what she did.

Then I'm picking up the phone to call them, not just to get revenge, but also because it's the truth, and as usual, there it is, festering in my mouth, waiting to come out, and if I don't call her parents right now and spit out every terrible thing she's ever done, then—

But the phone rings before I dial their home phone.

"Come over," Beck says on the other line. He is hushed and out of breath like he just worked out.

It's eight in the morning. Of course.

"Where are you?"

"My house," he says. "Just come over."

"I'm gonna have to walk," I say. He knows that means I'm in no state to drive and that I'm in full-on OCD mode right now, but he takes a breath and says that's fine. I can walk. He still wants me to come over. And walking feels good: my fingers, my toes, can all go numb and I can focus on nothing but one foot in front of the other. When I get to Beck's house on the other side of town, it's getting close to ten and I'm the kind of flushed-face-cold that looks totally pretty. Let's face it: I'm really pretty in the winter. I'm just that kind of girl. I catch my reflection in the window on his front door before I ring the bell, and underneath all the humiliation and nerves and anger there is that unmistakable feeling of being *pretty*. They should make a word for that emotion. It's like confidence but sweeter, more specific.

I check out the excessive Easter decorations draped all over the house while I wait for him to answer the door. Here's another useful SAT word for you: "gauche." I'm being hit over the head with it now, staring down a plastic bunny on his roof and Easter eggs in all sizes lined up on his lawn.

He takes forever to answer the door, and when he gets there, he does not look pretty. Or handsome. Or anything resembling the picture I have in my head of *Beck*. He's in jeans and one of his too-tight T-shirts, and he's scrubbed clean, which should be a good thing, but his skin is falling off in little sheets and what's underneath is raw and painful. His face, his hands, his forearms: All the parts of him that I can see are worn through from scrubbing.

"Wow," I say. It would be silly to pretend I don't see it.

"Yeah," he says. "Yeah, yeah, yeah, yeah, yeah, yeah, yeah." He's cringing as he hears the words coming out but he can't stop them. His head shakes as he does it, the deepest kind of self-hatred in that little movement.

"I'm bad too," I say. "I got caught. I mean, I know you

don't care. But Sylvia and Austin—you know, Tryst—they called Dr. Pat. They saw this notebook that I recorded all their therapy sessions in . . . I'll be having sessions *in my home* because I can't be trusted in a therapist's office. So. Nothing's more pathetic than that, right?"

He nods, but doesn't speak. I wonder if he can say anything less than eight times right now. From the way he's holding his mouth, I think not. Some serious struggle is going on behind those pretty lips. I'm caught off guard by the urge to kiss him. There's nothing actually sexy about the redness of his skin. But there's something sexy, I guess, in the fact that I had sex with him the other day.

Yep, that must be it.

"I can't hug you right?" I say.

He shakes his head, tears up.

"You going to invite me in?" And he does.

Being in Beck's room is not unlike being inside his head. It's a grid of organization and sparseness. There's none of my manic decorating, and there's no sign of recognizable boyness. No discarded pizza crusts or dirty underwear or clothes piled on clothes piled on a bed. There's just order. There's a place for his stapler, for his shoes, for his workout journal, for a photo of his sister. It's ninety-degree angles and a bed made with hospital corners and the fresh lines in the carpet from a vacuum cleaner. It smells like lemon and antiseptic.

It is the single most sterile place I've ever been.

In fact, I am the messiest part of it, in my red flannel pajama bottoms and a Harvard sweatshirt Lisha gave me a few months ago. My feet are stuffed into scuffed-up UGGs and I don't think I even managed to wash my face. I threw on lip gloss and had three mints, but that's about it. Maybe that makes me good for him, though. If Dr. Pat's theories are right, maybe my messiness will cure him.

So I do what I think Dr. Pat would want me to do: I throw myself on the bed and roll around in it a little like a deranged puppy dog and I grab the framed photograph of tiny eight-year-old Violet and I kick off my shoes, one on each side of the bed, and make myself at home. Just like that: impromptu exposure therapy.

"Hey—" Beck starts tapping his finger and swallowing in sets of eight.

"I get to stay here, you get to keep that pair of scissors in the little scissor space there on the desk. Then we're on equal footing and we can be psychos together," I say. The walk must have done something to me. My skin's prickling and I'm definitely sweating a little, but I'm doing an inward check on my anxiety levels and they're rising slowly, then leveling out, then sinking back down.

"I fucked up," Beck says. I don't know that I've heard him swear before. It doesn't suit him. That kind of thing should be reserved for obsessives like me and Rudy: the raw, whirling kinds of OCD kids. Not the neat-as-a-pin Beck.

"When?"

"At the concert. You were right. I hate that you were right. But you were," Beck says with a shake of his head. I sputter a little bit of laughter because I didn't think I was coming over here to get an apology. I am never right. I have OCD. I've pretty much come to accept that whatever is going on in my head is probably wrong.

"I was stalking people," I say, like he's forgotten. "We were on a date with the guy I was *stalking*." And though that's what I'm saying, I still have in me that flare of anger at the way I had to accept him while he never had to accept me.

"No," Beck says. It looks like he's swallowing down an impulse to just say it once. I get it. It looks the way I feel when I'm trying not to spit out the truth at ridiculous moments. "I mean, yes. That was weird. But not any weirder than the things I . . . *less* weird probably than most of the things I've done. So who the hell am I to—"

"Yeah," I say. There's that truth-telling again. Just hanging in the air. Just like that.

"Yeah," Beck says. He gets into bed with me: lies on top of the sheets I've properly messed up. We don't touch—things don't get solved that easily—but it's nice for a little to lie like that and stare at the ceiling. "You want to tell me about them?" Beck says. "The band? Dr. Pat's patients or whatever?"

I shrug.

"I'm sort of screwed," I say. I've tried not to think about

the next time the impulse hits me to see them because I know that's about to get much, much harder.

"What do you like about them?" Beck says. "What's so special about them?" It is a question I have asked myself, but no one has asked me out loud. Not even Dr. Pat. I think once you have that OCD label people stop asking for reasons, since everything you do is probably just from the disorder. I'm flummoxed. Speechless.

"When did you see them first?" Beck says. My jaw remains dropped because, again, no one has asked me this before. I've said the whole thing about magic eyes and people popping out at me from nowhere, and that's true, but I have a little fuzz along the edge of my answer, like there's more to it, more to uncover.

"God . . . I don't even remember . . . not long ago . . . ," I say. I scrunch up my eyes to make myself remember something more. "It's a recent thing."

"You just heard them or saw them one day?"

"I guess I heard them first. Before my session. Heard them talking about stuff . . ." For a moment I think it's there: a Reason. But then it fades back again and there's nothing. "I can check. It's probably in my notebook . . ." I almost scramble to my purse to get it, and the thought of flipping through it and putting pieces together makes me truly, truly happy for a moment. Like I'll get a real relief, the sort of relief that actually chills out my whole system.

But I don't have the notebook. Dr. Pat has the notebook.

"What if I never find out the reason?" I say. I don't know if he'll know what I mean, because I don't know if *I* really know what I mean. "Do you think I'll be okay if it was just a thing that happened? Would that be weird? What if there wasn't a real reason? I mean, maybe I'm just kinda crazy."

"Sometimes crap just happens," Beck says.

"Yeah, sometimes people just do really fucking weird things." I put down the photograph of Violet. "Sometimes there're real reasons, but sometimes maybe there aren't any."

"Yeah."

I touch some of the rawest parts of Beck's skin. His neck, the place where his thumb meets the rest of his hand, his chin.

"I'm sorry. This is, like, truly grotesque. My skin is falling off. I mean, this is not okay. There goes the theory that I'm less psycho than Jenny and Rudy. . . ." He's sort of tearing up. "I thought I was getting better."

I thought he was getting better too.

I thought *I* was getting better. This blows. And his sad, sad face hurts me. The scrapes on his skin, the dry patches in between each finger. I know how badly he wishes they could be hidden.

"I'm sorry," he says, "I'm sorry, I'm sorry . . ." I let him finish the eight times, but then I dive in. Because I can't fix the dried-up bits of him, the itch of too-clean skin, the haunting eyes of his little, gone sister, but I can do this, at least.

"I've got other stuff to tell you," I say. I have no interest in showing Beck how disgusting my thigh bruises have gotten. But something much deeper inside me doesn't want him to lie there thinking he's the only one whose crazed tendencies are showing up on his skin. So I unceremoniously take off my pants.

"Oh—" Beck starts. He thinks we're going to do it again, and I'm sure we will sometime, but I shake my head vehemently and hold up a hand to make him wait. He sinks back into the bed and my pants come off one leg at a time. I guess when we did this before—got undressed—we didn't take the time to inspect each other's bodies. I turn to the side so he can get the full effect of the black and blue and purple and yellow and red *thing* that is taking over my leg. There's no hiding his reaction—it's like a punch to his chest. But then he leans forward and touches it. Even just that light touch hurts, which is funny since I'm used to pinching it. But when I'm in the moment, compulsing, I'm far enough gone in the anxiety and the release that I don't think about the pain.

I'm not like a cutter. I don't *want* it to hurt. Jenny doesn't want that pinch of hair coming out. Rudy doesn't like the bit of blood that comes with the bit of pain when he excavates his face. These are things I don't have to say to Beck, who is nodding at the size and shape of the bruise, at the flush of my face.

"That it?" he says at last. And I guess it is.

"I think that's it. But I need you to come to Dr. Pat's with me."

"If we leave the house, does this count as a date?" Beck says. "Our seventh date?"

"Oh," I say. "I forgot you were counting."

He swallows eight times.

An hour later we're with Dr. Pat, at my house, in front of the fireplace. Dr. Pat must be from some kind of good New England stock, because she gets a fire going like only a real New Englander can: rolled balls of newspaper, strategically lit corners, a slow burn rising into a real flame.

"Cozy," Beck says a little sarcastically. I snort, *snort*, because Beck's dry moments of humor are so sparse and unexpected they always catch me off guard and I can't help the little noises my body makes in response to him.

Then Dr. Pat brings out that stupid pink notebook. My heart basically stops as soon as I see it. I want to devour it. I want to eat it, so that the words, the moments I captured, remain inside me. Safe. Just when I'm readying myself for the explosion of anxiety coming my way, my mother appears with a stack of notebooks, all mine, all filled with clippings. Months and months of collected data to protect me from the terrible things I could potentially do or become.

I go numb from anxiety. This is new: tingling fingers and a locked jaw. Awesome. I thought I'd experienced the full spectrum of symptoms, but there's always more. The numbness makes it hard to breathe, too, and Dr. Pat's saying over and over "What level, what level?" and Beck is looking me in the eye and it's a ten, a full-on TEN; this is definitely what a ten feels like. And Dr. Pat puts the pink notebook in my hand and my head is screaming at me to read through it, to take more notes, to try to remember and write down exactly what was said the other night when they caught me.

But I throw it in the fire instead. And we watch it burn.

My hands shake, and I have a cold flash. My limbs turn to ice. *This is new*, I think, and shiver from the sudden drop in temperature. The obese Anxiety Man sits on my chest, and I'm caught, paralyzed in that cold, weighted-down, shaking place for what seems like hours.

It is maybe seven minutes.

And then it drops. Slowly at first. I find myself at a nine, and then an eight, a seven-point-five.

I throw in the next notebook, and the next. I'm at a seven. A six-point-five.

A calm, normal-temperature six. The buzzing in my head stops. The pressure on my chest is still there, but lighter.

My mother makes hot chocolate and we experience the single weirdest afternoon of my life, watching my OCD notebooks smolder in the fireplace while stirring minimarshmallows into the Swiss Miss. Just me, my mom, Dr. Pat, and Beck.

♡ 25.

THERE'S NOT MUCH WE CAN DO BUT LOOK AT Jenny and her peach-fuzz head.

"Oh my God, that's a thousand times better," I say. It's not the same as a compulsion. This time I say it not because it's eating away at my throat or because it's of dire importance. I say it because she needs to know that I'd rather see her bald than to see her destroying herself. Rudy's eyes go huge from how pretty she looks. He's drinking her in and the rest of us relax, for maybe the first time ever, into our awkward metal seats. It's a weight off seeing her like that, clean and even and brand-new.

"Can I touch it?" I say with a grin. I don't know who I think I am. Beck's the one who made the breakthrough in group and Jenny's the one who has obviously made some kind of breakthrough at home, and I'm just the girl who yelled at everyone last time we were here. But Jenny nods and grins back and I rub her head before Dr. Pat can reinforce the rules.

"Good" is all Dr. Pat says. "Good." Then she pulls out a knife. Just like that. A knife that must be from her kitchen. It's sharp and real and glinting, but no one else is flinching. Just me. "This is for Bea," Dr. Pat says, and everyone nods and acts like the knife is some harmless mitten or banana.

"That's way worse than my Swiss Army knife, huh?" Rudy says.

"I'm sorry. I have to go," I say. It's a reflex, just the same as a doctor knocking your knee with his little hammer-thing. Just as automatic. I trust the reflex that says, definitively, *no.*

"Bea," Dr. Pat says. Just that. Just my name and the knife glinting at me as she holds it out. "Hold it to my heart," Dr. Pat says. This cannot be legal. I shake my head.

"Hold it to *my* heart," Beck says, and I know that's for sure not okay, because Dr. Pat puts her hand on Beck's back to tell him no. "Fine," Beck says. "How about just Rudy's knife? You know as well as I do"—Rudy is taking his little knife off his key chain and I'm shaking and I think this is actually somehow going to happen—"that this can't hurt anyone."

"Okay," Dr. Pat says. "Rudy? Can we . . . ?" But he's already handing it to Beck. I'm all sweat and fast breathing and when I look around the room, I expect the rest of them to have some kind of cloud of panic crossing their faces, but there's nothing like that. They're looking on with placid, matching smiles of support. I'd like to scream at them, show them my notebooks of research about normal-looking, even occasionally *pretty* girls just like me snapping, losing their minds all of a sudden, and killing people.

I mean, I have evidence showing what a bad idea this is. Evidence that shows just how unpredictable we all are.

But I don't have the notebooks anymore.

"Okay," Beck says. "Stab me." It's that dry humor again. The thing I love about him is now biting me in the ass. I'm breathing in short gasps, and when the knife is in my hand and erect, I'm shaking so hard I think I might drop it. Dr. Pat's kitchen knife lies beside me too, just to add to the stress. The journey of lifting the knife to Beck's heart is epic. And once it touches the hard mass of his chest, my anxiety is at a ten.

"I can't take it, I can't do it! It's a ten! Please let me stop!" I sob in Dr. Pat's direction, but she and the group only lift their shoulders and bite their lips and wait it out.

I'm going to kill Beck, I think. But I don't.

And then, like last night, the numbers start to drop. I do not spontaneously combust from the anxiety. It starts to subside. Like a toddler throwing a tantrum, it's worn itself out and is giving in. I'm at a seven. And I think: *I'm so not going to kill Beck.* And then: *I don't even know how to hurt someone with a Swiss Army knife.* I don't really get below a four and a half. I don't turn into some monk all of a sudden. And when Dr. Pat says I can take the knife away from Beck's chest, I'm relieved.

But. A little space has been created where I don't have to be afraid.

Then I'm thinking about shipwrecks on Caribbean islands, which I'm sure never happen. But I think about them anyway, as if they could. There's this horrible situation, and about a million very real things that could happen, and you're not exactly happy to be shipwrecked and you've got a lot of problems to solve and shit to work out. But you're on this island, and in the middle of building your hut and hunting for fish and, like, doing basic first aid on your injured friend, you take a break and lie in the sand and look at the way the palm trees swing a little in the warm wind. And the sound of the ocean hitting the shore is lovely, and you're in maybe the most beautiful place you've ever been.

So in the same moment you're terrified and amazed at the sobering reality of the world around you and the purity of the beauty.

Would you trade in that moment? Would you risk being shipwrecked to be able to see the most beautiful section of the human world?

I guess that's just a long way of saying I'm happy to be here. Beck and I are smiling goofy smiles at each other, and my stomach flips around thinking about getting naked with him on the mountain, and maybe again later in my room. It's like, I'm scared and there're a lot of ugly things, but I'd rather be shipwrecked on this lovely island than safe in a sad, gray cell. You know?

♡ 26.

THERE IS NO EIGHTH DATE. WE JUST SKIPPED IT.

Dr. Pat says you make your own decisions.

♡ 27.

MANY, MANY DATES LATER, LISH, BECK, AND I hang out in Harvard Square. There's a place called The Pit, and it's stoners and skaters and the three of us. We're people watching.

I'm taking notes, but it's okay because it's for a play I'm going to be costume designing at school. It's not a huge deal, just this student-run evening of short plays that other students wrote, but I offered to do the costumes and everyone was psyched, like it was obvious that I'd be great at that. Which I guess means I've been totally successful at having my outfits stand out from the sea of J.Crew sweaters and tight black pants that make up the rest of the student population at Greenough Girl's Academy.

One of the plays is about punked-out runaway kids, and I figured this was the place to find them. Jeff used to talk about coming here on the weekends, scoring Ritalin, and learning how to skate.

The memory of that doesn't scare me so much anymore.

But I told Dr. Pat I missed my compulsions. That sometimes I missed them because without them I was more anxious, but sometimes I missed them because they defined me. She recommended people watching. The winter is finally turning full-on into spring, and Beck, Lisha, and I can lean back and take in the crowds. It doesn't have the same euphoric, druglike magic of checking on Austin and Sylvia, but it's fun, catching snippets of conversation. I don't write them down (Dr. Pat's rules—I'm only allowed to write down costume ideas) but I share a smile and half laugh with Beck or Lish whenever we overhear a particularly good little moment between strangers.

"I'm thinking of getting back into shoplifting. Am I too old?" a brunette, superpierced chick says to her sad-eyed friend.

". . . should I go out with him even though he's ugly?"

". . . wish I just had one more purse, then I'd be in good shape."

"I'm thinking of moving to Sweden. I've heard good things. Healthcare and blondes and shit."

"You're a real dick most of the time."

"You're one beautiful bitch."

"I love you the most."

Lisha keeps smiling at the Harvard students that walk by since she's about to be one of them. She crosses and uncrosses her legs in an attempt to fit in and look like them. It's not warm between us, exactly, and we're not back to normal, and there isn't some perfect moment in the sun that fixes what's hurt between us. She sits a foot or two to our left and doesn't ever really talk straight to Beck, and she cringes when anything comes up that she thinks will trigger us: the number eight, soap, a sharp object, a guy in workout clothes on his way to the gym, a woman with fake breasts and gorgeous hair and dark eye makeup who could be Sylvia.

"Is that . . . ," Lish says, and I shake my head no, but then take a closer look and it *is*. It's Sylvia, and Austin beside her, and their hands are knit together and their pace is perfectly in sync, long limbs stepping in time to some song we can't hear. They share one pair of headphones between them and keep their heads close to listen to the music. Probably their own album. I want to point this out to Lish and Beck, who have both latched on to their presence, but then I remember they were never up in that apartment with me, and they wouldn't understand.

In some ways, Sylvia and Austin are still the people I know best in the world.

I miss them.

"You okay?" Beck says. There's a hint of green, green jealousy in his voice and in the space behind his eyes, but he's working hard to keep it in, to accept that handsome, string-bean, rocker-chic bit of my past. He's trying. I can tell because his clothes are a little looser on him than they were before. Not normal yet, but not straining against every muscle, not breaking at the seams. He had a whole series of button-down shirts with pulled-out threads along the sides, long slits where the fabric could no longer contain him.

He looks better now.

I keep my eye on the figures of Sylvia and Austin as they go into a café. I wait just enough time to not cause suspicion.

"You guys want coffee? I'm gonna go get a tea," I say, getting up, stretching my legs, pinning my sunglasses to my face.

"Black coffee," Lisha says.

"Latte," Beck says, and beams at me. He's working at breaking some of his rules, so green tea or bottled water is out. He's trying to enjoy the occasional vice. "With sugar," he continues, just showing off now.

I counter by dropping my notebook on his lap so he can see that every single line of scribble in there is about clothing ideas for the show. Sometimes progress becomes a minicompetition between us. One where everyone wins, I guess.

God, I sound like Dr. Pat when I get this way.

I make it all the way to the door of the café. Just a push of the door and I'll be in there, in line behind Austin and Sylvia. And I want it, maybe more than I've ever wanted anything. Maybe more than I want Beck and his deeply scarred but recovering hands on my body, or his eyes on mine.

There are huge windows and I don't hide, I just stand squarely facing them for long enough to breathe through and let go of the impulse.

I do not pinch my thigh, which is a strange brown-yellow in its latest stage of unbruising itself.

Austin's eyes find me there, outside looking in, like some puppy trying to beg through the storefront glass, practically panting. His hand goes to Sylvia's back and I think he's about to point me out but he doesn't. He just lets his hand stay there and he has the saddest eyes and a new tattoo on the back of that hand. I can tell because it looks raw and unfinished next to the expert patterns on his forearms.

They're so close, just behind the glass, that I can see every bit of him without straining. Every detail.

Or maybe it sticks out because it's a symbol I recognize: a small shooting star. This one is black, but the one it reminds me of was gold, embossed on the surface of a pink notebook I used to have.

A pink notebook I burned.

There's a squeeze in my heart with the realization that I may never know exactly what it means that he's tattooed himself with something that was on my notebook.

It could even be, I suppose, coincidence.

Dr. Pat says the human mind is a complicated place. That we hold on to things, images, words, ideas, histories that we don't even know we're holding on to.

Sometimes lines of poetry from that book Kurt gave me still flit through my head. It doesn't mean I'm going to call him and check to make sure he's still breathing. And even right now, I want to touch Austin's new tattoo, the one I think he got in my honor. I want to know how they're doing. The need hasn't vanished entirely, but it's become this thing I can dip into for a moment, and then dry off from.

Quick and dirty, that's what Beck calls it when we slide into a compulsion for one glorious moment and then save ourselves from the full immersion. I smile at the thought of it, because I like the turn of phrase. Austin smiles back. Guess he thinks I'm smiling his way, saying hello, but really, I'm not.

I don't go in. I don't have to.

ACKNOWLEDGMENTS

A huge, over-the-top thank-you to my amazing agent, Victoria Marini, whose support made me believe and whose insight helped me make it true.

I'm so lucky to have the honor of working with my fabulous editor, Anica Rissi, who gets me, challenges me, and inspires me.

Thank you to Monday Group and Thesis Group for reading, shaping, encouraging, and giving me deadlines: Dhonielle Clayton, Sona Chairapotra, Alyson Gerber, Caela Carter, and Amy Ewing.

I've been blessed with some unbelievable teachers in my life, and I'd like to thank all of them, but most especially Sandra MacQuinn, Dan Halperin, Hettie Jones, David Levithan, and Patricia McCormick. And an especially large thank-you to a truly amazing teacher and role model, Victoria Hart, who probably doesn't realize what a huge difference she made.

Thank you to Red Horse Café and Tea Lounge for making me mochas, playing good music, giving me distractions, and providing a cozy place to write.

So many people gave time and thought to this book and my particular journey to publication. A special thanks to Navdeep Dhillon, Michael Strother, Liesa Abrams and the rest of the Simon Pulse team, Kalah McCaffrey, Laura Schechter, and Danielle Chiotti.

I'm so grateful for my tiny, book-loving family: the Haydus: Dad, Mom, Andy, Jenn, Ellie, Gary, Marie, and Tina; the Spokeses: Dick, Carol, Suzie, and Jen; the Rosses: Judy (who is probably hand-selling this book right now), Doug, Cam, and Ian. And of course the grandparents.

And all my love and thanks to the ones who let me talk, cry, complain, exclaim, obsess, and celebrate:

The ten years or more club: Julia Furlan, Kea Gilbert, Mandy Adams, Honora Javier, and Tracey Roiff. I'm very lucky you've all put up with me and my crazy-writer ways for this long.

And the lovely rest who support me in so many unique ways: Anna Bridgforth, Pallavi Yetur, Leigh Poulos, Mark Souza, Michael Mraz, Brian Smallwood, Rachel Gordon Smallwood, Alisha Spielman, Meghan Formwalt Shann, Taylor Shann, Lizzie Moran, Katherine Jaeger-Thomas, Janet Zarecor, Jess Verdi, Lenea Grace, and Frank Scallon.

ABOUT THE AUTHOR

Corey Ann Haydu grew up in the Boston area but now lives in Brooklyn, New York, where she drinks mochas and uses a lot of Post-it notes, habits she picked up while earning her MFA at the New School. *OCD Love Story* is her first novel. Find out more at coreyannhaydu.com.